Coffee at
The Beach House Hotel

Judith Keim

BOOKS BY JUDITH KEIM

THE HARTWELL WOMEN SERIES:
The Talking Tree – 1
Sweet Talk – 2
Straight Talk – 3
Baby Talk – 4
The Hartwell Women – Boxed Set

THE BEACH HOUSE HOTEL SERIES:
Breakfast at The Beach House Hotel – 1
Lunch at The Beach House Hotel – 2
Dinner at The Beach House Hotel – 3
Christmas at The Beach House Hotel – 4
Margaritas at The Beach House Hotel – 5
Dessert at The Beach House Hotel – 6
Coffee at The Beach House Hotel – 7
High Tea at The Beach House Hotel – 8 (2024)

THE FAT FRIDAYS GROUP:
Fat Fridays – 1
Sassy Saturdays – 2
Secret Sundays – 3

THE SALTY KEY INN SERIES:
Finding Me – 1
Finding My Way – 2
Finding Love – 3
Finding Family – 4
The Salty Key Inn Series . Boxed Set

THE CHANDLER HILL INN SERIES:
Going Home – 1
Coming Home – 2
Home at Last – 3
The Chandler Hill Inn Series – Boxed Set

SEASHELL COTTAGE BOOKS:

A Christmas Star
Change of Heart
A Summer of Surprises
A Road Trip to Remember
The Beach Babes

THE DESERT SAGE INN SERIES:

The Desert Flowers – Rose – 1
The Desert Flowers – Lily – 2
The Desert Flowers – Willow – 3
The Desert Flowers – Mistletoe and Holly – 4

SOUL SISTERS AT CEDAR MOUNTAIN LODGE:

Christmas Sisters – Anthology
Christmas Kisses
Christmas Castles
Christmas Stories – Soul Sisters Anthology
Christmas Joy

THE SANDERLING COVE INN SERIES:

Waves of Hope – 1
Sandy Wishes – 2 (2023)
Salty Kisses – 3 (2023)

THE LILAC LAKE INN SERIES

Love by Design – (2023)
Love Between the Lines – (2023)
Love Under the Stars – (2024)

OTHER BOOKS:

The ABCs of Living With a Dachshund
Once Upon a Friendship – Anthology
Winning BIG – a little love story for all ages
Holiday Hopes
The Winning Tickets (2023)

PRAISE FOR JUDITH KEIM'S NOVELS

THE BEACH HOUSE HOTEL SERIES

"Love the characters in this series. This series was my first introduction to Judith Keim. She is now one of my favorites. Looking forward to reading more of her books."

BREAKFAST AT THE BEACH HOUSE HOTEL is an easy, delightful read that offers romance, family relationships, and strong women learning to be stronger. Real life situations filter through the pages. Enjoy!"

LUNCH AT THE BEACH HOUSE HOTEL – "This series is such a joy to read. You feel you are actually living with them. Can't wait to read the latest one."

DINNER AT THE BEACH HOUSE HOTEL – "A Terrific Read! As usual, Judith Keim did it again. Enjoyed immensely. Continue writing such pleasantly reading books for all of us readers."

CHRISTMAS AT THE BEACH HOUSE HOTEL – "Not Just Another Christmas Novel. This is book number four in the series and my introduction to Judith Keim's writing. I wasn't disappointed. The characters are dimensional and engaging. The plot is well crafted and advances at a pleasing pace. The Florida location is interesting and warming. It was a delight to read a romance novel with mature female protagonists. Ann and Rhoda have life experiences that enrich the story. It's a clever book about friends and extended family. Buy copies for your book group pals and enjoy this seasonal read."

MARGARITAS AT THE BEACH HOUSE HOTEL – "What

a wonderful series. I absolutely loved this book and can't wait for the next book to come out. There was even suspense in it. Thanks Judith for the great stories."

"Overall, Margaritas at the Beach House Hotel is another wonderful addition to the series. Judith Keim takes the reader on a journey told through the voices of these amazing characters we have all come to love through the years! I truly cannot stress enough how good this book is, and I hope you enjoy it as much as I have!"

THE HARTWELL WOMEN SERIES:

"This was an EXCELLENT series. When I discovered Judith Keim, I read all of her books back to back. I thoroughly enjoyed the women Keim has written about. They are believable and you want to just jump into their lives and be their friends! I can't wait for any upcoming books!"

"I fell into Judith Keim's Hartwell Women series and have read & enjoyed all of her books in every series. Each centers around a strong & interesting woman character and their family interaction. Good reads that leave you wanting more."

THE FAT FRIDAYS GROUP :

"Excellent story line for each character, and an insightful representation of situations which deal with some of the contemporary issues women are faced with today."

"I love this author's books. Her characters and their lives are realistic. The power of women's friendships is a common and beautiful theme that is threaded throughout this story."

THE SALTY KEY INN SERIES

FINDING ME – "I thoroughly enjoyed the first book in this series and cannot wait for the others! The characters are *endearing with the same struggles we all encounter. The setting makes me feel like I am a guest at The Salty Key Inn...relaxed, happy & light-hearted! The men are yummy and the women strong. You can't get better than that! Happy Reading!"*

FINDING MY WAY- "Loved the family dynamics as well as uncertain emotions of dating and falling in love. Appreciated the morals and strength of parenting throughout. Just couldn't put this book down."

FINDING LOVE – "I waited for this book because the first two was such good reads. This one didn't disappoint.... Judith Keim always puts substance into her books. This book was no different, I learned about PTSD, accepting oneself, there is always going to be problems but stick it out and make it work. Just the way life is. In some ways a lot like my life. Judith is right, it needs another book and I will definitely be reading it. Hope you choose to read this series, you will get so much out of it."

FINDING FAMILY – "Completing this series is like eating the last chip. Love Judith's writing, and her female characters are always smart, strong, vulnerable to life and love experiences."

"This was a refreshing book. Bringing the heart and soul of the family to us."

THE CHANDLER HILL INN SERIES

GOING HOME – "I absolutely could not put this book down. Started at night and read late into the middle of the night. As a child of the '60s, the Vietnam war was front and center so this resonated with me. All the characters in the book were so well developed that the reader felt like they were friends of the family."

"I was completely immersed in this book, with the beautiful descriptive writing, and the authors' way of bringing her characters to life. I felt like I was right inside her story."

COMING HOME – "Coming Home is a winner. The characters are well-developed, nuanced and likable. Enjoyed the vineyard setting, learning about wine growing and seeing the challenges Cami faces in running and growing a business. I look forward to the next book in this series!"

"Coming Home was such a wonderful story. The author has a gift for getting the reader right to the heart of things."

HOME AT LAST – "In this wonderful conclusion, to a heartfelt and emotional trilogy set in Oregon's stunning wine country, Judith Keim has tied up the Chandler Hill series with the perfect bow."

"Overall, this is truly a wonderful addition to the Chandler Hill Inn series. Judith Keim definitely knows how to perfectly weave together a beautiful and heartfelt story."

"The storyline has some beautiful scenes along with family drama. Judith Keim has created characters with interactions that are believable and some of the subjects the story deals with are poignant."

SEASHELL COTTAGE BOOKS

A CHRISTMAS STAR – "Love, laughter, sadness, great food, and hope for the future, all in one book. It doesn't get any better than this stunning read."

"A Christmas Star is a heartwarming Christmas story featuring endearing characters. So many Christmas books are set in snowbound places...it was a nice change to read a Christmas story that takes place on a warm sandy beach!" Susan Peterson

CHANGE OF HEART – "*CHANGE OF HEART is the summer read we've all been waiting for. Judith Keim is a master at creating fascinating characters that are simply irresistible. Her stories leave you with a big smile on your face and a heart bursting with love.*"

Kellie Coates Gilbert, author of the popular Sun Valley Series

A SUMMER OF SURPRISES – "*The story is filled with a roller coaster of emotions and self-discovery. Finding love again and rebuilding family relationships.*"

"*Ms. Keim uses this book as an amazing platform to show that with hard emotional work, belief in yourself and love, the scars of abuse can be conquered. It in no way preaches, it's a lovely story with a happy ending.*"

"*The character development was excellent. I felt I knew these people my whole life. The story development was very well thought out I was drawn [in] from the beginning.*"

THE DESERT SAGE INN SERIES:

THE DESERT FLOWERS – ROSE – "*The Desert Flowers - Rose, is the first book in the new series by Judith Keim. I always look forward to new books by Judith Keim, and this one is definitely a wonderful way to begin The Desert Sage Inn Series!*"

"*In this first of a series, we see each woman come into her own and view new beginnings even as they must take this tearful journey as they slowly lose a dear friend. This is a very well written book with well-developed and likable main characters. It was interesting and enlightening as the first portion of this saga unfolded. I very much enjoyed this book and I do recommend it*"

"*Judith Keim is one of those authors that you can always depend on to give you a great story with fantastic* characters. I'm excited to know that she is writing a new series and after reading book 1 in the series, I can't wait to read the rest of the books."!

THE DESERT FLOWERS – LILY – "The second book in the Desert Flowers series is just as wonderful as the first. Judith Keim is a brilliant storyteller. Her characters are truly lovely and people that you want to be friends with as soon as you start reading. Judith Keim is not afraid to weave real life conflict and loss into her stories. I loved reading Lily's story and can't wait for Willow's!

"The Desert Flowers-Lily is the second book in The Desert Sage Inn Series by author Judith Keim. When I read the first book in the series, The Desert Flowers-Rose, I knew this series would exceed all of my expectations and then some. Judith Keim is an amazing author, and this series is a testament to her writing skills and her ability to completely draw a reader into the world of her characters."

THE DESERT FLOWERS – WILLOW – "The feelings of love, joy, happiness, friendship, family and the pain of loss are deeply felt by Willow Sanchez and her two cohorts Rose and Lily. The Desert Flowers met because of their deep feelings for Alec Thurston, a man who touched their lives in different ways.

Once again, Judith Keim has written the story of a strong, competent, confident and independent woman. Willow, like Rose and Lily can handle tough situations. All the characters are written so that the reader gets to know them but not all the characters will give the reader warm and fuzzy feelings.

The story is well written and from the start you will be pulled in. There is enough backstory that a reader can start here but I assure you, you'll want to learn more. There is an ocean of emotions that will make you smile, cringe, tear up *or outright cry. I loved this book as I loved books one and two. I am thrilled that the Desert Flowers story will continue. I highly recommend this book to anyone who enjoys books with strong women."*

Coffee at
The Beach House Hotel

The Beach House Hotel Series
Book 7

Judith Keim

Wild Quail Publishing

Coffee at The Beach House Hotel is a work of fiction. Names, characters, places, public or private institutions, corporations, towns, and incidents are the product of the author's imagination or are used fictitiously. Any resemblance to actual events, locales, or persons, living or dead, is coincidental.

No part of *Coffee at The Beach House Hotel* may be reproduced or transmitted in any form or by any electronic or mechanical means, including information storage and retrieval systems, without permission in writing from the author, except by a reviewer who may quote brief passages in a review. This book may not be resold or uploaded for distribution to others. For permissions contact the author directly via electronic mail:

wildquail.pub@gmail.com

www.judithkeim.com

Published in the United States of America by:

Wild Quail Publishing
PO Box 171332
Boise, ID 83717-1332

ISBN# 978-1-959529-21-7

DEDICATION

This book is dedicated to you, my faithful readers, who love Ann and Rhonda as much as I do.

CHAPTER ONE

O n a beautiful spring morning along the Gulf Coast of Florida, with a soft breeze swaying the fronds of the nearby palm trees, I stood on the steps of The Beach House Hotel with my business partner, Rhonda Grayson. Greeting guests personally as much as possible was something we'd done together from the beginning.

Rhonda turned to me as we waited for the limousine to arrive with Bobby "Bugs" Bailey. Her dark eyes flashed as bright as the diamonds she wore in her ears, around her neck, and at her wrist. "I'm tellin' ya, Annie, that kid better not be the brat he's been made out to be. Famous football player or not, I'm not about to put up with any B.S. from him. I'm exhausted caring for my two younger kids and helping Angela with her three littles."

"You don't have to make excuses to me," I said. "With Robbie becoming more and more independent and having to help Liz with the triplets, I'm just about out of goodwill toward any misbehaved guest. The hotel business is tough enough without dealing with that."

"We never should've helped Amelia Swanson out a couple of times. She doesn't know when to stop asking for more help," said Rhonda. "Now, we're doing this for an NFL football coach who's a friend of hers. Gawd! I should've had that second cup of coffee."

"You must admit, it's quite an honor for the Vice President of the United States to trust us with difficult cases. If she didn't feel comfortable with The Beach House Hotel and how we run it, she wouldn't ask," I said, trying to make Rhonda feel better. But I knew she was as tired and irritable as I was, especially when we'd just found out that Brock Goodwin, our old nemesis, had emerged from past financial problems and was a newly appointed building inspector for the county.

A white limo entered the hotel property, passed by the wrought iron gates, and rolled to a stop in front of us.

"Here goes," I said. "Let's give the guy a chance to prove he isn't all bad." I'd been as exasperated as Rhonda by Bobby Bailey's bad behavior as reported in the press and thought it was a shame that young, talented sports figures were paid so much money. A little humility went a long way with me.

The driver exited the limo, hurried around the car, and opened the passenger door.

A hulk of a young man wearing a tank top and blue jeans emerged from the car and stared at us. His hands sat on his hips defiantly, and tattoos covered his muscular arms.

I could feel Rhonda tense beside me and spoke softly to her. "Easy. Let's start off with positive thoughts."

"I dunno. Maybe I should've had a third cup of coffee. Just looking at how he's staring at us with a big smirk, I want to wring his fucking neck."

Rhonda and I walked down the steps to greet him.

"Welcome to The Beach House Hotel," I said, forcing an upbeat tone to my voice.

"Yeah, yeah. I really had no choice, but I get it." He turned his baseball cap around to cover his face partially. "Where am I staying? Someone mentioned a special house."

"You'll be in one of our regular guest rooms on the second floor," I said, pleased Rhonda had refused to let him stay at the private house on the property.

"Okay." He turned to the limo driver. "My bags go inside."

I held up my hand to the driver to stop him. "Mr. Bailey can take his bags inside himself. But thanks."

Bobby looked surprised but picked up his two suitcases and headed for the door.

I paid the driver and followed Rhonda up the stairs. In her bright-green caftan and with her dyed blond hair, Rhonda was like a tropical bird while I, in my usual pastel colors, seemed pale in comparison. Of course, it had always been that way. At our first meeting, Rhonda even told me not to be so beige. After all these years of working together and becoming best friends, we were no more alike than we'd been then. Maybe that's why it worked so well between us.

When we went inside, Bernhard "Bernie" Bruner, our hotel general manager, was in the lobby about to greet Bobby when another guest interrupted him.

I approached the front desk with Bobby. "This is Mr. Bailey. Put him in Room 210 with no checkout time. That's to be determined."

The young clerk recognized Bobby and kept glancing at him as he typed on the computer.

I held out my hand for the room key and then gave it to Bobby. "This will allow you to use the facilities at the hotel as well as give you access to your room."

Bernie came over to us. "Ah, Mr. Bailey. Welcome to the hotel. I understand you will be working for us for the foreseeable future."

"Naw, I'm here to relax, have a good time," said Bobby taking off his baseball cap and smoothing back his long, brown locks of hair.

"Didn't your agent make it clear to you that you'd be working in the kitchen here?" asked Bernie, his eyes raised in surprise. "It's all been arranged."

"I can't work here. I need to rest to prepare for the next football season," Bobby said dismissively.

Bernie, Rhonda, and I exchanged glances.

"Guess you'd better talk to your agent," said Rhonda, pulling Bobby aside and lowering her voice. "There's no way you're simply staying here as a guest. We'll wait right here with you while you call him."

Bobby's shoulders drooped. "Shit. I thought he was kidding. What kind of trick is this?"

"I believe your coach insisted you needed to do something to improve your attitude," I said. "If you don't want to cooperate, we can call a taxi for you."

"This is effing B.S. I don't need any job here at the hotel," scoffed Bobby.

"If you'd rather work on landscaping, Manny can use some help," said Rhonda. "In fact, maybe that's where you should start. Then you'll appreciate working inside."

"Good idea," said Bernie. "I'll tell Jean-Luc to hold off on the kitchen training for a week or so. I'll explain the change to your agent and others," he told Bobby, whose face had turned white and then red again.

"Thanks, Bernie, for taking care of this," I said, taking hold of Rhonda's elbow and forcing her to come with me. She looked as if she was about to explode.

When we got inside our office, Rhonda whipped around and faced me. "That little prick! Too good to work? He'd better wake up and smell the coffee because an opportunity like this is saving his ass."

"I agree. Let's see what the next few days bring. It's going to be interesting, to say the least. He's in, or he's out." I didn't blame Rhonda for being angry. I knew she'd grown up in a tough neighborhood in New Jersey with hardworking parents, and though she was a multi-millionaire thanks to winning the Florida Lottery, she was a hard worker who respected that in others.

Rhonda plopped down in her desk chair with a sigh. "Let's ask Bernie to handle Bobby Bailey. After babysitting for Angela's kids last night, I couldn't get to sleep for the longest time. Now I'm pooped."

"How's Bella doing?" I asked. Isabella Ann Smythe was born soon after Liz's triplets and was a doll in every aspect but one. She was a light sleeper. Living with an active big brother and a noisy big sister often meant Bella was easily awakened. Then she became a cranky handful.

"She's doing better about chilling out. But I'm sure Bella will be like my Willow, never wanting to miss anything. But Evan and Sally Kate adore their baby sister. We all do. She turned out to be a sweet surprise."

"I hope Bella and the triplets become real friends one day." Liz's triplets— Olivia, Noah, and Emma, were now eight months old and crawling everywhere.

"Liz and Chad seem to handle the three of them very calmly. I don't know how they do it," said Rhonda.

"They have plenty of help during the day. The challenge has been nighttime. But, thank heavens, the babies are sleeping through the night, and Liz and Chad now have some privacy. And you know how much Liz wanted to be a mother. She's determined to prove to herself and everyone else that she's a good one."

"Funny, isn't it? We both wanted more than one child ourselves and couldn't, and now our girls are having so many." Rhonda shook her head. "It helps that they married good men."

"Yes," I said, my thoughts flying back to Robert, my ex. He'd never wanted to be involved with Liz's upbringing. He was too busy running the company I'd created, the company he claimed as his idea. I let out a sigh and pushed away bad memories. I was now married to Vaughn Sanders, a good man, a soap opera and movie star adored by all. He was a wonderful father to Robbie and Liz, and he loved "the Ts," as we sometimes called Liz's triplets.

"Will, bless his heart, dotes on our Drew and Willow, but finds the grandchildren a little overwhelming. But who could blame him? It's chaos at Angela's house." Rhonda's smile disappeared and morphed into a frown. "But getting back to our situation, do you think we're doing the right thing by forcing Bobby to work here? Of course, it was his coach's idea, but still, he's clearly a brat ...."

"After seeing his behavior so far, I think it'll be good for him to stay with us. And now that we've agreed to do it, we have our reputation and that of the hotel to uphold." I got to my feet. "Let's get that second cup of coffee."

"And one of Consuela's sweet rolls," said Rhonda, scrambling out of the chair, sounding more upbeat.

In the kitchen, Consuela greeted us. "Good morning. I hear we have a new staff member. Jean-Luc is grumbling about it already. And now, Manny has to deal with him."

"It'll be good for Bobby to work with Manny," I hugged her. Consuela and her husband, Manny, had worked for Rhonda before converting the seaside estate into an upscale hotel and were more like family than staff members. I adored them both, thinking of them as the parents I wished I'd had.

"He's a task master," agreed Consuela, automatically handing each of us a sweet roll on a plate. "Enjoy."

"You sure know how to make my mornings better," said Rhonda, throwing an arm around Consuela and squeezing her affectionately.

"For you, anything," said Consuela beaming at Rhonda. "How are all the babies?"

"Good," said Rhonda. "I was just telling Annie that Bella is learning to chill a bit."

"Time will take care of things," said Consuela. "She'll outgrow this stage."

"I hope so," said Rhonda, stifling a yawn.

I handed her a large mug of coffee. "Remember, we've got a meeting with Lorraine Grace this morning." Lorraine owned Wedding Perfection and worked for us, handling the many weddings held at the hotel each year.

Rhonda checked her watch. "We have time for a walk on the beach before meeting her. So let's do it."

We finished our sweet rolls and coffee and headed outdoors. Walks on the beach were a good way to relax and have private conversations. We did some of our best business strategizing there.

I took off my sandals and stepped onto the beach. Wiggling my toes in the sand, I paused to gaze at The Beach House Hotel. Like a pink flamingo sprawled on the sand, the hotel was a lovely landmark for all to enjoy. Rhonda bought the abused property after winning the lottery and brought it to life with a lot of money and care. Now, as a small upscale hotel for those seeking excellent food and privacy, it was a true gem.

Rhonda placed a hand on my shoulder and grinned at me. "Who'd a thunk it, huh? The two of us running a hotel, doing favors for the vice-president of the U.S., and hosting VIPs all the time."

"Your offer to go into business with you saved my life after Robert dumped me," I said with emotion.

"I couldn't run the place without you. It's a true partnership," Rhonda said. "But, Annie, I sometimes wonder how long we can keep it going before our daughters can take over for us. They've got their hands full with their families."

"If we need to hire more help before they can come into the business, we'll do it," I said. "I have no intention of selling the hotel again."

"Neither do I," said Rhonda. "Aubrey Lowell from the Sapphire Resort Collection almost ruined it. Good thing he's gone after the failure of his own hotel."

"But one of his partners isn't gone. So brace yourself; he's here now," I said, knowing we couldn't escape.

Brock Goodwin strolled on the beach toward us. Wearing swim trunks, he stood tall and handsome despite his gray hair turning white at the temples. To several single, older women in the neighborhood, he was the perfect person to add to dinner parties. I shuddered to think of it. I'd always remember how he'd treated me when I first came to Florida and had foolishly dated him. He wasn't the gentleman he wanted others to believe he was.

"Well, well," said Brock reaching us. "If it isn't the two biggest troublemakers in the neighborhood."

"Good morning, Brock," I said, holding Rhonda's arm to force her to stay with me.

"Who appointed you building inspector? That's what I want to know. How much did you have to pay them?" Rhonda exclaimed, making me wish I'd let her go on her way.

Brock squared his shoulders and glared at Rhonda. "The county is lucky to have me. They know how perfect I am for the job after working with contractors on The Sand Castle Hotel."

"The hotel that failed?" said Rhonda shaking her head.

"That wasn't my fault," said Brock. "I tried to tell Aubrey Lowell how to run it, but he wouldn't listen."

"Even with all your hotel experience?" Rhonda said.

I willed Rhonda not to say anything more. Like a spoiled child, Brock would only strike back at us in whatever way he could. As the former president of the neighborhood association, he'd been a thorn in our sides from the beginning. In his new position, he could be even more hurtful.

"We've got to be on our way," I said, giving him a quick wave. "The hotel is busy as usual."

"What's this about a football star being there?" Brock said.

"You know we can't talk about our guests," I said. Discretion and privacy were important components of the success of the hotel.

"I'll drop in at the bar and see what I can find out," said Brock giving me a triumphant look. "You can't keep me out."

"We'll see about that," said Rhonda. "Why aren't you on the job inspecting houses?"

"It's my day off," said Brock. "Remember, I can check hotels and business properties too. *Ciao.*" He tipped his hat and went on his way.

"What a prick," grumbled Rhonda. "Why would he have a day off in the middle of the week?"

"I bet his position is part-time. We'll have to ask Dorothy to check up on him." Dorothy Stern was an older woman who'd worked and fought hard for us from our first days. She was as short as Brock was tall and wore thick glasses that made her eyes look huge. But when it came to a battle of words with Brock, she usually came out the winner. We adored her.

"We can't let Brock interfere with our plans to build another small cottage on the property," said Rhonda.

"I know. I've worked the numbers, and it's a wise decision to go ahead with it," I said. The private house that used to be my home was a special location for VIPs and was used almost constantly. Tina Marks, a movie star we'd helped in the past and who was now part of what I called The Beach House family, was scheduled to arrive soon with her two children for an extended stay there.

"I can't wait to see Tina," said Rhonda. "Remember how she was sent to the hotel to hide while losing weight for her next movie?"

"She was tough to handle, but it ended well," I said. "That's why Amelia got the idea to have her own sister stay with us."

Rhonda faced me. "The hotel has become much more than simply a place to stay. Don't you sometimes wonder how we've pulled it off being hotel owners?"

"Truthfully, I have," I said. "But neither of us ever wanted to fail. Even when people told us they didn't think we could make it."

"Success is something we have to prove every day—good days, bad days, hard days, and easy ones," said Rhonda.

"Let's make this an easy day," I said. I walked down to the water's edge, where a variety of shore birds hurried along the water's edge, leaving behind small footprints in the sand.

Above us, seagulls and terns circled and screeched greetings. The water lapped the shore soothingly, kissing the sand and moving away as it had done for all time. This scene never failed to calm me.

"We'll check to make sure Bobby is working with Manny and then leave it up to Manny to handle him," said Rhonda. "What are we talking to Lorraine about?"

"We have an important wedding coming up. The governor's daughter is getting married here at the end of this week. We haven't talked about it much because it's been on the books for several months. But we need to make sure Lorraine has everything in order. The groom's father is a national television newsman, and we can't have anything go wrong."

"Right," said Rhonda. "Honestly, I'd forgotten all about it. I'd better have another cup of coffee."

I looped my arm around Rhonda's, and after putting shoes back on, we walked up onto the lawn to find Manny. He was the person Rhonda used to call her Manny around the house. Married to Consuela, he was a proud grandfather now and still a hard worker who would, I hoped, erase some of Bobby's sense of entitlement.

CHAPTER TWO

We found Manny and Bobby in the side yard and garden, which was a perfect place for weddings. Governor Daniel Horne and his wife Carlotta doted on their only daughter, Carolina, and they'd chosen to have her wedding in the garden. "Hey, Manny!" said Rhonda as we approached him. "How's the football star doing?"

Manny's face, half-hidden under his straw hat, showed his disgust. "He has a lot to learn. And I don't mean just about gardening."

Bobby meandered over to them from a corner of the garden. "Just to let you know, I've put a call into my agent. I'm not going to be anyone's gardener."

"What don't you get?" I asked, frustrated by his attitude. "You call yourself a football player, but basically, you're off the team unless you change or if they decide to put you back on it."

"As I said to Annie earlier, you'd better wake up and smell the coffee here at The Beach House Hotel. It may be your last chance to save yourself," said Rhonda. "You couldn't have a better teacher than Manny. We consider him a member of the family. No backtalk to him, or you can trot off home. Got it?"

"I don't know what your story is," I said. "But it would seem a waste to have you lose your job because you're too lazy to keep it. By the way, you might need something different to wear than a baseball cap. And be sure to put on a lot of sunscreen lotion." I knew I sounded like a mother, but I couldn't help it. Bobby seemed such a child. Right now, he looked as if he wanted to cry.

We left Manny and Bobby and headed indoors to meet Lorraine. A woman in her late fifties, she'd remained single for three years after her husband died. She was having too much fun, mostly with girlfriends and some dating, not because she couldn't get over her husband's death. Attractive, Lorraine dyed her hair a light brown with blond highlights and had a slim enough figure to wear younger-style clothes with grace. Her kindness made those working for her comfortable as she ordered them around. I'd always liked her and respected her business sense.

"Good thing Lorraine is on this wedding," said Rhonda. "It was a lucky day when she agreed to work for us."

"We have been lucky that way, haven't we?" I said, thinking of the staff members who'd stayed with us through the years. "She's perfect for what she does. I hope she never stops doing it."

"Me, too. Our wedding business has grown. Remember the royal wedding we were supposed to have at the Beach House Hotel?" said Rhonda. "This wedding and that of Amelia's sister are the closest we're likely to come to one."

"Oh, I don't know. I like to think of every wedding here as royal," I said, feeling romantic after welcoming Vaughn home from New York last night. He'd begun shooting some commercials and was very good at it. Hopefully, he'd start a movie soon. That's what he really loved to do.

"You're sweet, Annie. That's why we counter-balance each other," said Rhonda. "I can't help speaking my mind."

"You're a wonderful person," I said, quickly defending her. Beneath all her bravado, Rhonda was a sensitive woman who'd been teased about her size as a teenager. Today and at our ages in the mid-forties, women were kinder to one another.

"Before we meet with Lorraine, I have to tell you about a great idea I had last night," said Rhonda, giving me one of her impish grins that spelled trouble. "It came to me in a dream."

"Uh, oh. No matchmaking," I said. Rhonda thought she was terrific at putting people together.

Rhonda raised a hand. "Listen, Annie. You know I'm right on this. Lorraine has been alone too long. I've got the perfect man for her. Are you ready?"

"I guess. Who's the poor unsuspecting guy?" I knew Rhonda wouldn't give up until I allowed her to tell me about him.

"Arthur Smythe," Rhonda said triumphantly. "What do you think?"

I almost stumbled as we went into the back door of the hotel. I turned to face her. "You're trying to fix-up Angela's father-in-law?"

"It's been almost a year since Katherine died, and I know he's lonely. He's calling the kids all the time, and he will be coming to Florida soon. Perfect timing."

I shook my head. "What would Reggie think about it?"

Rhonda's face fell. "I'm not sure. Katherine and Lorraine are nothing alike. And no matter how terrible she was to me at first, Katherine and I became friends. Thinking about it, I think she would approve."

I felt my eyebrows shoot upwards. "You do?"

Rhonda shuffled her feet. "Well, maybe not. But I think it would work. Arthur isn't the type of man to forget the mother of his child, is he?"

I shrugged. "I can't answer that. But, Rhonda, I want you to know I want no part of this new idea of yours. It could spell trouble in all sorts of ways. And if it worked, then Arthur would be living here in Sabal. Do you want that?"

Her face formed a frown. "I'm not sure. Of course, I didn't

want Katherine here to begin with. But in the end, it worked out."

"Yes, because she's not here to interfere with your time with the family," I said.

"But now I wish she was," said Rhonda. "She'd be very happy with Bella. And you know how she felt about Sally Kate and Evan."

"True, but once again, I'm telling you I'm not getting involved in any matchmaking scheme of yours," I said with a determination I felt to my toes. "Okay, but I want you to take a careful look at Lorraine and tell me what you think," said Rhonda.

"No," I said, understanding how easily I could get sucked into this idea.

We entered the small meeting room where we were to meet Lorraine. As we walked inside, I couldn't help resting my gaze on Lorraine.

Her blue eyes lit at the sight of us. "Good morning! I'm glad we have this time to review the final arrangements for the Horne wedding. And then, perhaps, we can talk briefly about the small private wedding during the following week."

"Sounds like a plan," I said, pleased she was so organized.

"How's life?" Rhonda said to Lorraine, giving her a big grin. "Still having fun with your girlfriends? The dating scene?"

Lorraine returned Rhonda's smile. "There's a lot to do in Sabal, but it's nice to have some quiet time too. Thanks for thinking of me."

Rhonda shot me a look of satisfaction, which I chose to ignore.

"Let's talk about the wedding," I said. "We just saw Manny out in the garden. It looks spectacular. As long as the weather holds, it's going to be a gorgeous setting."

"Any weather reports?" Rhonda asked Lorraine.

"So far, I think we're in luck. No bad storms are predicted for the next seven days. Hopefully, that will stay the same," said Lorraine.

"Great. Let's go over the menu and the schedule for the wedding," I said. The timing of any wedding dinner was crucial. Especially because Jean-Luc, like many other chefs, wanted meals to come out piping hot or nice and chilled.

"Annette will be coordinating shifting people between the cocktail reception and the sit-down dinner," said Lorraine.

Annette, Bernie's wife, was an elegant hostess and had turned out to be a rare find for us. She'd become an integral part of the team.

"No problems with the meal selection?" I asked.

Lorraine shook her head. "Everything's in order. And when wedding guests arrive at the hotel, they'll be given a schedule of events. The morning of the wedding, they'll be directed to the garden for the ceremony and then brought back inside the hotel for the reception and luncheon. It should go smoothly."

"That's great. I'll leave it in your hands," I said. "If anything comes up, please let me know. Rhonda and I will be out of the office for the rest of the day, but you can always call us. And, of course, Bernie is on the property to handle the usual things."

"Okay, thanks for your time," said Lorraine getting to her feet as Rhonda and I prepared to leave.

On the way out of the office, Rhonda turned to me. "Are you headed to Liz's house?"

"Yes. I thought I'd stop by on my way home. Vaughn's in town, so I want to stay just long enough to see the babies and make sure Liz is set for tonight with a babysitter. Elena thought she could stay for the evening, but if she can't, I'll step in."

"Okay if I come with you? I *am* Noah's godmother."

I laughed. "Sure. You know how much Liz and the kids love to see you." Rhonda had been disappointed she wasn't asked to be godmother to all three of the triplets but understood that others needed to be included too.

"I'll stop by and then go on to Angela's house," said Rhonda. Angela, Reggie, and their three kids lived in the same neighborhood, which made it easy for Angela and Liz to see one another and continue their close relationship.

I pulled up to Liz's house and took a moment to study it. The one-story, four-bedroom home was a find because the interior had needed a lot of work and refreshing. Chad was handy, and before the birth of the triplets, he'd spent time repairing, painting, adding new features, and converting the house into something special. When the Ts were older, Liz and Chad would put in a swimming pool, but they didn't want to risk having one when the kids were this young. Besides, they had access to the neighborhood pool. In the meantime, the triplets would have a sizeable fenced-in backyard to play in.

Rhonda and I went up to the front door together. From inside came the sound of babies crying. Without waiting for someone to come to the door, I opened it and walked inside.

Elena, the young woman who was a part-time babysitter to Robbie, worked at Liz's house whenever I didn't need her, giving her a lucrative full-time job. Her sister, Rita, had the same situation with Rhonda and Angela.

In the kitchen, Elena was standing in front of three highchairs in each of which a baby fussed and cried.

At the sight of Rhonda and me, the babies stopped howling for a moment and then began again.

I hurried forward. "What's going on? How can I help?"

Elena gave me a look of relief. "I need to give them more

food. I gave them some Cheerios while I tried to fix each of them a plate of food. One cried, then the other two joined in."

"Where's Liz?" I asked.

"She's trying to take a shower and wash her hair," said Elena, handing a plate of food to Rhonda and me. "Here."

The plate held applesauce, small cubes of cheese and a dab of cottage cheese.

Feeding all three had been a real problem earlier. Now the babies could pick up some things with their fingers which kept them occupied while the other two were being fed other things. When people weren't there to help her, Liz had devised a seating arrangement with pillows on the couch where a baby sat with a bottle on either side of her while she held one. But I and friends and neighbors came on a rotating basis to step in and help. The three babies settled down with food in front of them and more being fed directly. They each had two adorable lower front teeth, which I could see as they smiled, as they were doing now as Rhonda made faces for them.

A few minutes later, Liz stumbled into the kitchen wrapped in a bath towel. Her blond hair hung wet to her shoulders. There were gray smudges of fatigue under her blue eyes. "Thanks for being here, Mom and Rhonda. I just wanted a shower." Tears seemed to surprise her. She swiped at them. "Sorry. It must seem stupid to you, but all I wanted was just a couple of minutes to myself. Ya know?"

I went over to her and gave her a big hug. "Honey, it's all right. Everything has been taken care of. See?"

The babies all lifted their arms to Liz, wanting to be held. "Thanks for helping," she said and hurried out of the kitchen, making all three babies cry again.

I picked up Emma; Rhonda took hold of Noah, and Elena lifted Olivia in her arms, bringing a peaceful silence to the room.

"Let's put the kids in the playroom," said Elena. "Then, if you two will stay with them, I'll clean up the kitchen."

Rhonda and I followed Elena to the playroom. Originally a den, the room was now converted to a wonderland of age-appropriate toys. The soft carpet on the floor meant that any falls were met with little hurt. A chair and a table with no sharp corners were the only pieces of furniture in the room. A television was mounted on the wall, and a speaker near it provided music through the blue tooth system Chad had set up for the house.

I stood with Rhonda outside the gated entrance watching the babies with interest. Emma seemed to be the leader of the three, but each had a personality of his or her own. It was cute to see them interact from time to time.

As we watched them play, Rhonda said, "Three at the same age is a lot to juggle. At least Angela has Evan to help her. At almost five, he can fetch things for her and entertain Sally Kate for a short while."

"Liz is going to be busy when the Ts all begin to walk. It's difficult enough now, but that will be even more so."

"Yeah, it's a good thing we can pay for help for them. Reggie makes a good living working for Will, but to get good full-time help, you have to do more than pay an hourly wage."

"Chad's doing a good job of running his own computer consulting company, but he's investing all he can into growing it. So I'm more than happy to take care of the babysitting expenses for them," I said, meaning it.

"It's good that we have a babysitting payback program for our hotel staff. We couldn't get the kind of help we have without it. Think of the single mothers working in the housekeeping department," said Rhonda.

"I love the fact of women helping women," I said. "And as we always say, staff is like family."

"Amen," said Rhonda. "I'll see you later. I'm going to check on Angela, and then while Drew and Willow are in preschool, I'm going to take a nap."

"Enjoy," I said. "I promised Vaughn I'd go sailing with him and Robbie later today."

I walked Rhonda to the front door and turned as Liz approached us.

She hugged me and smiled at Rhonda. "Thanks for stopping by. Two of the T-team will come and help give the babies their bottles so they can go down for a nap. Sorry to be emotional, but I'm exhausted."

I stepped back and gazed at her. "Liz, sweetie, it's okay to be tired, crabby, emotional, and not perfect. I know how much these babies mean to you, to all of us, but no mother is perfect. So, cry if you need to."

Rhonda winked at her. "Your mother's right, you know. Motherhood is the hardest job you'll ever have. That's why we still fuss over you girls. You're our babies."

Sniffing, Liz nodded. "Thanks. Chad and I are going out to dinner tonight. That'll give us some time alone."

"And remember, call me for help anytime," I said, giving her a hug. "Vaughn is home, so I'm going to go."

"Say hi to him and thanks again, you two," Liz said. A smile spread across her face. "Noah and the girls call me Mama. Isn't that adorable?"

Smiling at the switch in mood, I said, "Of course. They're my grandbabies."

I was still smiling when I left the house with Rhonda, but I turned to her outside. "Do you think Liz is okay? She does look exhausted."

"She's fine. She's young. Not like me when I had Drew and Willow. The good thing is that Liz knows there's help anytime she needs it. That's a huge blessing for any young mother."

"Right. She knows to call me if she needs me," I said, feeling better about seeing my daughter stressed out.

"Say hi to Vaughn for me," said Rhonda. "I'll talk to you later. I'm glad Lorraine is so competent. We don't have to worry about the Governor's family if she's in charge." A sly grin crossed Rhonda's face. "I will suggest Arthur come down to Florida for a few days. Maybe I can introduce them then."

"Now, Rhonda," I began ..." and ended up laughing with her.

CHAPTER THREE

My heart lifted as I drove into the driveway of the house I shared with Vaughn and Robbie. It was a home full of love and trust. With Vaughn's work as a well-known television and movie star, it was important to us that it remains that way.

Trudy, a black-and-tan, smooth-haired dachshund, barked and ran toward me. I leaned over to pet her. We'd adopted her from Bernie, who couldn't keep her at his condo. She was a fantastic addition to our family, especially because she and Robbie had been close friends from the beginning. As I stroked her head, I noticed the gray around her muzzle and realized she was getting old. I wondered if it was time to add a puppy to the family, some little imp to keep her young.

Trudy followed me into the silent house. I knew where to find my family on a sunny day like today. I stepped outside onto the lanai and gazed across the lawn to the dock where Vaughn's 34-ft. Pearson named *Zephyr* was tied up. Vaughn and Robbie loved working on the boat and sailing her. When I saw them together now, my heart filled with gratitude. Robbie, the child of my ex, Robert, and his young wife, Kandie, was a much-loved child we'd adopted when he was just two, following his parents' deaths. He was a happy boy who'd learned what living in a peaceful home was like.

Seeing me now, Robbie waved and ran toward me. He was eight now and full of energy, questions, and a love of all electronic games like every other boy his age. But he also loved being outside and playing sports.

"Hi, Mom! Dad said when you arrive, we can go sailing. He said we'd eat on the boat. Okay?"

"Sure. Sounds like fun. I already planned a picnic supper." I hugged him to me, grateful he still allowed me that privilege. His brown eyes sparkled below a shock of dark hair that covered part of his forehead. Sometimes, seeing an expression like Robert's cross Robbie's face was jarring, but I'd come to accept my ex was part of who he was.

I looked up as Vaughn approached. My heart raced at the sight of him. He was tall and trim with dark curls and chocolate brown eyes that his fans adored. But, more than that, he was a good man—kind, thoughtful, and loving.

"Hi, sweetheart." He swept me into his arms.

Robbie groaned, "Oh, no," as Vaughn lowered his lips to mine and gave me a kiss that made me wish it was bedtime already.

When Vaughn pulled away from me, he tousled Robbie's hair. "Someday, you'll find a woman as wonderful as your mom, and then you'll want to give her kisses too." Vaughn gave me an amused look and wrapped his arm around my waist. "Let's get ready for a sail. The wind is up a bit, and it should be great."

"It'll be nice to relax. But I have a feeling the next few days at the hotel will be hectic. We have the governor's daughter's wedding on the weekend, and in the meantime, we're 'babysitting' Bobby 'Bugs' Bailey."

"The football player? When did that happen?" Vaughn asked.

"It's another of Amelia Swanson's requests. This time for a friend, an NFL football coach who's a friend of hers. It's a challenge we felt obligated to take on for PR purposes and as a favor to Amelia."

"I've heard Bobby is a problem, but it's got to be difficult for a kid from an underprivileged background to suddenly have a lot of money, publicity, and adoration. No wonder he's messed up."

I nodded thoughtfully. Vaughn was right. Bobby might need more than a bit of humility. I'd have to look further into the situation.

Inside the house, we packed up a picnic, plenty of cold drinks, and a bottle of wine for Vaughn and me. It would be pleasant to drop the anchor in a quiet spot and share a meal on the water.

"Where's Trudy?" I asked and then looked at my feet, where she looked up at me with a hopeful look. She loved to eat.

"Time for a boat ride," I told her and went to get her life jacket. She'd fallen off the boat once, and though we were pleasantly surprised at how easily she swam, we didn't want anything to happen to her.

Vaughn carried the cooler and the canvas boat bag to the dock, and while Robbie put his life jacket on, we stowed the food inside the boat. Big enough to sleep four, the interior of the boat had a sizeable refrigerator which made it easy to keep things cold for longer trips.

"Get the bow line, Robbie," Vaughn said, "then jump aboard. Mom will get the stern line." He started the engine, and after he made sure Robbie was aboard, he signaled me.

I tossed the line on board and followed, landing in the cockpit as Vaughn headed out of the inlet where our house and dock were located. We'd go through the nearby pass and onto open water where we could hoist sail.

Sailing without the noise of the engine and hearing the hiss of the water as the bow sliced through the water never failed to relax me in a way nothing else could. The warm air, the sun, and even the raucous cries of seagulls above us blended to make the sights, sounds, and smells memorable. Vaughn and I looked at one another and grinned at our pleasure.

Robbie was turning into a good sailor, and as soon as Vaughn felt it was safe, Robbie took over the helm, checking to see that the sails were properly filled and we were heading in the right direction.

Vaughn had taught his own children, Ty and Nell, to sail too. His deceased wife hadn't loved sailing like I did, but she'd encouraged it for the three of them.

We sailed down the coast and back up toward Sabal. Outside the Sabal pass, we anchored the boat and bobbed gently in the water. While Vaughn and I had wine, Robbie sipped on flavored water.

I studied him sitting opposite me, caressing Trudy. "Trudy is beginning to show her age. So I thought it might be time to add a puppy to our house to keep Trudy company and help keep her young."

Robbie frowned. "Is Trudy going to die?"

"I hope not for a long time. But eventually, she will. She's in good health, though, and I suspect it won't be anytime soon." Robbie knew about death because of the death of his parents and the story of how he came to be ours.

"I'm gone so often that it's up to the two of you to decide," said Vaughn. "How do you feel about it, son?"

A wide grin spread across Robbie's face. "I like the idea. Another dachshund just like Trudy." He patted the dog's head. "Right, Trudy?"

Trudy barked, and though she didn't know exactly what Robbie had said, I felt she agreed with the decision. It used to be that Robbie spent a lot of time with her, but now, with all his activities away from the house and with my work and Vaughn's absence, Trudy was often alone.

"Can I pick out the puppy?" Robbie asked.

25

"Sure, but I want to be sure Trudy will be happy, too," I said. "I'll start searching for information this week." I had nothing against fostering or adopting, but I thought a dachshund puppy would do best in this case.

"Another baby to think of, huh?" teased Vaughn.

I laughed. "Thank goodness Liz doesn't have a dog to worry about. I'm sure she'll end up with one after the Ts are older, but that poor mom has her hands full." I told him about my visit that morning, and he gave me a sympathetic look.

"As Rhonda says, our two families have blossomed with Angela's and Liz's children. I admit that though I love them all and love to visit, I'm relieved I don't have the day-to-day care of them."

Sitting beside me, Vaughn leaned over and kissed me. "You're the most beautiful grandmother I know."

My heart warmed. Vaughn made it very clear how he felt about me. When we'd first met, I wasn't sure whether he was saying something from one of his shows or from him. Now, I knew I could trust him to speak from his heart.

I got up to serve us our dinner. I'd made a chicken salad with a lot of fresh pineapple and a gingery sauce. Soft dinner rolls and plenty of carrot and celery sticks accompanied it. Some of Consuela's cookies, previously frozen for such occasions, were for dessert.

Robbie gazed at the food, shrugged, and dug in. Being the only child at home, he'd learned to eat a lot of food other kids might turn down. But then, one of Consuela's cookies was an enticement to eat a good meal.

"How did your last commercial go?" I asked Vaughn as we ate.

"Good," he said. "Fortunately, I was in this one alone and didn't have to retake the scene more than a couple of times."

"Not like the days with Lily Dorio," I said, mentioning the

woman who'd caused us a lot of personal trouble in the past.

"I hear Lily has quit the business and is now going into the agenting end of things. I can't imagine she'll do well, but I don't think many acting jobs were coming her way." Vaughn shook his head. "I'm happy I don't have to worry about her anymore. I have enough problems as it is getting people to quit calling me the mayor from the soap. I want to expand into different kinds of roles."

"I understand," I said, "but you were beloved in that role. Do you want to play a villain?"

Vaughn grinned. "It might be a lot of fun. When Tina Marks comes for a stay, I hope the whole family will come. I want to talk to Nick about it." Nicholas Swain, Tina's husband, was a well-known film director.

"I'll be sure to set up a dinner party for him after he arrives," I said, pleased to think I could help. Though Vaughn was good about finding interesting projects to fill his time at home, he loved acting jobs.

After eating, we headed back. Dusk was near, and we wanted to be able to see clearly. The air had chilled, and we were all anxious to get home.

After getting Robbie in bed, Vaughn and I settled in the den. In the summer, no one used that room much, but, in the spring, like tonight, we could watch television here or read books. Tonight, Vaughn and I were content to sit on the couch reading with Trudy stretched out between us.

"Do you think Trudy is going to enjoy having a puppy?" Vaughn asked, petting the dog.

"She's very spoiled, but I think she'll like having a companion." I lifted her face and gazed into her eyes. "I suspect she'll be a good mother to any pup."

Trudy wagged her tail and barked.

"See?" I said, laughing. "That's twice she's barked about it."

"Guess that's it," said Vaughn grinning. "But let's make the puppy Robbie's project. At his age, Robbie should have a responsibility like that."

"Did Nell and Ty have dogs?" I asked.

"Yes, we had two. Black labs." Vaughn said. "Ellie loved dogs, and they loved her."

"It's very sweet that you have such fond memories of Ellie," I said wistfully. "I wish I felt the same way about Robert."

Vaughn reached over and took my hand. "We're making new, sweet memories. I feel very fortunate to have found you."

"It was a lucky day for me when the soap decided to film *The Sins of the Children* at The Beach House Hotel. Brock Goodwin tried to undermine us, but Rhonda and I persisted. Having the show here was the beginning of the best time of my life."

Vaughn grinned, and seeing it, an image of him smiling just like that on television flashed in my mind. That smile had made women all over the country swoon a bit. It used to bother me to share that image of him with others, but now I knew his smiles for me were special.

He rose and offered his hand.

Knowing what lay ahead, I took it. He was a most generous lover.

CHAPTER FOUR

The next morning, I awoke and snuggled up against Vaughn. As he'd proved to me earlier, he was in great shape for a man in his fifties. He turned over and faced me. "Hi, beautiful woman." He pressed his lips against mine, and my heart filled with gratitude for all we shared.

The bedroom door opened, and Robbie and Trudy jumped up onto the bed.

"Are we having pancakes?" Robbie asked.

"No reason we can't," I said, rising. "We have time before you go to school."

I slipped on a silk robe and walked into the kitchen, pleased to have breakfast with "my boys" before heading to the hotel.

I'd just served up the pancakes when my cell rang. *Liz.*

"Hi, Mom. Any chance you and Vaughn could come over? Elena will be unexpectedly late today, and I need help with the Ts."

"Sure, we'll come over as soon as we drop Robbie off at school."

"Thanks. It shouldn't be for too long," said Liz. "I really appreciate it."

"No problem. I understand, honey." Liz felt bad about asking for help, but I always tried to accommodate her.

Vaughn looked at me. "A 'T Help' run?"

"Yes, just for a short while," I said and turned as my cell rang again. *Rhonda.*

"Hi, Rhonda. What's up?"

"That snake, Brock Goodwin, is trying to involve himself in

the plans for the new house we're building on the hotel property. I got a call from Doug Friedrich, my friend on the planning board, who told me about it."

"But surely, he knows a building inspector's job doesn't involve any input on the planning board. So his job comes later."

"Brock doesn't care. He's just gearing up to make trouble for us. So I asked Doug to help us. If Brock continues to be a problem, I'm going to ask Mike Torson to take action." Mike was a very clever lawyer who helped us buy the hotel back.

"One step at a time with Brock. I'm stopping at Liz's for a while on my way to work. See you soon. We'll talk then." I ended the call and shook my head. It looked like we were right back to our usual routine of fighting with Brock. How was it he always survived one financial disaster after another?

"Bad news?" asked Vaughn. "I take it Brock is up to his old tricks."

"Oh, yes. But this time, Rhonda and I must find a way to end it. I'm not certain, but I believe our newly elected female mayor may be eager to side with us after winning a political race against Brock for the position." Rhonda and I had held private parties at the hotel in support of her candidacy, more than eager to do anything to prevent Brock from winning the election.

Still disgruntled by the phone call, I turned to Robbie. "Time to brush your teeth and get ready for school. Dad and I will drop you off."

"Okay. Are we going to get a puppy today?" Robbie gave me a hopeful look.

"Not today, honey. We have to find the one we want. And if the puppy is still a baby, it can't leave its mother until he's ready. So we'll work on this together, though it probably won't be today."

"You and I have a dinner date tonight with Darla and Meredith to discuss their video production company," said Vaughn. Darla Delaney had been a co-star on *The Sins of the Children* with Vaughn, and she and her wife were forming a production company to make videos for music stars.

"Right, I almost forgot. But remember, I'll be involved in a big wedding at the hotel this weekend. Even though we have good people doing most of the work, Rhonda and I have to be present. This is a big PR opportunity for us. A bridal magazine is doing a spread on the wedding."

A few minutes later, I left the house with Vaughn and Robbie, dropped Robbie off at school, and drove to Liz's house.

Liz greeted us at the door wearing pajama bottoms and a tank top and was holding two babies.

"Where's the little guy?" asked Vaughn, taking one of the girls from Liz's arms.

"He's crawling around the kitchen," said Liz, handing me the other girl and making a dash for the kitchen.

I glanced over at Vaughn smiling at Emma. He was such a natural dad.

Olivia placed a hand on my cheek. I took hold of it and kissed it, tasting some of what I thought was cereal. Then, chuckling to myself, I went into the kitchen to find Liz wiping Noah's hands.

"They're starting to get the idea of a spoon, but it's easier for them simply to grab some in their hands." Liz finished with Noah, kissed him, and reached for Olivia.

I handed Olivia to Liz and picked up Noah to give him a snuggle. He gave me a two-tooth grin and then wiggled to get down. Of the three of them, he was the most active this morning.

"Will you dress him?" Liz asked me.

I took Noah to the large room with three cribs in it. A dressing table sat against one wall with a mobile hanging above it. Liz had put out clothes for the babies, and I snatched an outfit and took off Noah's pajamas. He loved the freedom and began to kick like crazy. Gazing at that blond boy, my heart filled with love. He reminded me of Liz when she was that age. She'd been as active as he.

As soon as I finished changing and dressing Noah, Vaughn took over the space.

After all three children had been dressed, the kitchen cleaned up, and Liz had taken a shower, I checked my watch. It was mid-morning, and I was already tired.

Elena rushed into the house. "Sorry I'm late, but I had to handle some personal business. Troy is buying the spa in town, and I had to sign some papers." Troy Taylor had worked in the spa at the hotel when it had first opened and then had decided to open his own. This would be the second spa for him. Rhonda and I were happy for him and Elena—they were a cute, hardworking married couple.

"Thanks for coming as soon as you could," Liz said to Vaughn and me. "I have a doctor's appointment later this morning."

"Do you want us to stay?" I asked Elena.

She shook her head. "No, the babies should be napping then. But thanks. They're good little ones. Just busy."

I hugged her. "You're fabulous with them. How's night school going?"

Elena grinned. "Good. I'll be helping Troy more after I get certified as a massage therapist. Chad is setting up our Wi-Fi systems for free." She winked. "It pays to know the right people."

I laughed. Many of our staff members at the hotel had become part of our families in ways we'd never suspected.

I entered the office I shared with Rhonda at the hotel carrying a cup of coffee. I knew I'd need it. We had a meeting with the architect to go over the final plans for the small house we were building on the hotel property.

The new structure would be similar to the house we had, the place that had been mine when I joined Rhonda in the business. Originally a caretaker's cottage, we had transformed it into a modern home with a private swimming pool. VIPs often requested it and were willing to pay a high price for it. Adding one like it was a smart business decision.

The office was quiet. Wondering where Rhonda was, I took a sip of coffee, set down the cup, and went outside. Before I reached Manny's small office in the outbuilding, I heard Rhonda's voice.

"Well, I'm glad he's gone," Rhonda said as I approached the open door.

"Who's gone? What's going on?" I asked.

"Bobby up and quit," said Rhonda, a disgusted look on her face.

"Really? What happened?" I asked, seeing how upset Rhonda was.

"I told him he had to obey Manny, that Manny was the boss, and we didn't allow name-calling," said Rhonda. "The kid's got a filthy mouth and a nasty attitude. First, he called me an 'effin' bitch.' And then, when he called Manny something worse, I kicked him out of the office." Rhonda's voice quivered with outrage.

"I agree we can't have someone like that around here. But, Manny, I'm sorry," I said.

Manny placed his hands on his hips and shook his head. "I don't care if he's some football big shot. He's not working for me unless he agrees to change. I don't think Jean-Luc will want him in the kitchen either."

"Let me go talk to him. I assume he's back in his room packing."

"Yeah, I think you'll find him there."

I went into the hotel, trying to figure out what to say. Rhonda swore occasionally, but she didn't call anyone bad names to their faces. Not even Brock Goodwin. What she said privately was another matter. As angry and upset as she sometimes got, she chose to think of herself as a lady when dealing with others. The thought made me smile.

I knocked on Bobby's door.

"Go away," he called.

"It's Ann Sanders. I need to talk to you. I'm asking you to open the door."

A few minutes later, the door opened. "Yeah?"

"We need to talk," I said. "May I come in?"

He shrugged and stepped back.

I looked at him. His long, brown hair was dirty, and he had a shadow of whiskers on his face. I knew it was the style for that kind of man look, but his was scruffy and uneven. He'd tossed clothes on a chair and wore a bathing suit.

"Why are you dressed to swim? I thought you quit your job," I said. "You can't stay here without a job."

"I quit. Manny didn't like the work I was doing. So, eff it."

"I understand you called him a disrespectful name. Rhonda too. What's that all about?" I asked calmly, though I wanted to shake him.

"This whole thing is B.S., and I'm not taking part in it."

"So, how does your family like you playing football?" I asked, taking another approach.

He blinked in surprise. "They love it. You should see all the things I can buy for them. I bought my dad a truck."

"Ah, that must be a good feeling. So, they're proud of all your hard work on the football field?"

Bobby grinned. "My dad and my brother came to my last game."

"The game where you threw down your helmet and got into a fight?" I asked. "They liked that?"

"Well, not that part. My dad tore me ..." Bobby stopped. "Sorry."

"Okay, I'm hearing your family doesn't like temperamental, bad behavior any more than we do. Am I correct?"

"Yeah. Especially my mom." He looked away and kicked a bare foot at the carpet.

"Then why would you give up the chance to be a football star and help your family simply because people are making you follow the rules? Being a football star isn't everything to everyone, and it doesn't give you the right to treat others badly. Am I making myself clear?"

"It's not fair," grumped Bobby. "The coach has it in for me. He's not making the others work at a job like this."

"Why do you suppose he's making *you* do it?" I asked, seeing a troubled look cross his face.

"I dunno. He's just mean," Bobby said.

"I happen to know that's not true. He sees the kind of player, the kind of man you can become. He believes in you enough that he wants you to understand how lucky you are, and he wants you to stop the B.S. so you can succeed. Is that clear?"

"Yeah? How's a job going to do that?" Bobby scoffed.

"It's going to teach you to respect others and yourself for doing a good job no matter what it is. Manny is a fine man, a good, hard-working one. If you're lucky, you could become a man almost as honorable as he. But it will take a change in attitude and a lot of work on your part."

He stared out the sliding glass door to his balcony.

I came up behind him and put a hand on his shoulder. "You can do it; make a change, Bobby. I believe that with my whole heart. Don't become less than you are because that's easy. Do the right thing."

He was silent, but I could tell he was thinking.

"I'm going to wait in the hallway while you get dressed for work, then you and I are going back to Manny's office, and you're going to apologize to him and Rhonda. Agreed?"

Bobby let out a long breath. "I guess."

I beamed at him. "That's a very good beginning. Get ready, and we'll go."

Rhonda glared at Bobby when we walked into Manny's office.

I nudged Bobby, wondering if he'd respect our agreement. It would tell me a lot about him.

"I'm sorry I said those things about you. Both of you. My mom would be very upset with me."

Rhonda gave him a nod of approval. "It's about time you woke up and smelled the coffee because if you do it right, you have a great life ahead of you. So, shake hands with Manny, and let's start over."

Bobby shook Manny's hands and murmured. "As I said, I'm sorry."

"Okay, *Amigo*, let's get to work. The longer we wait, the hotter it'll get."

Rhonda and I left them.

On the way to the office, I said, "I'm very pleased Bobby

honored our agreement for him to apologize to you and Manny. That speaks well of him."

"Yeah, it's a shame he's been made to believe he's better than anyone because he can play football well. The fact that he cares what his mother thinks is a big plus for me," said Rhonda. "But, honestly, a swipe alongside his head wouldn't hurt."

I laughed. "Let's hope things are off to a different start with him. He's a good-looking, street-smart kid who, as you said, could have a bright future ahead of him."

We'd reached the door to our office when Dorothy Stern came running toward us.

"Wait up, girls! I've got news!"

Dorothy was maybe one inch taller than five feet and was a bundle of energy. Now, she seemed breathless.

"Come in, sit down, and catch your breath," said Rhonda.

Inside the office, I pulled out a chair for Dorothy.

She sat, fanning her face while she slowed her breathing.

"Okay, what's the news? I hope it doesn't have anything to do with Brock Goodwin," said Rhonda.

Dorothy's eyebrows rose above the top rim of her glasses. "I'm afraid it does. The president of the neighborhood association is too ill to continue, and Brock has requested the job. He's been circulating why he's qualified for the position, including his appointment as a building inspector. Many people like the idea that he'll keep our neighborhood up to par."

"Don't they understand how difficult he's been to deal with in the past?" I asked.

"How can he do both jobs?" asked Rhonda.

"His job as building inspector is a part-time one. No matter what he says about it, I know that to be the true situation because a friend of mine works in that office," said Dorothy.

"But after campaigning for the job of president of the neighborhood association, it's pretty much Brock's. No one else wants to do it."

"How about you?" said Rhonda. "Would you consider it?"

"No," said Dorothy firmly. "It would take up too much time. I want to be here to help you girls, and I have other volunteer work. I just wanted to make sure you knew about the change. But I'm here to help you. What do you want me to do?"

Sighing at the news, I said, "Thanks, Dorothy. Lorraine asked for help assembling the gift bags for the guests' rooms for the wedding this weekend. The bride has picked out several treats and small gifts for each room."

"Oh, what fun. I'll be delighted to help her." Dorothy got up and waved goodbye. "See you later."

After she left, Rhonda plopped down in her desk chair and gave me a woeful look. "What are we going to do about, Brock? You know he loves using any excuse to bug us."

"All we can do is keep a careful eye on things," I said, exhausted already to think of what might lay ahead.

CHAPTER FIVE

A couple of days later, I met with Rhonda, Wilson Carruthers, our architect, and Jeff Zimmerman, our builder. A tall, older man with an easy-going manner, Wilson was easy to talk to, flexible, and creative. He knew my old house well because his company had designed its renovations. He'd made a few changes to the original drawings of the new house and thought it would be an easy build.

Jeff Zimmerman was a no-nonsense man who said little but got a lot done. His company, Zimmer Construction, was the most favored builder in the area. We were lucky to have him.

As we began the meeting, Rhonda said, "You probably should know that Brock Goodwin is going to try to interfere with whatever we try to do. Especially because he's about to become president of the neighborhood association again."

Wilson shook his head. "Brock Goodwin is a donkey, but we'll have to work with him if he raises any issues. I've gone before the planning board with these, and they're approved, so I don't think he can say much about it. When is construction going to start?"

"With this final approval, I can begin now," Jeff said. "Any delay might be a chance for that troublemaker to interfere. But, it's a well-drawn plan, with enough detail that any competent builder wouldn't have any difficulty knowing what he needs to do to get the job done."

Wilson looked at me. "I understand you'll have the same

tasteful interior finishes as in the original house."

"Yes, we've selected them already," I said. Rhonda and I worked together on that project and were looking forward to seeing our choices on display.

The men stood along with us.

"Thank you for coming. We appreciate it," I said. "We'd like to offer you both lunch in the dining room."

"You don't have to ask me twice," said Wilson grinning. "My wife and I planned to eat here anyway."

"This will be on us," I said.

Jeff shook his head. "Sorry. I'll have to take a rain check. I was serious about getting this job underway. I want to complete the house by summer's end before we bump into hurricane season."

"Thank you." I held out my hand, and Jeff shook it. "Let us know if any trouble occurs with you know who."

He tipped his cap. "Will do." He and Rhonda shook hands, and then he left.

I walked Wilson out to the lobby, where a pretty, older woman stood and waved.

"Hi, Leslie; nice to see you," I said. She was an important social organizer in town, and she'd held several charity events here at the hotel.

"I understand you've got a busy weekend ahead of you. Wilson and I are invited to the wedding. It should be a lovely affair."

"Lorraine at Wedding Perfection does such a beautiful job," I said. "As long as the weather holds, we'll be fine. Even then, it'll all work out. She's that clever."

Wilson turned to his wife. "We've been invited to lunch here. Shall we?" He offered his elbow, and Leslie took it.

"Thank you, Ann. That's very sweet of you," said Leslie.

"I'm happy you're here. Enjoy!" I responded, anxious to get

to the office to take an aspirin.

When I arrived, Rhonda was leaning back in her chair, mouth open, snoring softly.

Amused, I tiptoed away. But later, I wondered how long we could keep going at this pace. Maybe it was time for each of us to have a break.

That night, Vaughn and I talked about going on a mini vacation somewhere after the wedding. We discussed a European trip and a trip to New York. But, in the end, we decided to take a long weekend at one of our favorite spots, The Palm Island Club. Even though it was part of the area, vacationing there made us feel as if we were thousands of miles away.

After that decision was made, I slept so well I had a hard time waking up. I stared at the empty place beside me and then heard Vaughn and Robbie in the kitchen. Stretching happily, I smiled at hearing their voices. Robbie had been such a surprise in our lives, but Vaughn and I wanted him to become our son. It allowed us to have a child together even if that child wasn't ours biologically.

I opened the blinds and gazed at the bright sunshine, pleased it was a good day for the governor's daughter's wedding party to arrive. Tonight, the groom's family was hosting a dinner at the hotel. Tomorrow, the bride's family was putting on a bridal lunch. With a guest list of just 120 people, it was a very manageable number, which is what the bride and groom wanted. While the hotel could handle bigger groups, I liked that we could provide better service with a gathering of this size.

"Hello, Sleepyhead," said Vaughn when I walked into the room. He put his arms around me and kissed me.

When we pulled apart, I went over to Robbie and hugged him. "Daddy fixed you breakfast? How nice."

"Yeah, it was good," said Robbie. His sturdy frame seemed to have no problem keeping weight off no matter what he ate.

"Looks like a good day to start the wedding weekend," said Vaughn. "Guess we won't see much of you for the next day or two."

"I'll be here from time to time, but the wedding is very important. Rhonda and I will be at the hotel most of the weekend."

"Got it," said Vaughn agreeably. "Robbie and I are going to spend time with *Zephyr*. Right, Bud?"

Robbie looked at Vaughn. "Trudy too."

Trudy's ears perked up at hearing her name, but she remained at Robbie's feet, hoping for a morsel to drop in her direction.

I headed back to my room to take a shower and dress in something comfortable but professional. Then, Rhonda and I would greet the guests. For those who came early, in addition to offering coffee to our guests in the lobby, we'd set up a small coffee reception in the library with an abundance of Consuela's famous sweet rolls and other sweets she'd baked.

After a light breakfast, I kissed Vaughn and Robbie goodbye and headed to the hotel full of excitement. I loved these big, challenging occasions that tested us. Each success proved how right we were to take back the hotel even while our families were growing, and they needed us too.

At the hotel, a festive feeling hung in the air as two limousines unloaded well-dressed guests at the front entrance. Rhonda and I greeted them and escorted them inside with directions to their block of rooms and the coffee reception in the library.

An occasion like this brought out Bernie's leadership as he made sure all departments were on duty and alerted to requests. When we first opened the hotel, Rhonda and I decided The Beach House Hotel would be upscale. But after we'd taken in a couple of VIPs, we learned we had to provide that kind of service unobtrusively and with discretion. If a VIP came with someone unknown in the family, it wasn't our business. And if government officials met secretly, we would keep quiet about it. That's how the hotel earned its reputation as a safe place for the famous to stay.

Now as I spoke to the governor's wife, Carlotta said, "It's lovely to be back. We're very happy Carolina has chosen to have a small, elegant wedding at the hotel. Her in-laws wanted them to be married in New York City, where Gregory works, but I explained we would never take our business out of Florida."

"We're pleased you didn't," I said. Not only would the wedding help us, but it would also help all the other associated enterprises.

"I've planned a day at the spa with Caro and her friends. I'm glad you expanded your spa."

"Thanks, we are too." It had been one thing we'd done over which Brock had no control because it was just a matter of shifting the small laundry to another location in the same building.

A while later, Carolina arrived in a white limo with her three bridesmaids. They were still holding glasses of champagne as they exited the car. Seeing their young, innocent faces, I thought of Liz. So much had happened to her since she was that age.

Carolina was a lovely young woman who looked like her mother, with dark, almost black hair and delicate features.

From her father, she'd inherited blue eyes.

"Hello, Carolina, Welcome to you and your wedding party," said Rhonda standing next to me.

"We've ready for you," I added. "We want you all to enjoy this special time."

"We already are," said one of the bridesmaids, giggling.

I glanced at Rhonda and then said to the young woman. "We have plenty of coffee available too."

The other bridesmaids chuckled. "See, Chrissy; we told you to slow down."

Carolina took hold of Chrissy's arm.

"Thank you," said Carolina. "I'm happy we could have my wedding here."

Rhonda led them inside while I stood by to make sure all the suitcases and other gear were put on the luggage cart.

As someone approached, I turned. Holding in a groan, I faced Brock. "Hello, Brock. Why are you here?"

"Is that a way to greet a guest?" he said, his eyebrows raised in astonishment. "I'm an old friend of Governor Horne's. I thought I'd stop by to see him."

"It's a family time for him," I said. "We probably shouldn't disturb him."

"We'll see," said Brock, walking past me and up the stairs.

I wanted to call him back, but other wedding guests were arriving carrying wedding gifts, and I had to let him go.

Inside the lobby, Carolina and her bridesmaids were gathered in a group, laughing and chatting as they waited for their registration to be completed. Bernie was at the front desk taking care of details, shifting room selections as requested by two girls who'd decided to switch rooms at the last minute.

I noticed Brock walking toward the group and quickly followed.

"Hello," Brock said to the young women with a lecherous smile. "As neighborhood association president, I'm happy to have you here."

Rhonda emerged from behind the group. "Don't mind him, girls. He thinks he's important, but it's a job nobody else wanted."

Brock's body stiffened as the women giggled.

I took hold of Brock's elbow, and though he tried to shake me off, he allowed me to continue walking him away from the group.

We stopped at a distance, and I turned to face him. "What were you doing? You can't harass our guests! Either leave now on your own, or Bernie will see that you do."

"You can't decide who walks into your hotel," huffed Brock.

"We can and will remove disruptive persons," I retorted. "I don't understand why you continue to try to do harmful things to Rhonda and me."

"Did you hear what Rhonda said?" He jabbed a finger in her direction. "Just because she has money, she thinks she can say anything she wants."

My laugh was bitter. Brock had failed at many enterprises. "You know that's not true. In addition to being a friend to all who deserve it, Rhonda never pretends to be anyone but a hardworking businesswoman. But she won't tolerate lying or cheating from anyone. And as you know, she'll call you on it. Every. Time."

Bernie came over to us. "Everything all right here?" Bernie wasn't a fan of Brock's.

"I believe Brock is about to leave," I said, walking away.

I followed the bridal group to their rooms and helped see them settled, checking to make sure they had their special welcome bag of gifts from Carolina. I'd already seen the sterling silver heart necklaces she'd given to each of the bridesmaids and knew they would love it.

Rhonda and I said goodbye to the group and headed to our office.

"That Brock Goodwin is a total ass," grumbled Rhonda. "Acting like he was someone who should welcome them to the neighborhood. I'm tellin' ya, Annie, I will bring him down one day."

"Best to just leave him alone. As we both know, he can be very vindictive."

"Yeah, I'll lay in the weeds until I have my chance to pounce," said Rhonda. "What a lech. The way he was looking at those girls was sickening."

"They're a wild group. I already can't wait for this wedding to be over," I said. "By the way, Vaughn and I want to plan a trip to The Palm Island Club after this week if that's all right with you."

Rhonda gave me a thumbs-up sign. "I'm glad you brought it up. Will wants to take an Alaskan cruise. I was going to check dates with you."

"That sounds terrific," I said. "We'll go over the calendar and work both times in. We each deserve a vacation."

We walked into the kitchen to grab a cup of coffee.

Consuela greeted us with a smile. "Hectic time, but the coffee reception is going well." She glanced over at Jean-Luc, busy with his crew prepping for tonight's dinner and the luncheon tomorrow. "Not a good time to talk to him."

"Thanks for the warning," I said, filling a cup with coffee and handing it to Rhonda before getting my own.

"Thankfully, the bride has chosen a simple wedding cake," Consuela said.

Carolina and her groom had chosen a lemon cake with a lemon cream frosting. In addition, dessert for the bridal luncheon included individual servings of flan, Carolina's favorite dessert, garnished with fresh flowers.

Jean-Luc gave us a nod of his head. Since marrying Amelia's sister, Lindsay, he'd softened a lot from the crusty French chef Rhonda and I knew well and loved.

I took Rhonda's arm, and we left the kitchen. When we'd first started the hotel, it had been difficult for Rhonda to give up her kitchen to Jean-Luc. They'd fought over recipes until she and I realized Rhonda could no longer be part of the kitchen crew.

In the office, we reviewed a checklist I'd developed for overseeing weddings.

"The idea for a coffee reception is working out well," I said. "It makes the guests feel part of the entire weekend, not just the wedding tomorrow."

"I think so too," said Rhonda. "And for later arrivals, wine and beer served around the pool is a good choice. I'm happy Carlotta and the governor were open to both options. Not everyone can afford to do it."

"Lorraine makes it an easy choice when she presents it as a weekend wedding. She's very clever."

"And pretty and strong," said Rhonda. "I spoke to Angela about my idea of having Arthur come for a visit and introducing them to one another. She thought it would be nice. She knows how lonely Arthur has been since Katherine's death."

I lifted my hand and stepped back. "I'm having no part in your matchmaking. Does Reggie know about your idea?"

"No-o-o-o. And I don't want him to," said Rhonda. "This is women's work."

"Women's work? Is that what you're calling it?" I asked, laughing in spite of myself.

Rhonda elbowed me. "Have a little faith, Annie. It'll work out. I just know it."

Still shaking my head, I looked up as Manny entered the office.

"What's up?" I asked him.

He took off his hat and held it in his hand. "I just heard from my nephew, Paul. He wants to come back here and work for me at the hotel. He and the girl he thought he'd marry have split up, and he's coming back here."

"I'm sorry about the relationship, but it's wonderful news that Paul wants to come back on staff. Ever since Jax left, we've thought you were understaffed. Are you excited about having Paul help you again?"

Manny's dark eyes lit. "*Si.*"

"How soon will he be back?" Rhonda asked.

"He's here now," said Manny. A smile creased his tanned face, exhibiting white teeth.

"God knows we can't let Bobby anywhere near Jean-Luc until this wedding is over," said Rhonda. "Let's have Paul start on Monday, and we'll keep Bobby with you, Manny, for a few more days."

"That sounds good. Thank you. I wanted to be sure you're okay with it."

"I'm delighted to have Paul back with us. He was with us initially, and like you, we think of him as family." I walked over to him and gave him a hug. He was such a good man.

Rhonda patted him on the shoulder. "*Familia.*"

He tipped his head and left us, a smile lingering on his face.

"Good news," I said.

"Wonderful," agreed Rhonda. "Rita says the whole family has been worried about him. They want him home."

"And now the real challenge for Bobby will begin. If he thinks it was hard working outside with Manny, wait until he works with Jean-Luc in the kitchen," I said.

"I see a few life lessons coming up for him," said Rhonda

chuckling. "Jean-Luc won't put up with any shenanigans."

A thought suddenly stopped me. "I hope the bridal party doesn't discover Bobby is staying at the hotel too. That could be a disaster."

CHAPTER SIX

I was walking through the lobby to check on the coffee service we provided guests when I heard a shriek from outside. I hurried out to the pool area to see what the problem was.

Chrissy, the bridesmaid who'd been tipsy earlier, was standing by her lounge chair pointing at a figure trimming the bushes outside the screen. "Omigod! That's Bugs Bailey, the football star."

Several people turned to stare at him.

Bobby picked up the basket of trimmings and jogged away.

I walked over to Chrissy. "Please sit down. I need to talk to you."

She folded herself onto the lounge chair and looked up at me. "I'm sorry."

I squatted beside her and spoke softly, firmly. "As part of your arrangements to stay here, you signed an agreement that you wouldn't draw attention to any other guest who might be at the hotel and would respect their privacy. That same consideration should be given to people you might see working here."

"But it's Bugs Bailey," she said in a stage whisper.

"Exactly. So, give him the courtesy of privacy."

Carolina came over. "What's going on?"

"I'm trying to explain the agreement you all signed to show respect for the privacy of our other guests or even, as in this case, those who might be working for us. It's just a reminder, that's all."

"Chrissy, you should understand we can't do that here."

Chrissy rose. "Guess I'll go get a drink in the bar."

Carolina put a hand on her arm to stop her. "Let's go to the beach. We can party there."

They picked up their towels, and at a signal from Carolina, the three other girls followed her out of the pool area.

I watched them go, hoping I hadn't been too forceful. But a matter of privacy was important to many of our guests.

Inside the lobby, one of the dining room staff was changing out the coffee service for containers of cold water with cucumber slices and pitchers of icy lemonade.

I thanked her and went to the library to ensure the coffee service had been shut down. Lorraine was there when I arrived.

"How did it go?" I asked her.

"It's a nice addition when several guests are arriving from out of town," she said. "Well worth the small amount of money we charge for it. Such goodwill for the hotel."

"I think so too," I said. "We'll set it up for tomorrow morning too. Right?"

"Yes, the governor requested it then too."

Thinking of Rhonda's plan, I studied Lorraine. She was an attractive woman with hair curling softly above her shoulders. She had lovely taste in clothes that fit her attractive figure perfectly. From the moment I'd met her, I had the impression of elegance in both looks and manner. And, more importantly, she was both kind and smart.

"And how are the rest of the plans coming along?" I asked. "I saw on the news that rain is expected on Sunday, but that shouldn't hamper the wedding in the garden."

"I'm not concerned about it. As long as it holds off until then, it won't be a problem. And, I suppose, if it didn't, we'd make do with something in a quiet corner of the lobby. We've done it before."

I clutched my hands and made a wish that wouldn't happen. It was never quite the same.

Lorraine gave me a quick hug. "Don't worry. These kids are in love."

"Have he and his family arrived?"

"Not yet. Their flight from New York was delayed, but I got a text from Brandon that they'd taken off."

"Gregory Forrest and his wife, Vivian, are used to being catered to," I said. "He sent a list of special requests—a brand of bubbling water, special soap, and certain snacks in their room. Nothing big but fussy about the detail. I want to do a great job for them because, as a national television commentator, he could direct business our way."

"Their son, Brandon, is easy-going, very likable. He and Carolina are an adorable couple."

"Good. That makes me feel better. I don't know why some weddings make me nervous."

Lorraine gave me an encouraging look. "Don't worry. This will turn out alright because all the bride and groom care about is being married. They're headed to Paris for their honeymoon."

"That sounds delightful." Maybe someday, when the babies were older, I could think of a long faraway vacation. Right now, my mother vibes told me to stay close.

Rhonda entered the room. "There you are, Annie. I've been looking for you. Hi, Lorraine. Nice to see you. How's the dating going?"

As Lorraine blinked in surprise, I longed to reach over and pinch Rhonda.

"Going, I guess," Lorraine said, a little flustered.

Rhonda grinned. "Glad to hear it." She turned to me. "We have a small problem. The governor now wants to give the presidential suite to Brandon's parents and take the private house for Carlotta and him."

I sighed. That would mean a refreshing cleaning of the Presidential suite when the staff was already busy with other rooms. "We're fully booked. Is there any way to talk him out of it? We thought the private house would be perfect for the Forrest family."

"I told him we'd talk it over and get back to him. But everything you said is right. We don't have flexibility. Come with me while I explain that, okay?"

"Sure." We hated disappointing our guests, but we had to be practical too. The house was scheduled to be used by Gregory and Vivian, Brandon, and Brandon's sister, Hazel."

A few minutes later, Rhonda and I knocked on the door to the Presidential Suite. Originally Rhonda's private quarters, it was perfect as our finest suite. The furnishings were gorgeous and served the space well. The oversized bathroom even had gold faucets. Best of all, it had a beautiful view of the Gulf at one end and a lovely side view of the garden from a balcony.

Governor Horne answered the door. "Are you able to arrange a move for us?"

I swallowed hard. "I'm afraid we can't. The hotel is fully booked, and the entire Forrest family, including the groom, his sister, and his grandmother, is scheduled to stay at the house. We can't come up with the two extra rooms required to make that move. Besides, it will be easier for you to be near the action within the hotel."

"I hope you understand," said Rhonda, looking worried.

"No problem," said the governor. "I should've thought of it earlier. I don't want anything to ruin my baby girl's wedding."

"No, of course not," I said, feeling my shoulders tense. As I'd told Lorraine, something about this wedding put me on edge.

With the Forrest family due to arrive at any minute, Rhonda and I stood with Carolina at the top of the stairs to greet them. Carolina was a pretty, soft-spoken girl who I knew from reading about her was a brilliant law student.

"I understand you and Brandon met at Columbia Law School," I said to her. "That should make it interesting going forward."

She laughed. "Brandon is into politics; I'm most definitely not. I'm interested in Family Law. We don't always agree on issues but are open to new ideas. Unfortunately, his parents and mine have totally opposite ideas about how this country should be run. It can make it difficult. Brandon and I have each warned our parents about keeping things nice for the weekend by avoiding such discussions."

Rhonda and I exchanged worried looks. Weddings brought out the best and the worst in people.

Observing the black limo rolling toward us, Carolina hurried down the stairs. Rhonda and I followed slowly to give her time to reunite with her fiancé.

The tall, sandy-haired man who emerged from the limo was striking as he swept Carolina into his arms. The way he was kissing her warmed my heart. As Lorraine has mentioned, they were a darling couple.

The driver held the door for the other passengers, and Gregory Forrest, a well-known financial commentator on television news, stepped onto the pavement and held his hand out for his wife. With his gray hair, fine features, and glasses, the word best to describe him was aristocratic. Standing beside him, his wife, Vivian, seemed small but vivacious, with an easy smile. To me, she was a younger Martha Stewart look-alike with that same air of confidence.

An older woman appeared next. It was easy to see where Gregory got his looks. His mother was as imposing as he.

Last to exit the limo was a young woman I assumed was Hazel. Heavy-set, she remained in the background as if that was her normal place. She had a pretty face with shoulder-length chestnut hair and green eyes that appeared to study everything around her. I waited to see the interaction between her and Carolina.

Carolina greeted Brandon's parents and grandmother with handshakes and awkward hugs before turning to Hazel with an affectionate smile. "Glad you're here. As soon as possible, join my friends and me at the beach. Okay?"

Hazel's face brightened, and she nodded.

"Welcome to The Beach House Hotel," Rhonda and I said together, greeting Brandon's parents and grandmother. "We hope you have a pleasant stay," said Rhonda.

"I hope everything is exactly the way I want it for tonight's dinner," said Vivian. "I left specific instructions with Lorraine Grace as to how everything should be."

"Lorraine is very good at her job. I'm sure you'll be satisfied," I said, though looking at Vivian's impeccable linen suit, her perfectly applied makeup, and the way she held her body erect, I was worried that she'd find something not to her liking. I turned to Gregory.

"After you register, the driver can take you to the house. It's been prepared for you."

He turned to his family. "It'll only be a minute."

Brandon elbowed his sister. "C'mon, Haze, let's you, Caro, and I jog over to the house."

A smile of gratitude filled Hazel's face, and the three of them took off.

"We're trying to get my daughter to exercise more," said Vivian with a sigh.

I studied Vivian's rail-thin figure and hid my dislike. It was no mystery why Hazel liked to hide behind others. I glanced at Rhonda and knew she felt like I did about a mother belittling her child.

"It looks like the weather may hold for the wedding," I said. "I think you'll be pleased with all the details."

Vivian shook her head. "Weddings are for the groom and his family, too. People seem to forget that."

We looked up as the governor and his wife descended the stairs.

"Welcome!" said the governor, smiling as if he were on television. That was the Daniel Horne we Floridians knew all too well, but the man many liked.

"We're happy you're finally here," said Carlotta, pressing Vivian's hand between hers before shaking hands with the older woman at Vivian's side. "It's such a beautiful place. I'm sure you're going to love it here."

"I know about The Beach House Hotel, of course," said Vivian. "It's too bad we won't be able to stay long. That was the reason we wanted the wedding in New York."

"I understand, but Florida is Daniel's state, and we are loyal to it." Carlotta had always been known to be kind and gracious. She was doing an excellent job of it now, I thought.

The two strong women continued to face one another until Gregory's mother interceded. "As you said, Carlotta, it is a lovely place."

Rhonda stood talking to the governor about a political issue while I stayed with the women wondering how I could help relieve the tension between them.

"Thank heavens Carolina decided on a garden wedding. Beach weddings sound delightful, but they can be very messy," said Vivian.

I knew from the tight expression on Carlotta's face that she was trying not to respond.

"It's good that the hotel can accommodate both beach and garden weddings," I said. "The important thing is for the bride and groom to have it their way."

Carlotta shot me a look of gratitude, and I knew I'd just made a friend. I was relieved Rhonda wasn't part of the conversation. Vivian reminded me of Katherine Smythe when we'd first met Reggie's parents, and at first, Katherine and Rhonda did not do well together.

Gregory returned to the group, and after chatting about the weather and the timing of events, he got into the limo with his wife and mother, and they took off for the house.

Rhonda and I watched them leave.

"I don't know, Annie, but this wedding is a tough one. No fist fights or anything like that, just a bad undercurrent," said Rhonda.

"The bride and groom are adorable together. That's got to mean something," I said, praying that would help.

"Let's hope. Think we'd better give Lorraine a warning?" Rhonda asked.

"It might not be a bad idea," I said. It seemed only fair.

CHAPTER SEVEN

Inside, while Rhonda went to talk to Lorraine, I headed into the kitchen to make sure the preparations for dinner were going well. Vivian had ordered a choice of filet mignon with bearnaise sauce or grilled sea bass for dinner. Both main courses were easy to prepare but depended on precise timing to be served piping hot, something Jean-Luc worried about. As Lorraine had already indicated, Bernie's wife, Annette, would oversee the seating of guests to help with that issue, but it was always a problem.

Jean-Luc was mixing a rub for the fish when I stopped by. "How are you doing? Is there anything I can do for you?"

He shook his head. "No, it's all a matter of having things ready for the guests as they finish their salad course. Both the beef and the fish look great, so we're good to go."

"The desserts too?" I asked.

"*Mais oui*," he replied, a little irritated.

"Thanks. See you later." I left him and walked into the dining room. The large room was versatile with the ability to shape different spaces using special room dividers. In this case, the front half of the dining room was open for our regular guests, while the back was blocked off for the wedding party with floor-to-ceiling fabric-covered dividers.

I went into the reserved area. Pretty pink linen tablecloths covered the round tables for eight. A small bar was set up in a corner of the room. A staff member from Tropical Fleurs was busy filling vases with pink and white lilies. I noted the battery-lit candles in matching cut-glass containers and thought the effect would be stunning. Vivian Forrest entered the room as I was talking to the woman from Tropical Fleurs.

I heard her gasp and turned to her. "Is something wrong?"

"I didn't order pink tablecloths. I want white."

"Oh, I'm sorry," I said. "Let me call Lorraine. She'd never make a mistake like that." I got her on my cell. "Lorraine, can you please come to the dining room? There is some question about the use of pink tablecloths. We need to clear up this issue with Mrs. Forrest." I clicked off the call and turned to Vivian. "She's on her way."

Lorraine and Rhonda appeared moments later.

"Who told you to use pink tablecloths?" Vivian asked, her cheeks flushed with anger. "I never would've chosen them."

Lorraine gave her a practiced smile. "But, of course, I had your approval. Brandon told me you'd agreed to the idea. Both he and Carolina wanted it to keep to her color theme for the wedding."

"Brandon told you I'd agreed to it?" Vivian said, surprised.

Lorraine held out a checklist. "See, the date and his initials are posted under dining room décor."

"Well, I don't know what to say."

"It looks nice. Don't you agree? And it's what the bride and groom wanted," said Lorraine. "The menu looks superb, and I'm confident it'll be a lovely occasion for everyone in the party."

Vivian's shoulders went limp. "All right. We'll let it go. But this wedding is not at all what I expected. It's a good thing I have a daughter. Maybe then, I'll have a real voice in one."

"You know the old saying about weddings and grooms, don't you?" I said, trying to inject some humor into the situation. "All the groom has to do is show up and say, 'I do.'"

Vivian didn't laugh; she sighed. "I suppose you're right. I'll go talk to the kids."

Later, while Rhonda and I were checking the garden, we heard voices from inside the gazebo.

We stopped and listened.

"I wish we'd never agreed to have a wedding. I wanted to elope, remember?" came a voice I recognized as Carolina's.

I glanced at Rhonda, and we both held our breaths, waiting for a reply.

"We can elope anytime. Say the word, and I'll do it," said Brandon.

"Let's see how the rest of the day goes. For heaven's sake, I've never been so chastised and over the color of tablecloths. No wonder our parents don't get along. Mine would be furious to know what scolding took place."

"Give my mother a chance. She's always trying to make my dad proud of her. Unfortunately, this is just one of those times when she feels she has to be perfect."

"And the way she treats Hazel? No wonder Hazel tells us she wants to run away from home. At sixteen, she still has some growing up to do, but Brandon, she's a wonderful person."

"I know, I know. Let's get back to the group. And if you decide you've had enough, I'm in."

Rhonda grabbed my arm and yanked me behind some bushes lining the garden.

We heard rather than saw the two of them walk away, talking softly to one another.

After they left, Rhonda and I stepped from behind the bushes and stared at one another.

"How do you like them apples?" Rhonda said. "What are we going to do?"

"We can't do anything about it. We were snooping. Besides,

it's not our news to spread. Like any other guests, Carolina and Brandon deserve privacy. In any case, the wedding plans must go forward. It's just wild bride talk."

Rhonda thought a moment. "You're right. We can't say a word about it. But it's a shame the two families can't be friendlier. Those poor kids."

"I'm going home for a break and will come back in time to oversee the cocktail reception and dinner," I said. I could hardly wait to get out of my dress and shoes and wiggle my toes.

"Sounds like a plan. I'll tell Bernie we're leaving and meet you back here." Rhonda gave me a little salute, and we headed in opposite directions.

At home, I greeted the dog, took off my dress and shoes, and decided to change into my swimsuit. Exercising in the water was a good way for me to relax. Though the temperature was cool for March, the pool was heated.

When I stepped outside, I saw Vaughn and Robbie in the distance and waved. They stopped working on the boat and headed my way.

"Hi, Mom!" cried Robbie running toward me. "Guess what? Dad found a kennel online with dachshund puppies. Can we go get one?"

"Give me a chance to relax, and then we can talk about it."

"How are things going?" Vaughn asked me. He was wearing swim trunks and a T-shirt, which he took off before diving into the pool with me.

Robbie sat on the edge of the pool, stroking Trudy's head. "We found a dog just like Trudy. I want to go get it."

I turned to Vaughn as he swam over to me. "Better tell me about this."

"It's a kennel in Orlando, and as Robbie says, they have some pups like Trudy—smooth black-and-tan, small standards. It's a reputable place, and the pups are gorgeous. But I don't think we should wait long. I had a hard time finding doxie pups."

"Okay, call them and see what's available," I said. "But I won't be able to go see the puppies until after the wedding. If it ever takes place."

Vaughn frowned. "What do you mean if?

I told him about the conversation that Rhonda and I had overheard. "I must say Vivian Forrest is difficult. But then, her husband is too."

"I imagine the governor and his wife are used to being in control, too," said Vaughn. "I guess it's going to be one of those weddings you have to put up with. And in this case, I understand why. The parents are influential people."

"Yes, that's why I needed a break. The timing for dinner is crucial, and we have to keep Jean-Luc happy by respecting it. Thank God Lorraine is handling the details. She's a gem."

"Okay, tell you what. I'll handle the information on the puppies; maybe we can plan to see them on Sunday. Okay?"

"Yes. With the wedding scheduled for late morning tomorrow, most of the chaos will be ended by evening, and we can all rest easy, and I can easily have Sunday off. Thanks, hon."

He tugged me to him, threw his arms around me, and pressed his lips on mine. At the comfort he gave me, the tension in my shoulders eased. He was the person who made me stronger.

"Love you," I murmured, looking into his eyes and loving how he gazed at me.

"So, we can get a puppy?" asked Robbie, breaking into that quiet moment.

"I'll make some calls, and we'll see if any are available," said Vaughn. "If this doesn't work out, we'll keep looking. But, I think it's time for Trudy to have that playmate we were talking about."

"Yay!" cried Robbie. He jumped into the pool, and we laughed even as water splashed over us.

"He's getting so big," I said, seeing how long his limbs were getting. A pang of sorrow hit me at that thought, and then I felt better. I had Liz's three babies to fuss over.

I entered the hotel refreshed and ready for an evening of celebration for the bride and groom. I looked around the cocktail reception to make sure they were there. Seeing Carolina standing with Brandon talking with the governor, I let out a sigh of relief and walked over to greet them.

"Good evening. Lovely party," I said.

"Yes, indeed," said the Governor holding a drink in his hand.

"Are you all set for tomorrow?" I asked Carolina.

"I think so," she replied, turning to Brandon and smiling at him.

Satisfied, I moved on to other guests, welcoming them to the hotel and ensuring they had everything they needed for a nice stay.

Rhonda was standing with Vivian and another woman. When she saw me, she rolled her eyes and then excused herself from the two of them.

She walked over to me and said softly, "I'm doing my best to keep Vivian out of the kitchen. She wants to direct when everyone should move to the dining room for dinner. I told her we would take care of that. The thing is, she wants to play a major role in the wedding, and as the groom's mother, there's not much for her to do."

"Hopefully, the party will get into full swing, and it won't remain an issue. Let's make sure everyone is having fun."

In a half hour, it became apparent I needn't have worried. People who'd been out in the sun were enjoying the evening and were partaking of the hors d'oeuvres and drinks offered to them.

The bridesmaids, Hazel included, were talking to some of Brandon's friends. They were a good-looking bunch—healthy, happy, and laughing. I noticed Chrissy making her way to the bar, and though I was tempted to warn her about drinking too much, I refrained.

Later, as the space became crowded with more and more revelers and the noise level rose, I watched, horrified, as Chrissy staggered on her 4-inch sandals and then fell, hitting her head on the side of the pool, as she glided rather than splashed into the deep end of the pool. No one paid attention to her as the crowd watched the entrance of the bride and groom.

I kicked off my heels and jumped into the water. As I reached for her, the smell of alcohol hit me. "Chrissy, I'm helping you out of the pool," I said as calmly as I could as she began to flounder.

"I tripped," she said.

I grabbed her under her arms and dragged her toward the side of the pool, where a gentleman pulled her out. Another gentleman helped me out of the pool.

"She hit her head. Is there a doctor in the group?" I asked, kneeling beside her. Chrissy was sitting up now and looking around, dazed.

A woman and a man stepped forward.

"I can take a look," said the woman. "I'm Dr. Roberts."

Rhonda pushed her way through the crowd gathering

around us. "Are you okay, Annie? Is Chrissy okay?"

"I think so," I said, getting to my feet. "It's another case of her having too much to drink. I should've spoken up earlier, but I didn't. After we're sure she's all right, I'll go home to change and be right back."

"Don't worry. I'll hold the fort here," said Rhonda. She gave me a worried look and lowered her voice. "Let's hope this is the end of those bad feelings you've had."

"I hope so too."

The doctor beside Chrissy rose and turned to me. "She's had a good bump to the head but nothing severe, though she may have a sore spot for a while. She'll be fine once she sobers up."

Vivian approached us. "Thank you, Ann, for your help. I'm sorry you've ruined your dress. Chrissy's parents aren't here, but I'll tell them about the accident. She said she slipped on the wet pavement."

I bit my lip and then spoke. "That isn't true. Chrissy had too much to drink and tripped in her spike heels. I saw it clearly." No way did I want anyone to think the hotel was at fault.

"I see," said Vivian, glancing at Chrissy. "I know she likes to have a good time, but ..." she let her words hang in the air.

I gave her a steady look. "We'll fill out a proper accident report, but I assure you that what I said was true."

Someone handed me a beach towel and my shoes.

I excused myself, wrapped the towel around me, and headed for my car parked in the back of the hotel. My sleeveless linen dress would be all right, but it would take some time to dry my hair and put on makeup.

All the way home, I whispered a prayer that this incident would be the worst thing about the wedding.

I returned to the hotel to find the guests being seated for dinner. As usual, Annette was doing a beautiful job of directing people to their seats. Her skill in handling guests was inborn in her.

Rhonda and I stood by and watched everyone enjoy their salad course. Later, after clearing those plates, the main course was about to be served. We had several part-time waiters who were happy to help with weddings, a short-term job that assured them of a nice tip. Now, they worked together to place the food in front of the guests at the same time at each table. Like a conductor, Annette helped orchestrate them.

Waiters and waitresses next served the wine. Vivian had been very specific about wanting a choice of Chandler Hill wines, both red and white.

Gregory got to his feet. "While everyone is enjoying their food, Vivian and I want to welcome you to dinner. It's a big day when a family gains a daughter, a woman as beautiful and bright as Carolina."

I saw the pained expression on Hazel's face and cringed. She obviously wasn't the recipient of such words.

Gregory continued. "We ask you to enjoy the meal with us before the excitement of tomorrow." He lifted his glass in a toast. "Here's to Caro and Brandon."

As Gregory sat down, Daniel Horne got to his feet. "I just want to add that we are delighted to bring Brandon into our family. As many of you know, he and I have become close working together on my next political campaign. So, Brandon, we welcome you."

From my position next to the wall, I saw a look of frustration and hurt cross Vivian's face and realized she was jealous of that relationship. I glanced at Rhonda. She'd noticed it, too, and was shaking her head.

"Please get us through this wedding," I said to whoever might listen. Fortunately, the guests seemed unaware of the friction I felt between the two families.

I noticed some commotion at Vivian's table and saw a waiter take her plate away. I hurried out of the room and stopped him. "What's wrong?"

"I was told the fish was overcooked."

"Oh, boy! You'd better let me take that back to the kitchen. Jean-Luc is going to be upset."

I took the plate and hurried to the kitchen. There, I explained what happened, and both Jean-Luc and I poked the fish with a fork. A soft, white fish that melts in your mouth if cooked properly. This looked perfect to both Jean-Luc and me.

"Let's put it on a fresh, hot plate, and I'll sauce it. This fish is ... is *magnifique!*" Though Jean-Luc hated criticism, he had no problem admitting when something wasn't up to his standards.

"Okay," I said, praying it would pass inspection by Vivian. Unfortunately, several guests had changed their minds about their order, and we had no other pieces of sea bass available.

I picked up the hot plate of food and carried it back to the room to Vivian. "I apologize. I think you'll find this better. *Bon Appetit.*"

"Thank you," said Vivian, lifting her chin. "Now, about the wine. My husband ..."

Gregory put a hand on her arm to stop her. "Vivian, the wine is fine."

She gave him a look of surprise.

I let out my breath and moved away, wondering what was going on between Vivian and her husband. He seemed to be the one in control. Not her.

At the other end of the room, Rhonda was speaking quietly to the governor, holding up a bottle of wine to allow him to read it. He nodded and lifted his glass. Rhonda signaled the waiter, and a fresh bottle was brought to the table.

As we stood aside, observing the wedding party guests, Rhonda said, "Annie, this is the worst group we've had in a while. No wonder the kids want ..." She stopped talking as Carlotta walked by.

I took Rhonda's arm. "Let's get out of here."

We went into our office.

"We need to follow up with Vivian and Chrissy's parents to make sure no blame is placed on the hotel for Chrissy's fall. Let's ask Bernie to come in here while I describe exactly what happened. We can record it, and then a security officer can fill out an accident report."

"Good idea. You do that while I check on the delivery of the next course," said Rhonda. "Just give me a moment to catch my breath. If I sit too long, I'm afraid I'll fall asleep."

I laughed and then sobered. A vacation couldn't come soon enough,

CHAPTER EIGHT

After filling out the accident report, I returned to the dining room in time to see the group break up. The fresh fruit sorbet cups with chocolate curls for a topping appeared to be a choice people loved. I noticed that both the bride's and the groom's parents made no effort to communicate but stood talking in two different groups. Carolina, her four bridesmaids, and Brandon and his four groomsmen were laughing and talking in another group. Pleased that they seemed to be having fun, I began to relax.

Rhonda came up beside me. "I think things have settled down enough that we can go home."

We left the dining room and went to our office to gather our things.

"Tomorrow will be another busy day, but I promised Will and the kids I'd have breakfast with them before returning to the hotel," said Rhonda. "Bernie and Lorraine can handle the breakfast scene here."

"Absolutely. Relax with your family. I'll come in because I won't be here on Sunday. We're going to look at a puppy for Robbie. Or maybe I should say, a puppy for Trudy."

"You're doing it, huh?" said Rhonda, shooting me a look of surprise. "I'm sticking with two cats. Then, when the kids are older and can take care of it, we'll think about a dog. That Trudy sure is cute."

"Vaughn is determined that Robbie learn to take care of the puppy. He's good with Trudy already." The more I thought about another puppy, the more I liked the idea. My strict grandmother had never allowed me to have a pet, and I enjoyed Trudy.

Rhonda and I said goodnight to one another, and I headed home feeling better about the wedding party. Carlotta was a much easier person to deal with than Vivian. Tomorrow should be easier.

The next morning, I awoke to the sound of rain pounding the tiles on the roof. Startled, I jumped out of bed and raced to the sliding door that led to the small patio outside the master bedroom. Pulling aside the drapes, I stared with dismay at the tropical downpour.

Vaughn stirred, and I quietly told him I had to get to the hotel. I quickly showered, dressed, and headed there. The only good thing about a downpour like this was that it usually didn't last long. The downside was the heavy rain could damage the landscaping.

I drove behind the hotel, parked, and then hiding under a golf umbrella, went to the side garden. Manny was already there.

"How are we doing?" I asked him.

"We'll lose a few blossoms, but if it stops raining soon, we'll be okay. The sun is supposed to come out this morning. With luck, it will, and most of the lawn will be manageable. We'll wait until the last minute to set up the chairs. Paul's in town, and I'll have Bobby help the usual crew, too."

I looked up at the gray sky, praying Manny was right and the sun would come out in time to dry things up. Then, leaving him, I went into the kitchen to check on the guests' coffee service and the wedding crowd's coffee reception.

Consuela and the sous chef who handled breakfast were already in the kitchen. Consuela saw me, looked up at the sky, and made a sign of the cross. I hoped that would help because it might otherwise be a mess.

I helped myself to a cup of coffee and went to check the pool area. Through the sliding glass doors to the outside, I saw that staff had already spruced up the space after last night's party. I spoke to Ana, Consuela's neighbor, who also was head of the housekeeping department.

"Good morning. Thanks for getting right on this cleanup last night. Except for the rain, it looks good."

"You're welcome. I know how important this wedding is for the hotel." Her eyes shone with humor. "Bernie made that very clear."

I chuckled. When Bernie first came to the hotel, his brusque manner and German accent were a bit intimidating. Though he'd never have a Southern drawl or totally relax, he'd mellowed a lot.

"I haven't checked the library yet, but I assume that's also been cleaned."

"Oh, yes," said Ana. "We're on standby to make sure it and the lobby are spotless in case the wedding is moved indoors. But the weather forecast said the rain would quickly move out."

As she said the words, I spied a spot of blue in the sky and clasped my hands. "Look! I think you may be right."

Ana left me, and I stared out at the Gulf water. The surface had calmed, but the waves continued to roll in and move away, giving me a sense of peace. Finally, it looked as though things were going to be okay.

I turned to leave and saw Vivian approaching me. "Good morning," I said, noting the worried expression on her face.

"I hope so. Brandon didn't come back to the cottage last night. I'm angry he'd do that to me the night before the wedding."

"He's probably with his friends," I said, trying to edge away. I didn't want to get mixed up in that fight.

"We were trying to make it a family time with him," said Vivian. "Hazel is with the other bridesmaids, and now he's gone."

"I hope you're enjoying the guest cottage," I said. "It's very peaceful there."

"With this rain, how will the wedding ever go on? My husband wanted the wedding in New York. Carlotta probably should've listened to him."

"I saw a bit of blue sky earlier. I'm sure things will work out," I said. "Have you helped yourself to coffee and sweets in the library?"

"No, I should get some," said Vivian, heaving a noisy sigh.

"Enjoy. I must check on other things," I said, happy for any excuse to avoid more of her negativity. I was already on edge.

Later, I was in the dining room inspecting the settings for the bridal luncheon when Carlotta came in. "Oh, good. Everything looks fine. I thought it was very sweet that the dinner décor last night used Carolina's colors. Today, the white tablecloths, pink napkins, and pink flowers are perfect."

"Lorraine does a fabulous job of coordinating weddings. We're lucky to have her," I said.

"And you and Rhonda are lovely hosts," said Carlotta. "Now, to see to my daughter. After that, it's a morning of makeup and hairstyles for all in the party."

"Malinda at Hair Designs and her staff always do a lovely job." I laughed. "Don't look at my hair. I got up in a hurry."

We shared smiles, and I went to check on the coffee reception, hoping I wouldn't bump into Vivian.

A short while later, the rain stopped, and I walked outside to see Manny and the crew in the side garden. Paul trotted over to me. "Hi, Ann. I'm glad to be back. Thank you."

I hugged him. "Welcome home. Manny and we are delighted to have you on the team again."

I noticed Bobby watching us and waved. "Thanks for the help."

He shrugged and turned back to his job of picking up debris among the flowers.

"What do you think, Manny?" I asked him. "Is it going to be all right?"

"We have almost four hours. I think we'll be fine."

"Good," I said, pleased. The wedding was planned for 11:30 A.M. because of Gregory's schedule. Not an ideal time, but workable. Especially for those staying on after the wedding. They'd have another lovely evening to enjoy at the hotel.

Thinking of the timing, I understood why Carolina and Brandon had considered eloping. Unfortunately, it seemed as if the wedding they wanted had been overtaken by accommodating Brandon's parents. No wonder the families were not getting along.

I went inside to my office to check on the billing for the rehearsal dinner. I wanted to make sure all was in order so Gregory would have no complaints when they checked out.

Carlotta rushed into the office and faced me with an expression of horror. "Have you seen Carolina or Brandon? No one can find them. Oh my God! Do you think something bad has happened to them?"

I stood and paused, not knowing how much to say. "I'm sorry; I haven't seen them. But, with all the discord in the families, do you suppose they might have ..."

"Oh, my God! Caro told me they might consider eloping if things didn't get better." Tears spilled onto her cheeks. "I thought she was kidding. What are we going to do now?"

"Hold on. I'm sure they wouldn't have gotten far. They were both drinking last night and would be smart enough not to go any distance. Let me check with a few other hotels in the area."

"Would you?' Carlotta said, clutching her hands. "That would be helpful. I'd better tell Daniel about this possibility. He'll be furious."

She left, and I picked up the phone to call The Sanderling Cove Inn. Smaller than we, they were similar in style and with an excellent reputation as a wedding venue.

When I explained the situation, one of the owners, Grace Hendrix, said quietly, "They're here but haven't been married yet. Why don't you have the bride's parents give them a call? I heard last night that the groom's parents are the problem."

"Thanks for the news," I said. "I'll speak to the bride's mother now."

I rose, then sat down and picked up the phone.

"What's up?" asked Rhonda when she answered the call.

"It's me. You'd better get here. Carolina and Brandon are trying to elope."

"Oh, my God! We knew something bad was going to happen!" cried Rhonda. "We've got to save this wedding, Annie!"

CHAPTER NINE

Carlotta rushed into the office. "Daniel said we can't cancel the wedding. The bridal magazine is going to cover it."

Before I could say anything, Carlotta's cell rang. She glanced at it. "It's Caro." She clicked onto the call. "Caro? What's going on? You must come back here to the hotel." Carlotta held up a finger and then punched in speaker phone.

"Mom? I'm sorry. Last night I panicked." She sniffled. "Vivian scolded me about the table linens, and all these plans for the wedding aren't what I originally wanted. We changed them to make Brandon's family happy. I've always wanted a beach wedding."

Carlotta looked at me. "Can you do it?"

I gave her a thumbs up. Though it would take some work, we could move the wedding to the beach.

Carlotta said, "I have Ann Sanders here with me. She's indicated you can still have a beach wedding if that's what you want. Please, come back to the hotel right now, so we can all get ready. I've been worried sick about you. And please, have Brandon call his mother. She's worried too."

"I'm sorry to upset you and everyone else. But I wasn't sure I could go through with all those preparations. Brandon and I just want to be married without any fighting."

Carlotta drew herself up. "I will speak to Vivian and Gregory. It's time this nonsense stopped."

"I know Vivian is trying hard to please Gregory, but this is my wedding, Brandon's wedding, ours."

"Exactly. Ann said you're not that far away. So get here as quickly as you can. Don't worry. We'll work things out at this end."

"I love you, Mom. Tell Dad I'm sorry. But, when it came down to it, I didn't want to marry Brandon without you two there."

Carlotta clicked off the call and turned to me with a look of determination. "I should've stood up to Vivian and Gregory from the beginning. What can I do to help you? You said we could change locations?"

"Yes. We have a large deck used to watch the sunsets in the evening. We'll set up chairs there facing the beach for those who can't or who are uncomfortable walking on the sand. The area in front of the deck is where we'll have the wedding."

"What about all the sand on people's feet?" asked Carlotta.

"We have several water faucets for that purpose at the end of the boardwalk ..."

Rhonda burst into the room, stopping me. "Okay, what are we doing?" I filled her in.

"I'd better go tell Vivian about the change," said Carlotta. "As long as the wedding can still take place at 11:30, we'll be fine."

"We'll make it happen," I said brightly while Rhonda rolled her eyes.

After Carlotta left, we called Bernie, Lorraine, and Manny to our office and gave them the change in plans. "We'll need the staff that was going to set up on the lawn to set up chairs on the sunset deck," I said.

"And we'll need to use the portable altar," said Rhonda.

"Also, The Bride magazine will be here taking photos, so we want everything to look its best," I mentioned.

"I'll be in touch with Tropical Fleurs immediately," said Lorraine.

The three of them left, and Rhonda and I sat in our chairs facing one another.

"Well, Annie, you were right. This wedding is a stinker. But we'll make it work." Rhonda shook her head. "I'm glad I'm not the one telling Vivian Forrest about the change in plans."

I chuckled. "Carlotta won't need any help doing that. She's mad at herself for not putting them in their place earlier."

At 11:15, Rhonda and I stood by as the first wedding guests began to trickle into the sunset deck. We'd put up a sign for our regular hotel guests to please use a different section of the beach. From the edge of the lawn, an outdoor carpet led to the sunset deck, where plenty of seats were placed. In front of the deck, a small altar sat on the sand between two white concrete stands, each holding a floral bouquet. Tropical fleurs had cooperated with the change of plans and, instead of more elaborate indoor bouquets, had created baskets of pink and white flowers perfect for this occasion.

From the buzz of conversation, guests seemed excited about the change. While some chose to sit on the deck, others took off their shoes and headed out to the beach, where a section had been cordoned off.

On the sunset deck, a harpist and a guitar player began to play music.

I gazed around, remembering my own beach wedding. I loved the idea of something as special as a wedding celebrated with nature. Even now, the cries of the seagulls above us sounded like blessings from the heavens. The sound of waves meeting the shore and pulling away seemed another way to bless the marriage with wishes that the bride and groom would be as constant in their love.

Brandon arrived, and he and his four groomsmen stood

beside the altar wearing khaki Bermuda shorts and pink golf shirts, which they'd planned to wear in the garden.

After the guests were in place, Gregory walked his mother to the sunset deck, then turned back and escorted Brandon's mother to a chair beside her in the front row on the deck, and they both sat.

Daniel escorted Carlotta to the sand in front of the altar and returned to the bridal party.

Anticipation built.

The four bridesmaids, one behind the other, walked onto the beach and stood opposite the altar from the groomsmen. They looked young, fresh, and beautiful, dressed in pink sundresses in different styles.

The music changed to the Whitney Houston song, "*I Will Always Love You.*" My eyes filled as I watched Carolina and her father walk down to the beach with happy smiles.

Carolina wore a long, silk, sleeveless white dress and carried a bouquet of pink lilies, hydrangeas, white roses, and freesia. She wore a crown of the same flowers on her head, which stood out in sharp contrast to her gleaming black hair.

The photographer from the magazine was taking pictures with Carolina's every step, but she didn't seem fazed by it. Instead, she kept staring at Brandon with such love that tears filled his eyes.

Teary-eyed, I exchanged glances with Rhonda, who was trying not to make too much noise as she sobbed into a handkerchief she'd brought.

Observing how Brandon held his hand to Carolina, I knew they'd be all right. Even Brandon's parents and grandmother seemed touched by that moment.

I eased away from the ceremony to ensure staff was standing by with towels at the beach's edge to help people rinse the sand off their feet.

Inside, the dining room looked perfect. We'd taken over the entire dining area so a cocktail reception could be held at one end before lunch was served at the other end.

Annette approached. "How did it go? I saw the bride before she went outside. She's stunning."

"Yes, she is. She's so happy that her wedding turned out to be what she wanted. I am too. Weddings are for the bride and groom."

"I'm glad you could accommodate the change in plans," said Annette.

We turned as the photographer from the magazine hurried toward us. "I need to get a couple of shots of the luncheon setup."

"No problem," said Annette. "Let me show you."

As she led him away, I silently blessed her and the rest of our staff. We couldn't run the hotel without them.

Rhonda came into the dining room as the crowd descended. "Well, we did it! I was worried, but that wedding was one of the best. Even Brandon's parents are raving about how sweet it was."

"Really? That's a change," I said, wondering what Carlotta had said to them to bring about that new attitude.

We stood by and watched as people came in, found their seats in the dining section, and then enjoyed drinks at the reception. All seemed in order.

I saw Vivian and went to speak to her.

"Hello, it was a lovely wedding," I said brightly. "We've kept right to your schedule. So you'll be able to catch your flight back to New York."

Tears filled Vivian's eyes. "Actually, I wanted to stay, but Gregory insisted he get his mother back home." She clasped my hand. "I'm very sorry about the mix-up. I didn't realize Caro was so upset about the wedding plans."

"I'm happy we could accommodate her and Brandon and make it the wedding they wanted. I understand they'll spend a night or two in Miami before taking off for Paris. That should be a pleasant break from the wedding activities."

"Oh, my husband is signaling me," said Vivian. "We're to have our photographs taken with some other people. Thanks again for your help."

As she walked away, I found myself feeling sorry for her. Her husband dominated her.

The luncheon was a lovely affair. With family tensions eased, the room filled with conviviality.

A green lettuce and strawberry salad preceded the main course starting the meal with a touch of sweetness. For the main course, the bride and groom had chosen cold poached salmon with a lemon and caper sauce, grilled asparagus, and a tart potato salad with a vinegar and dill dressing that complimented the fish. For those who didn't like salmon, a cold poached chicken breast with a watercress sauce was offered.

Because much of the prep work could be done beforehand, it was a relatively easy meal to serve.

Rhonda and I left the guests enjoying their food and went to the office to reconcile the billing. With the parents of both the bride and groom leaving that afternoon, we wanted to make sure we'd captured most of the expenses. Though we'd follow up with any additional costs, we'd found it left a better feeling for members of a wedding party to pay while they still experienced an appreciation for all we'd done for them.

"We oughta add a surcharge for all the aggravation they've

caused us," grumped Rhonda. "This wedding had the makings of a disaster."

"Sh-h-h," I whispered. "No bad luck. We won't celebrate until the parents and most of the guests are gone."

"Right, right," said Rhonda. "Good thinking."

A short while later, Lorraine joined us. "The wedding party is finishing their dessert now."

"Okay, we'll come to say goodbye to those who are leaving," I said. Though we didn't always have the opportunity to thank hotel guests as they were leaving, we tried to do it for our wedding parties.

When we arrived in the dining room, I saw Gregory, his mother, and Vivian talking to Carlotta and Daniel. We went over to them.

The photographer said, "May I have a picture of you and your business partner with the wedding parties?"

"Sure," I said and cooperated as he formed us into a group and took a photograph. It would look as if we were a friendly group when it had been anything but.

While Rhonda spoke to Daniel and Carlotta, I thanked the Forrests for taking part in the wedding at the hotel. "I hope you found everything to your satisfaction."

After a pause, Gregory said, "It was nice."

I was irritated by Gregory's hesitation. Was it difficult simply to thank us? I glanced at Vivian, and a flash of understanding passed between us. She, no doubt, was used to living with this domineering man who paid more attention to his mother than to her. I'd seen Vivian talking to Caro and Brandon earlier. They'd all looked very serious.

Vivian shook my hand. "I appreciate all you did to make the kids happy. The wedding turned out to be lovely."

"Very nice, indeed," said Gregory's mother quite stiffly.

A feeling of disquiet seized me as they left the dining room to get ready to go. I'd seen something on Vivian's face that told me she was as annoyed by her husband's behavior as I was.

Sometime later, Rhonda and I were in the office when a knock sounded at the door, and Vivian poked her head inside the room.

"Any chance I could have a room at the hotel for the rest of the week? I've decided to stay, after all."

Rhonda and I looked at one another and grinned.

"We certainly do," Rhonda said. "Brandon and Caro already spoke to us about the possibility, and they hoped you'd agree to some well-deserved time to yourself."

"They did?" A smile broke across Vivian's face, and I realized how beautiful she was without a worried look marring her features. A shiver crossed my shoulders, and I had a fleeting thought that she might one day become a member of the hotel family.

"I'll walk you to the lobby," I said, "to make sure your luggage gets to the right room."

"Thanks. I've got a lot of thinking to do," Vivian said.

As Rhonda and I later agreed, weddings brought out the best and the worst of people. Maybe this was one of those times when good would follow a bad beginning.

CHAPTER TEN

That night after Robbie was asleep, Vaughn and I took a swim in the heated pool. It was a good way to relax after a stressful day, and if it led to a night of sex, so much the better.

I swam briskly for a few laps and then went and sat on the steps in the shallow end. Vaughn joined me and tugged me onto his lap facing him.

"How are you?" he asked. "You've been pretty quiet."

"I've had a lot to think about. The mother of the groom reminded me of how I constantly tried to keep Robert happy, even though he was a hard man to please. That, and then the contrast of remembering our beach wedding and how special that was." I wrapped my arms around his neck and lifted my face to kiss him.

His lips met mine, and I closed my eyes, drinking in the taste of him, the touch of his skin against mine. I was very lucky to have found a man like Vaughn, who encouraged me to do whatever I wanted to be happy. He worked with beautiful women every day in his work but never made me feel less than what he truly desired.

I nestled against his broad chest. "I love you so much," I murmured.

"Love you too," he said, nuzzling my neck.

Laughing at the tickling sensation, I pulled away and looked up at him. "I can't wait until we go on our mini vacation. We should be able to set one up soon."

"Can we still go if there's a puppy in the house?" he said.

"Elena is good with dogs. She's already excited by the idea of a puppy because Troy won't let her get one."

"Okay, then. It's a go if we find the right little pup. Robbie is very excited about it. I hope we won't be disappointed when we see them."

I chuckled. "I've never known of anyone walking away from a Dachshund puppy."

"You're right. We'll just assume it's going to happen."

The next morning, Robbie was pumped up with adrenaline as we ate breakfast. Our trip to Orlando would take approximately two to three hours.

On the drive, we let Robbie talk about how good he was with dogs and how he'd take care of the puppy. When I asked him what names he had in mind for a dog, he surprised me by saying, "Baxter."

"Where did you get that name?" I asked.

He shrugged. "One of the kids in my class has a dog named Baxter, and I like it."

"What kind of dog does he have?"

"He looks sort of like a Dachshund, but he has long legs," said Robbie.

"Do you mean a Doberman?" I asked.

"Yes, that's it. A Doberman."

"That's a name for a boy dog. Is that what you want?" Vaughn asked.

Robbie smiled and nodded. "He can be Trudy's boyfriend."

I glanced at Vaughn and held in a laugh.

"I see," Vaughn said. "Well, they would be brother and sister too. What about another female? That would give Trudy a sister."

"Maybe," said Robbie. "When are we going to get there?"

he asked for what seemed like the twentieth time.

"Soon," I said, excited as he to see the puppies.

We arrived at a house in the suburbs, a pretty, one-story beige stucco house. As we got out of the car, we could hear dogs barking.

After we rang the bell, a woman came to the door, holding a puppy. "Are you the Sanders family?"

"Yes," I said as Robbie moved restlessly beside me.

"Hi, I'm Laura Smith. I believe I talked to you, Mr. Sanders." She blinked in surprise, and I could tell the moment she realized who she was talking to. She waited until we all were ready, then opened the door, urging an adult Dachshund at her feet to stand back.

"Come in. We have the mother and the babies out back. Here." She handed the puppy to Robbie, who grinned as if he'd just received a gift from Santa. We followed the woman through the kitchen to a sunroom where the pups' mother sat on a pile of blankets on the tile floor while four other puppies played around her.

"Here they are," Mrs. Smith said. "All five of them have had their shots at ten weeks, have been microchipped, and are pretty much house-trained." She took the puppy from Robbie and set it down with the others. "Go ahead, sit on the floor, if you like, and see which puppy you want," she said to Robbie. "One of the female pups, the one over there, has already been spoken for. That leaves two boys and two girls."

Robbie sat on the floor and giggled as all the puppies ran over to him, stumbling against each other in their haste.

"As you can see, they've been raised as family pets. My two teenagers help."

Vaughn took pictures of Robbie surrounded by puppies.

This was a time we'd all remember. I knelt beside Robbie and laughed when one of the pups scooted up into my lap.

"What do you think, Robbie?" I asked.

"I like this one," he said, giggling as the puppy covered his cheeks with kisses. "Look! She loves me!"

The look of joy on his face made my eyes sting with tears. "You're right; she's a girl. Are you sure? You told us you wanted a boy."

Robbie drew the puppy to his chest in a protective gesture. "She's the one I want. Trudy needs a sister like Dad said," he said with quiet confidence.

I gazed at the puppy's sweet face. Her brown eyes seemed to look right inside me, and she was wagging her tail so fast it was a blur. "She's a beauty."

"We call her Cindy, but you're free to change the name," said Mrs. Smith. "She's very cuddly and loving."

"Cindy is a perfect name for her," declared Robbie, and I was amused at his change of heart. But then, the puppies were all adorable, and the pup also needed to choose Robbie.

"As I told you on the phone, we have an older female Dachshund at home. Any problem having two females in the house?" asked Vaughn, smiling at Robbie and the puppy.

"Usually not. It depends on the temperament of the dog," said Mrs. Smith.

"Trudy is very loving and is wonderful around human babies," I said.

"Well, then, it sounds as if that won't be a problem. Like I told Mr. Sanders earlier, we don't let our pups go to just any home. The fact that you already have a Dachshund whom you love is very important to me."

"Her name is Trudy, and she's definitely a member of the family," I replied, eager to get her approval.

"If you're sure this puppy is the one you want, I can get

started on the paperwork," said Mrs. Smith. "The pups' father is off the premises, but he's a real beauty. I'll give you pictures of him. You can see for yourself how lovely our Sadie is. She has the papers to prove she comes from a good line. He does too."

While Vaughn dealt with the paperwork and paid, I listened as Mrs. Smith rattled off a list of instructions. "Don't worry. I've written down everything. We send the puppies home with a blanket that smells of Mom and a favorite toy. In addition, we recommend a stuffed toy with a heartbeat to help the puppy through the transition period. Will you be keeping her in a crate most of the time?"

Vaughn and I looked at each other.

"I think it's a good idea," I said. "We can bring the crate into Robbie's bedroom at night, so he can get up and let her out when she needs to go outside."

"It sounds as if you've already thought this through," said Mrs. Smith giving us a look of satisfaction.

I returned her smile, but I realized that having a new puppy was a whole lot like bringing home a human baby.

"We'll stop by the pet store on our way home," said Vaughn quietly.

"Stay here in the kitchen, and I'll bring the puppy to you," said Mrs. Smith. "And then you can leave quietly and quickly. It's easier on Mom."

I felt a pang at the thought of Cindy's mother missing one of her pups.

A moment later, Robbie held the puppy. We left the house and went to the car. I held the puppy while Robbie buckled into his seat in the back of the car, and then I handed the puppy wrapped in the blanket to Robbie.

Robbie looked up at us. Tears filled his eyes as he hugged Cindy close to him. "Thank you. I can't believe she's mine."

"She truly is," I said, realizing we'd all have to remember this sweet moment as we trained her. Dachshunds, we knew, could be stubborn.

Mrs. Smith stood by as we got settled in the car, and then with a sad look, she waved goodbye and turned to go back into the house.

"Okay, Robbie," said Vaughn as we drove away. "We'll go to the pet store on our way home and pick up the items Mrs. Smith suggested. And then your job as owner of a Dachshund puppy will begin."

"Can Cindy sleep in my room with Trudy and me?" asked Robbie.

"I think that might be the best solution. But the puppy should remain in her crate at night for training purposes," I said.

"You'll need to get up with her at night, if necessary," said Vaughn. "She'll need to go outside early morning, too."

Robbie, bless his heart, nodded agreeably, but I wondered if he knew what he and all of us were getting into.

When we finally walked into the house with the puppy, we faced our first test when Trudy and the puppy nosed one another. The puppy, playful as always, bounced around Trudy.

Trudy looked up at us with a look of surprise, and then I swear a pout appeared on her face. She studied me with an expression that said, "Really? You're doing this to me?"

I sat on the floor with Trudy and wrapped my arms around her. "It's okay. You're going to love having your little sister around. Isn't she adorable?"

The puppy came over to us, stared at Trudy, and let out a small yip.

Trudy barked, and the puppy edged away, then rolled over submissively.

"She's a baby, be careful," I warned Trudy. I glanced at Vaughn and Robbie, waiting to see how Trudy reacted next.

Trudy trotted over to the puppy and began to lick her face.

The three of us released sighs of relief. It was going to be all right.

That evening when Robbie went to bed, Trudy stretched out beside him. The puppy lay in the crate with the blanket, her favorite toy, and the special stuffed dog with a heartbeat. We kissed Robbie goodnight, reminded him to come to get us if there was a problem, but told him if the puppy whined to go outside, he should take her.

Vaughn made sure our automatic outdoor light system was in order so Robbie could see in the darkness, and then we retired to our bedroom. I knew that even though the puppy was Robbie's responsibility, I'd be half-awake most of the night to be sure everything was going well.

Sometime in the night I awoke with a start. The house was silent. I decided to go see what was happening with the puppy.

I opened the door to Robbie's room and peered inside. With the help of a nightlight, I spied Robbie sprawled on the bed. Trudy lay at his side, curled up with the puppy.

I couldn't help smiling. Dachshunds had a talent for getting their way. Even a puppy as young as Cindy.

But there was something special about seeing a boy with his dogs. Growing up in a cold household alone, I wished I'd had the chance for a warm, cuddly puppy.

Alert now, Trudy stared at me, but I silently closed the door and walked away, leaving them to a peaceful night.

CHAPTER ELEVEN

The next morning, I slid onto my chair in the board room at the hotel just as Bernie was about to start his weekly staff meeting. I couldn't wait to show him pictures of the puppy. Trudy had been his dog before she came to live with us, and I knew how he felt about Dachshunds.

Beside me, Rhonda asked, "How did it go with the puppy?"

"The good news is that it went well. The puppy slept with Robbie and Trudy. The bad news is that now she won't want to be crate-trained at night. We'll see what, if anything, might change going forward, but it will take some work to train that puppy. She is too darn cute."

"Ready to begin?" Bernie asked, and my mind turned to business and a review of the wedding as I sipped on my second cup of coffee.

As the meeting was about to end, I said," I wish to thank all of you and those staffers you supervise for the help you gave us with the last-minute changes to the wedding plans. Without you, we never could've pulled it off."

"Yeah, we had bad vibes from the beginning of the weekend, but it turned out right because of you," said Rhonda. "I just hope our next wedding isn't as difficult."

"As we've often said, weddings bring out the best and worst in people." Lorraine's lips curved. "But we've got an older couple coming in for a very small, intimate wedding next weekend, so it should be a very different event."

As the meeting broke up, I hurried to Bernie to show him pictures of the puppy and Trudy together.

As expected, he lit up at the sight of them. "I still miss Trudy, but I know she couldn't have a better home than with you. Are there more puppies available? I might be able to talk Annette into one."

"When we left the house, there were three puppies still available. I'll give you the number of the owner if you want." I'd always been grateful that Bernie had given us Trudy because she had helped Robbie make the transition to our house. I looked up the information on my phone and gave it to him.

"Let me see," said Rhonda.

When I showed her the pictures, she sighed, "Adorable. You're forbidden to show those photos to anyone in my family."

I laughed. "The only reason we got a puppy is that Trudy is starting to show her age. We thought a puppy would keep her young. And it's a good lesson for Robbie to have the care of a puppy. He's old enough."

"Willow and Drew are still too young," said Rhonda. "It's sometimes hard for me to believe I'm the mother of pre-kindergartners."

"The time is going by fast," I said. "I wonder if Willow will be married at the hotel one day."

"Thank goodness, you and I will be long retired by then. Once that girl makes up her mind about something, that's it. Willow now wears her ballet outfit with her brother's cowboy boots and refuses to take them off. She says they are her high heels." Rhonda shook her head. "I admit she reminds me of me. That's what makes it scary."

I laughed because the two of them were alike in many ways.

We headed to our office and stopped when Vivian approached us. "I've just had the most marvelous walk on the beach. I met a very interesting neighbor of yours. He's offered to give me a tour of the neighborhood."

A cold chill ran down my back. "Are you talking about Brock Goodwin?"

"Why, yes. That's his name," said Vivian smiling.

I gave a warning glance to Rhonda and said, "He isn't someone we consider reputable. I suggest you stay away from him."

"Oh? Well then, no worries. I'll cancel my appointment," said Vivian. "Thank you for telling me. He seemed like a very charming man, eager to help me."

Rhonda rolled her eyes and clamped her mouth shut.

"It's a lovely day. Have a pleasant one," I said, leading Rhonda away before she could burst out with her personal selection of descriptive words to describe Brock.

Inside our office, Rhonda clamped her hands on her hips and faced me with a look of disgust. "That's it, Annie. Brock's now harassing our guests. It's got to stop."

"I'm as mad as you are," I said, "but we cannot prove it. Vivian was pleased by the attention and his offer of help."

Rhonda let out a long sigh. "You're right. We'll have to catch him in action or find someone annoyed by his stunts like this."

"It's going to be difficult. As Vivian said, Brock can be very charming. Forget him. Let's go and see how Bobby is doing with his introduction to working with Jean-Luc."

When we walked into the kitchen, Consuela looked up at us and glanced in Jean-Luc's direction. Bobby stood by as Jean-Luc explained that he would start as a pot washer. Then, if he showed interest, he could do some other jobs.

"*Comprenez vous?*" Jean-Luc said, giving Bobby a steady look.

Bobby said, "I'm not sure what you just said, but okay. My agent told me I won't be here that long."

Jean-Luc frowned. "Whether it's a day, a week, or a month, I'm the chef."

Bobby shuffled his feet, let out a long sigh, and nodded.

Rhonda and I approached.

"Good morning, Bobby. Congratulations on doing a great job for Manny. It will be good to work for Jean-Luc. You can learn a lot from him. You'll also get a chance to taste some delicious food."

"If it's not a burger and fries, I'm not interested," said Bobby, shaking his head.

Jean-Luc looked as if Bobby had slapped his face. He held up his hands. "No, no! I can't have someone in the kitchen who doesn't care about food."

"Hold on," said Rhonda. "We all have to learn about food somewhere. Who better to teach him than you, Jean-Luc?"

"You have such a special ability to make everything taste delicious," I began ...

Jean-Luc turned and went into his office, mumbling to himself.

"Guess he doesn't want to work with me," said Bobby with a shrug.

"Oh, he's gonna work with you," Rhonda said. "I know that look. Try to stay on his best side. That's all I'm sayin'."

We left the kitchen before getting more involved. Working with Jean-Luc would be a bigger lesson for Bobby than we'd thought.

When I got home that afternoon, Vaughn and Robbie were sitting on the lanai playing with the dogs. It seemed such a normal, calm scene I was happy to leave the hotel troubles behind. The lure of a few days off would keep me going forward. That, and knowing that Tina Marks was arriving tomorrow with her two children to stay in the house on the hotel property. After getting off to a rocky start with Tina as a spoiled movie star, we'd come to her defense against an abusive mother and taken her into our hotel family. She was now like another daughter to me.

"Hi," I said, lowering myself onto the tile floor and giving Trudy an ear rub. Cindy left Robbie to trot over to me, wanting attention too. I took her into my lap, letting her get used to me. "How's she doing?"

"She's very smart," said Robbie. She knows when I take her outside and say, "Get busy," as Mrs. Smith told us, she'll go to the bathroom."

"I've had to make a couple of dashes outside with her," said Vaughn. "But since Robbie is home from school, she's stayed with him the whole time."

"We must remember she's still a baby and needs lots of sleep," I said, rising. "When she settles down for a nap, we need to leave her alone." I turned to Vaughn. "Any resolution on the crate training at night?"

Vaughn shook his head. "As long as she is trained to be comfortable in the crate during the day, I have no problem with Cindy sleeping with Trudy and Robbie at night. She got up only once during the night and then again early morning. Robbie did an excellent job of taking care of her."

"I'm really a good dad," said Robbie seriously, making me laugh and hug him.

"You're terrific with Trudy and now Cindy," I said, affirming what he'd said.

I left them and went to change into something more comfortable. Rhonda and I made sure to dress comfortably and professionally, but there was nothing better than pulling on a pair of shorts and a T-shirt for total relaxation.

Vaughn walked into the room as I finished.

"Bad day at the hotel?" he asked, wrapping his arms around me.

"Lots to think about. Brock has been approaching some of our guests, which Rhonda and I don't like. Bobby has started working with Jean-Luc, and I'm not sure it will work out. I'll check in with them tomorrow. A bright note is that we got a preview of the magazine article about Carolina Horne's wedding, and it's spectacular. A great piece of PR for us."

"As it should be," said Vaughn. "The care and attention you give to weddings are worth every penny people spend."

"We couldn't do it without our staff. Our Spring Brunch is coming up, and I want to make sure the employee party following it is especially nice."

"I should be around for it, though, as I mentioned, I'm going to approach Nick Swain about any upcoming roles that might be suitable in one of his movies. If it means going to California to audition or speak to people, I will."

"Understood," I said. "In the meantime, a few days at the Palm Island Club sounds better and better. Hopefully, after our Spring Brunch."

"Let's have a glass of wine before I grill up some chicken. I even made a special salad dressing today," he said.

"My! You really are becoming domestic," I teased before his lips met mine, and my body relaxed in his arms.

CHAPTER TWELVE

The next morning before I walked into the office, I stopped in the kitchen, hoping to see Bobby.

I served myself a cup of coffee and turned to Consuela. "Any sign of Bobby?"

"He's not due in for a while," she said. "He worked late last night."

"Any word on how it went?" I asked her.

She shook her head. "It's Jean-Luc's day off, so we won't know for a while."

"When Bobby comes in, will you please send him to my office?"

"Sure thing. I see on the guest list that Tina Marks is returning. I can't wait to see her. Her latest movie was terrific." Consuela smiled. "But it's really her baby I want to see."

"Me, too. Hard to believe that she has another little boy, and Victor is almost four."

"Happy changes," said Consuela. "She was such a lost soul when she first came to the hotel."

I left the kitchen with thoughts of Tina and the horrible mother who would do anything to secure a movie role for her daughter.

Rhonda called to say she was running late, so I was in the office alone when Bobby came to see me.

"How's it going?" I asked him. "You worked late last night." I indicated for him to sit in a chair.

He plopped down into it and stared out the window. "The whole week I was working for Manny, we talked. I mean, he talked, and I listened. If I quit now, I would never be able to face him. As you said, he's a good man. He didn't take any bullshit from me. Did you know when he first came to the States to work, he and Consuela had only ten dollars?"

"He and Consuela have worked hard all their lives and raised a wonderful family," I said, surprised by Bobby.

"Jean-Luc isn't easy to work with, but I'm going to try." Bobby shook his head. "He wants me to taste everything he's cooking. What's that all about?"

"To eat tasty, healthy food is one of the pleasures of living. 'Live, love, eat' is a motto for many. For Jean-Luc and others who feel like him, presenting someone with good food is a gift they're willing to share. It's an insult to him if someone is close-minded enough to refuse to taste something new."

"We never had fancy food at home," said Bobby. "It was easy to grab a hamburger and fries."

"Do yourself, Jean-Luc, and us a favor and try to go along with his ideas. I think you will surprise yourself with how much you like it."

Bobby sighed and moved restlessly. "This whole thing is stupid. But, as you asked, I'll give it a try. I'm not the only one in the kitchen Jean-Luc yells at, but nobody seems to mind."

"All chefs are a bit temperamental," I said, remembering the arguments Jean-Luc and Rhonda used to get into. They'd sometimes made me laugh. Especially when she'd called him a fuckin' French frog, as only she could and get away with it.

"How's the kitchen schedule going to work out for you?" I asked. "You should have most afternoons off, which will give you time to relax or do exercises or whatever you do to prepare for another season."

"I jog in the morning before it gets hot, and then later, I get to relax before I have to go to work. I'm getting paid for all this work, aren't I?"

I shrugged. "I don't know. That's between you and your coach."

Bobby made a sound of disgust and shook his head. "It's not fair."

"Talk to your coach. We're just doing a favor for him."

"Why? What's in it for you?"

"Just helping a friend. And now, you. That's all. Someday, you'll thank all of us for believing in you."

Bobby let out a long sigh and got to his feet. "Gotta go to work."

I stood too and placed a hand on his shoulder, inches above me. "You're doing well. I'm proud of you for sticking it out."

He bobbed his head and left the office. In the short time he'd been at the hotel, I'd seen nice changes in him and hoped he'd realize that many people cared for him without wanting anything in return but respect.

Rhonda burst into the office a short while later, gave me a triumphant smile and said, "Guess who I just picked up from the airport?"

A sneaky suspicion filled my mind. "Arthur?"

"Yes. When the time comes, he'll be interested in meeting Lorraine. We had a chance to talk privately on the way home from the airport, and he admitted he's lonely and ready to date."

"Did you tell him about Lorraine?" I asked, dismayed by Rhonda's boldness.

"Not exactly. I want them to think they made it happen, not

me. Ya know?"

"What I do know is that I'm not getting involved. We have enough going on." I held up my hand to stop her from trying to change my mind. "You're on your own. You can handle Reggie. Not me."

"I know Reggie loved his mother, but hopefully, he'll realize his father is lonely. If he sees how happy his father is, he won't have a problem with it." Rhonda waved away my concern. "You know how good I am at this. Bernie and Annette, Lindsay and Jean-Luc, Jax and Mandy, Debra and Whit are just a few examples."

I rolled my eyes. Rhonda took credit for those relationships, but she had little to do with those people falling in love.

Rhonda threw an arm across my shoulder. "You know I love people to find love."

"That's the only part that's true," I said. "But be careful. Arthur and Lorraine are two strong people who surely have their own ideas. And you don't want Reggie angry with you. That would make Angie and Will upset too."

"Yeah, it's risky, but I know it'll be worth it. I heard you had a talk with Bobby. How'd that go?"

"Surprisingly well. Manny had quite a bit to say to him as they worked together. Of course, Bobby doesn't want to disappoint him. I don't think he's had much guidance from his father, and he seems to have taken Manny's advice to heart."

Rhonda said, "Jean-Luc is an entirely different challenge. That will make or break Bobby's determination to see this job through."

"And say a lot about the man we think he can become. He's a good kid who doesn't know how to respect others at every level."

"His coach must be one of those people he does respect, or

he wouldn't stick it out here," said Rhonda. "How's the puppy doing? And what will you do about her when you leave for the Palm Island Club?"

"Cindy is adorable, and Robbie is proud to be a "good dad" as he calls himself."

Rhonda laughed. "It was such a lucky day for Robbie when you adopted him. Vaughn has been a good influence."

"When the time comes, Elena will check on Cindy during the day, and then she'll stay at the house with Robbie and the dogs after leaving Liz's house in the afternoon." I emitted a worried sigh. "I need to find a relative or friend of hers to take over if she goes to work for Troy."

"Has she mentioned it?" asked Rhonda.

"Not yet," I replied, dreading the thought.

"I've given Rita another raise. With my two active kids, she deserves it. Having children in your forties is a far cry from having a child in your early twenties."

"We'll take it one day at a time." I checked my watch. "Tina should be arriving soon." My cell rang. *Paul. Calling from our limo.*

"Hi, Ann. We're approaching the hotel," Paul said quietly.

"Thanks." I grabbed Rhonda's arm. "They're almost here. Let's go."

We hurried to the front steps.

Waiting for her to arrive, my thoughts flew back to the sassy, obnoxious young woman Tina was when she first arrived. Now this happy, successful woman was coming home to the only family she had, and I couldn't wait to see her.

Rhonda nudged me with her elbow. "Here she is!"

She took off down the stairs, and I hurried behind her.

Paul pulled the limo to a stop in front of the hotel. Before he could go around and assist her, Tina opened the back door and climbed out of the car into our arms for a group hug.

"It's so wonderful to see you!" I cried. "Let us get a good look at you."

She was of medium height with a curvy figure and striking facial features. Her straight hair hung at her shoulders in a chestnut brown that suited her and matched her eyes. Her face was even more beautiful as she neared her thirties and enjoyed a happy life as a wife and mother. It did my heart good to see her this way.

A little boy climbed out of the limo and stood facing us.

"And this must be Victor," I said, lowering myself to his height. "Hi. Do you remember me? I'm Auntie Ann."

"And I'm Auntie Rhonda," said Rhonda bending down to him from behind my shoulder. "I'm Drew and Willow's mommy."

Victor smiled at us.

"He's such a nice big brother to Tyler," Tina said, placing a hand on his shoulder and smiling at him before being handed an adorable baby boy dressed in navy shorts and a navy and white striped T-shirt.

Last to emerge from the limousine was a young woman with blonde hair and striking blue eyes. Short and thin, I guessed her age to be late teens or early twenties.

"This is Sydney Harris, my very capable nanny. We all love her," said Tina, giving her an affectionate look.

A flush of pink covered Sydney's cheeks.

Victor tugged on Sydney's hands. "Syd. I wanna go to the beach."

"Not yet. We have to unpack first," said Sydney, laying a gentle hand on his head. "You can help carry in things from the car. Right?"

Victor nodded agreeably, and Rhonda and I exchanged quick glances at Sydney's calm authority. For such a small person, she exuded a lot of control.

"Why don't you take the boys over to the house, Sydney, while I sign us in? It won't take me but a minute. I'll meet you there."

Sydney took the baby from Tina and helped Victor back into the limo. After Paul drove them to the house, I shook my head. "Your nanny is a wonder."

"It's a long story, but she's grateful to live with us. She escaped a verbally abusive mother, something I could totally relate to."

"We were talking about you earlier," said Rhonda. "We remember what you were like when you first arrived at the hotel."

"Don't remind me. I was such a brat," said Tina.

"We have someone like that here at the hotel now. A certain football player," said Rhonda.

"He's coming along, working for Jean-Luc to gain some humility and appreciation for others," I said. "We're doing another favor for Amelia Swanson."

Tina's eyes rounded. "Really? After the last two times, I thought you decided not to get involved with requests from her."

"Honestly, how do you say no to the vice president of the United States when she asks you for help?" I asked.

"At least this time, there's no sister hiding from an abusive husband," said Rhonda. "Being shot at took years off my life."

"How are all the babies?" Tina asked. "It's hard for me to believe you each have three grandchildren."

"It's a trip, especially for me, with Willow and Drew at home," said Rhonda. "But I love them all, children and grandchildren."

"And Liz? How's she handling three at once? I can't imagine it," said Tina shaking her head.

"Liz is doing well with 'the Ts,' as we call them, with a lot of help from friends and neighbors, who love coming in occasionally. But Liz tends to put a lot of pressure on herself to become the best mother ever. I hope she'll give herself a break and ease up."

"All these babies are wearin' Annie and me out," said Rhonda. "Who'd a thunk it? And now you're here with two babies of your own. It must be something in the Gulf waters."

Tina laughed. "I'd better check in and get to the house. I don't want to leave Sydney with two travel-weary kids for too long."

"I'll go with you," said Rhonda. "Annie can check on the kids. All right?"

"Sure. That'll give me a chance to see the boys again." I headed to the house I'd loved as my own. It was the first house I'd ever owned. Vaughn and I had courted there, made love there.

As I approached the house, I could hear laughter coming from inside. It made me happy to hear it.

I knocked on the door and went inside.

Sydney was on the floor playing with the boys, tickling them.

When she saw me, she stood. "I'm trying to give them a chance to let off some steam. The flight from the coast was long."

"Tina will be along shortly. Is there anything I can do to help you?"

"As soon as I can, I'll unpack the boys' things and then my own. Tina's bags are already in her room." Sydney picked up the baby and gazed around. "This house is beautiful."

"Thanks. I wanted to warn you about the pool. We have the safety gates around it, but be sure Victor can't figure out how to open it. We don't want any tragedies."

"No, of course not. I plan on taking Victor to the beach as

often as possible, especially when Tyler is down for a nap. He'll have plenty of space to run around there." She smiled. "Don't worry. Tina made sure I had lifeguard training."

Victor walked over to Sydney and wrapped an arm around her waist. Her face lit with affection, and she hugged him to her.

Tina arrived, and Victor ran to her. Tyler held out his arms to her.

Beaming, Tina took Tyler from Sydney and ruffled Victor's hair. "We're all going to sleep well tonight. The smell of the salt air always makes me relax."

"I'll leave you to it. Let us know if you need anything." I gave Tina a quick hug. "Welcome Home."

CHAPTER THIRTEEN

The next day, Vaughn left early for New York to tape a public service ad that came up at the last minute. He'd also check on his condo there. He asked me to go with him, but I had to say no. A senator and his wife hosted a private party at the hotel, and Rhonda and I agreed to attend. It didn't happen often, but this VIP couple had supported us and the hotel from our early days. They were more like friends now, and I didn't want to disappoint them.

After dropping Robbie off at school, I decided to walk on the beach. It was a good way to gather my thoughts, and it would be a test for Trudy and Cindy to see how they'd handle themselves gated into the kitchen. Cindy was still enough of a baby to require naps, which suited Trudy perfectly.

I pulled up to the back of the hotel and parked. It was early enough that it was quiet, with only a few guests walking the grounds. I took off my sandals and headed across the grass to the beach.

Vaughn had told me the producers of *The Sins of the Children,* the soap opera Vaughn had starred in for several years, wanted him to come back for a few cameo roles, which meant he'd be staying in New York for a while. I didn't mind, except he'd be working with Lily Dorio again. She'd never hidden the fact that she wanted Vaughn. She'd even accused him of impregnating her in a wild scheme gone wrong. It was all foolish nonsense, but it still bothered me.

The sand still held a coolness from the night as I stepped onto it and wiggled my toes.

I saw Bobby jogging toward me and waved and then turned as Sydney approached me.

"Good morning. I see you've found some free time," I said, smiling at her.

"Fortunately, the boys are good sleepers, and Tina likes to get up early with them. It gives me a chance to walk the beach."

Bobby sprinted up to us. "Good morning, Ann." His gaze rested on Sydney, and his eyes lit with interest.

"Bobby, this is Sydney Harris, a nanny for one of my friends." I turned to her. "And this is Bobby Bailey. He's helping us around the hotel for a while."

"Nice," said Sydney. "You're lucky to be able to work at a place like The Beach House Hotel. It's beautiful."

He gave her a thoughtful look. "Guess you're right."

"What do you do at the hotel?" Sydney asked him, and I waited to see how he'd answer.

"I work in the kitchen," he said, giving nothing away.

"Another lucky break. The food here is to die for. Simply delicious. I hope you get to eat some of it. What's your favorite?"

"Uh, I'm still trying to decide," Bobby said, avoiding the answer. "I'll let you know. Do you always walk the beach in the morning?"

"As often as I can," she said. "I'm back here in the afternoon with my charges—two little boys."

"Okay, I'll look for you," Bobby said, giving us both a salute as he began to jog away.

I waited to see if Sydney showed any sign of recognition, but she didn't seem to know who he was. She simply said, "Wow! He's pretty big."

"Are you getting settled at the house?" I asked.

"Yes, it's going to be a great stay. Tina is very happy to be here, and the boys love it. That makes my job easier."

"How long have you been working for her? Tina hasn't been here for almost two years, and you weren't with her last visit."

"I started with her a few months before Tyler was born." She gave me a wistful look. "In some ways, he feels like my baby. I've spent so much time with him."

"I can imagine. My daughter, Liz, had triplets about the time Tyler was born. You two will have to meet. Maybe we can arrange a luncheon. Something fun to give you both a break. Rhonda's daughter, Angela, too. I know you'd all get along."

"That sounds nice," said Sydney. There was a note of sadness in her voice I found intriguing. I decided to ask Tina about it. I left the beach, grabbed my sandals, and headed to the house. I loved having coffee with Tina during the rare opportunities given to us.

Tina was in the kitchen with her children when I arrived. Victor looked up at me and smiled, matching the one on Tina's face. My heart filled with love for the woman who'd needed Rhonda and me to help her. Now, seeing her with her boys, Tina looked as happy as I'd ever seen her.

She hugged me. "You're in time to share a cup of coffee with me. Tyler is fine in his highchair for the moment, and Victor is done with his breakfast, too."

"Thanks. I'd love it. I saw Sydney on the beach and thought I might have a chance to chat with you alone. You mentioned she has quite a story, and I'm curious."

Tina poured me a cup of coffee and handed it to me black. "Still the same?"

I nodded. "Thanks."

Tina said, "This is so much fun. Let me get Victor settled in front of the TV for his morning show, and I'll be right back. Tyler likes to play with his toys in the highchair while I clean up. He'll be fine for a while."

While Tina was with Victor, I played a game with Tyler, who was using Cheerios to make designs. The "Ts" liked to do the same thing.

Tina returned to the kitchen, grabbed a cup of coffee, and sat at the table with me. "I've often told you and Rhonda how much it meant to me to be rescued from my mother's control. Since then, I've tried to be aware of other young women in trouble. I was in a coffee shop and overheard Sydney telling a friend she was saving money to leave home, that her mother's cruelty was out of control." Tina shook her head and let out a long sigh. "You can imagine how I must have felt hearing that."

"Oh, yes," I said.

"At the risk of frightening the girls, I asked if I could speak to them. They were open to it. I queried them about the situation at home and ended up offering Sydney a job. While her mother wasn't as bad as mine, Sydney was being blamed for her mother losing her latest boyfriend, a man Sydney said had tried to abuse her sexually. He was gone, but her mother wasn't happy about it."

Seeing tears fill Tina's eyes, I placed my hand on Tina's arm to comfort her. That was just a portion of what Tina had faced with her mother. "So, you saved her," I said.

"She's a lovely person—bright, capable, hard-working. Her father wasn't ever part of the picture. Her mother doesn't want communication. So, she's embraced my family. We made a big deal out of her nineteenth birthday, and she loved it."

"She looks young for a nineteen-year-old," I said. "Maybe it's that fresh, California look about her."

Tina's lips curved into a warm smile. "She's beautiful, isn't she?"

"Yes, she is. No trouble with boys?"

"No. Though she dates, Sydney is reluctant to get too close, too fast. Understandable, considering her background," said Tina. At Tyler's cries, Tina rose, took him out of his highchair, and set him down on the living room rug near Victor.

I was going to mention Sydney's meeting with Bobby but stopped as Sydney walked into the house.

"Ah, Syd, can you please take Tyler? I want to talk to my friend," said Tina.

"Sure. Ready, Sweetie?" cooed Sydney, picking him up and hugging him.

Watching her, I was touched by Sydney's gentle way with the baby she knew very well. He obviously adored her.

"Are you up for a walk on the beach?" Tina asked me.

"I'd love it. It's been too long since you've made the trip to Florida, and I want to get caught up on all your news."

Tina and I left the house and headed to the beach.

She turned to me. "I want you to be among the first to know I'm taking a break from starring in movies. Nick and I talked it over, and we both think it's a good move for me to spend time with the boys even as I learn some of the behind-the-scenes business."

"Marvelous," I said, meaning it. Tina had started as a child star and deserved this different kind of life.

"How is Vaughn doing being out of the show?" Tina asked.

"He's enjoying it, but he's been asked and has agreed to do a few cameo appearances. Lily Dorio will be part of that." I shook my head. "She seems to keep appearing in our lives."

Tina shook her head. "I saw her not too long ago. She's had so much plastic surgery you almost wouldn't recognize her. Over the top."

"Vaughn is interested in doing another movie. He's hoping to talk to Nick about it."

"Excellent, because Nick has something in mind," said Tina. She took hold of my hand and squeezed it. "It was such a lucky day when I was sent to The Beach House Hotel."

"We have someone in-house who was sent here," I said. "In fact, Sydney met him this morning. He's a football star working on his attitude. But I like him. He's a good guy who's been overwhelmed by fame and fortune. Sydney didn't even recognize him, which was good for him. I'm not about to clue her in."

Tina grinned. "Sydney is very down-to-earth. She has no interest in flashy men. They remind her too much of her mother's boyfriends."

"Hm-m-m. Good thing Rhonda isn't here. She'd want to play matchmaker. As it is, she's trying to get Reggie's father together with our wedding planner."

Tina laughed. "Rhonda is a hoot. I hope she never changes."

"Me, too," I said, chuckling with Tina. Rhonda was irrepressible.

As if our words had conjured her up, Rhonda walked onto the sand and turned toward us.

We waited for her, and then she and Tina embraced.

"What'cha cooking up?" Rhonda said.

"I was telling Ann about my new life changes," said Tina. She filled Rhonda in on her news and said, "I'm not making a big splash about it, but letting it evolve. Because you two are like my special mothers, I wanted you to know about it."

"I'm happy for you, honey," said Rhonda. "Every day around here feels like a life change with our growing families. Yours, too. Your two boys are adorable."

"Thanks. Nick and I have talked about another one. We'll see. We'd both like a girl, if possible."

"This is a special place to try and make it happen," said

Rhonda bluntly. "We have babies everywhere."

"I can't wait to see all the little ones. Sally Kate looks very grown-up in photos."

"She's way ahead of her years," bragged Rhonda. "She's always trying to keep up with her brother. It was just the opposite in my house with Drew trying to keep up with his sister."

"Victor is very sweet with Tyler, showing him all kinds of things." Tina turned to me. "Does that happen with all of Liz's babies being the same age?"

I smiled at the memories. "Oh, yes. When one of them discovers something, the other two quickly learn. Right now, they're crawling. But I saw Emma trying to pull herself up to a standing position by a table. The others will soon follow."

We continued to stroll along the beach, enjoying the sun on our shoulders. I stepped into the cool water and turned to face the Gulf waters as the foamy waves met my feet. Tina waded in beside me, took hold of my hand, and offered a hand to Rhonda. We stood side by side, three women united by love.

"I remember how you taught me just to stand quietly, listen to the sounds around me, and discover the beauty here," Tina said softly.

"It's something Vaughn and I still do when we're together at the beach," I said. "It brings back happy memories of our early romance. In those quiet moments, I learned to trust Vaughn."

I looked up and groaned as a familiar figure strolled toward us. "Oh, no! Does he never work?"

"How can a day that started so beautifully turn into this," growled Rhonda staring at Brock Goodwin.

"Oh, dear, that horrible man," said Tina. "I can't believe a group of women haven't reported his behavior. He's way too slimy."

Oblivious to all the bad thoughts directed at him, Brock continued to advance toward us.

"We could simply ignore him," said Tina, facing the water again.

"Not a chance," said Rhonda. "That rat bastard doesn't miss a chance to harass us somehow."

"Morning, ladies. I saw that the foundation for the new house on site had been poured. I can't wait to uncover what you're planning. I intend to inspect it."

"I talked to someone in your department, and our property isn't assigned to you and won't be," I said calmly.

Deep lines marred Brock's forehead, and his smile evaporated. "You have no right to talk to anyone in my department about me."

"Believe it or not, Brock, this isn't about you," said Rhonda. "It's about running a successful business."

"A business that abuses people like me by over-reacting to the neighborhood rules," he said, sounding like a sullen schoolboy.

I sent Rhonda a silent message to let it go.

Rhonda glanced at me, sighed, and said, "Bye, Brock," as she looped her arm through mine before walking away with Tina and me.

"Annie, you owe me one," Rhonda muttered. "I had a lot I wanted to say to him."

"Don't I know it," I said, "which is exactly why I didn't want you to do that. Brock already has our new building on his radar. I have a feeling he's going to interfere no matter what."

"That man still gives me the creeps," said Tina.

"Good thing he didn't recognize you with that hat and those sunglasses," I said. "Let's go back to the hotel. We can talk there."

"I have to go back to the house," Tina said. "I have an online meeting in a short while and want to be ready for it. But let's try to meet up like this again."

We all exchanged quick hugs, and while Tina went on her way, Rhonda and I headed indoors.

"I have an appointment this morning and need to go over a few things with you before then," Rhonda told me.

We went through the back of the hotel and into the kitchen. While I got ice water and Rhonda got a cup of coffee, Jean-Luc walked into the room.

"Good morning," I said, pleased to see him happy. Since he'd married Lindsay, he was a changed man.

He bobbed his head. *"Bonjour."*

"How is Bobby doing?" I asked him.

A smile spread across his face. "We're making progress. He asked me if he could taste some different foods."

I held back a chuckle. I knew very well why Bobby had done that, and it had more to do with an attractive young lady named Sydney than anything else. "Every little thing counts."

"Yes, but he still has much to learn about cooking and food," said Jean-Luc. I won't give up on him, though I won't make it easy."

"Good for you," said Rhonda. "That young man still has a lot to learn about life and other people."

We left Jean-Luc and went to the quiet of our office.

I sat in my desk chair and faced Rhonda. "What did you want to talk to me about?"

"Will and I have decided that instead of an Alaskan cruise, we want to return to Tahiti, where we honeymooned. Sort of a revival of our marriage." Rhonda sighed. "Some of that magic is gone. We want to get it back."

"Your marriage isn't in trouble, is it?" I asked, concerned.

"No," said Rhonda. "But I remember how things were when we first married. Now, it seems like we are just managing to get through life. We each have our own business, the kids demand a lot of attention, and now the grandchildren do too."

"That's called life," I said. "Anything beyond that?" Rhonda was usually upbeat.

"Well, you know how I never believed I was okay body-wise. Now, it's worse. Gravity is taking hold, and when I look into the mirror, I want to run away and hide. It's especially hard when we live in an area where young, skinny women are everywhere, flaunting their bodies. I know how awful I must sound, but I feel old, fat, and ugly."

"I wish I could say I don't understand, but I get it because it's hard getting older, seeing my body and face change shape. But I keep telling myself, it's life."

"Annie, you're in far better shape than I am," said Rhonda. "I just want to feel attractive to Will."

"Have you seen the way he looks at you?" I countered. "The man has been in love with you since you met."

"I want him to show it more," said Rhonda. "Ya know?"

I hugged her. "I think you're right. A vacation is what you need. A chance for you and Will to be together without interruption. Remember all those pieces of sexy lingerie you bought for your honeymoon?"

Rhonda let out a soft giggle. "The ones I didn't even bother to put on?"

"That's right," I said. "We'll pick out a few more and see where it takes you."

Rhonda got up from her chair, did a little shimmy and danced across the floor. When she held out her hand, I grabbed it, got up and danced with her.

"What are you girls doing?" asked Dorothy Stern, beaming at us, her eyes shining behind her glasses as she walked into the room.

Laughing, Rhonda and I stopped and faced her.

"Just getting ready for some vacation," I said. "As soon as we can fit it in, Vaughn and I are heading to The Palm Island Club for a few days, and Rhonda and Will plan to return to Tahiti."

"Wonderful! You both deserve a break," said Dorothy. "When you have exact dates, give them to me, and I'll set aside extra time to come in to help."

"Deal," said Rhonda, puffing as she took her seat again.

We gave Dorothy her assignment for the morning—working on invitations for our Spring Brunch, and then alone in the office once more, I said to Rhonda. "What appointment do you have?"

She shook her head. "Just my annual physical. Nothing I'm worried about."

"Good. Do you have time to walk to the new house before leaving?"

Rhonda checked her watch and stood. "Let's make it quick."

We walked over to the northeast corner of the property and beyond the house already there to where a new foundation had been poured. It would be another small but well-designed house with a pool landscaped for privacy.

When we arrived, one of Jeff's workmen was there.

"Hello," I said. "We're here to see what's been done. We've talked to Jeff, who said he can start the framing soon."

"Yup. That's on the schedule," the man said.

"It's important for you to know that we don't want Brock Goodwin to be here for any reason. He's a part-timer in the Building Inspector's office, but he's out to get us."

"We've already spoken to the department about the problem but thought you ought to be aware."

"Is he a tall man with gray hair?" the man asked. At my nod, he continued, "He was here a short while ago."

"Dammit!" said Rhonda. "I'm going to get security to post Brock's picture at this site warning people to send him away." She chuckled. "A Most Wanted Away poster."

I laughed. It would serve Brock right.

That afternoon, I was going over monthly financials for the hotel when my cell rang. *Rhonda*. I picked it up. "Hey, you! Are you coming back this afternoon?"

Silence met me; then I heard a soft sob. "Rhonda, what's wrong?"

"Oh, Annie, the doctor found a lump in my breast. I'm at the mammography center now. But I don't think it's good. They're doing an ultrasound next. I think I'm going to die."

"Whoa, don't even go there," I said, my heart pounding with alarm. "I'm coming down to the center to stay with you while you wait for results."

"Thanks," Rhonda said softly and hung up.

I turned off my computer, grabbed my purse, and took off.

CHAPTER FOURTEEN

When I walked into the waiting area of the mammography center, Rhonda looked up at me and dabbed at her eyes.

I went over to her, sat in the empty chair beside her, and held her hand. "Everything's going to be all right. This center is state of the art, thanks to some donations from you."

"I'm glad I helped pay for their new machines. It's amazing what they can discover." She hiccupped. "But I didn't want them to find anything on me."

"But that's exactly what we'd want. Early detection. Had you felt anything yourself?"

Rhonda shook her head. "No, but I haven't been looking. I'm not sure I could've felt it anyway." Her eyes filled again.

"Rhonda?" a nurse asked from the doorway.

"Come with me, Annie. I can't do this without you," said Rhonda, giving me a pleading look.

I rose and followed her and the nurse into an exam room. "Dr. Perkins will be with you shortly," announced the nurse before she left us alone.

"Oh, Annie, what if it's cancer? A bad kind? I don't want to leave Will, my kids, Angela's family, or you."

"Let's think happy thoughts," I said. "Tina would tell us not to send any bad vibes to the universe."

"Right, right," said Rhonda. She stopped talking but wiggled one foot nervously. When she spoke, her voice was full of regret. "I never should've complained about my life. Maybe I'm being punished for not being grateful for it."

"No," I said softly. "We're not going there either. That's not how it works."

"Hello, Rhonda. Who is this?' asked an attractive, middle-aged woman wearing a white coat.

"Hi, Dr. Perkins. This is my best friend, Ann Sanders. She's here to give me support. What's the news?"

Dr. Perkins sat on the edge of her desk and faced Rhonda. "After viewing the ultrasound, I'm convinced we need to take a biopsy. It could be just a type of cyst, but it looks a little off, and I want to make sure that it's nothing more than that."

"What does having a biopsy mean exactly?" said Rhonda. Her face turned white.

"We'll do a lumpectomy to remove the lump and examine it. It's a simple surgery. While we're in there, we'll check for any signs of trouble, but I don't anticipate that. This is just a cautionary measure."

"If you find signs of cancer, what then?" I asked, feeling sick at the thought.

"Then we'll decide how extensive the treatment should be and whether more surgery is necessary. But I'm hopeful that it won't be the case. Today, we treat breast cancer much more effectively without the mutilation that sometimes happened in the past." Dr. Perkins frowned. "I'm here in this business because of what my mother went through when I was a child."

"I'm pleased that many women like you are dedicated to treating breast cancer. It's every woman's worry," I said.

"I understand," said Dr. Perkins. "As I said, with new medications and procedures, we beat it back much more effectively than before." She placed a hand on Rhonda's shoulder. "You're in good health. That's a big plus. It would be best if you didn't worry unnecessarily. We're going to take good care of you."

"How soon can the surgery be done?" I asked.

"You'll have to talk to my office staff to arrange it, but it probably won't be for a couple of weeks. I'm fully booked, and this is a very early-stage situation. If I thought this was cancer, I'd push for an earlier date, but as I mentioned, this procedure is only for clarification." Dr. Perkins rose. "I'll see you soon. Take care, Rhonda. Nice to meet you, Ann."

When Dr. Perkins closed the door behind her, Rhonda turned to me.

"What if Dr. Perkins was just being nice to me? What if I have cancer, and they can't beat it? What if I die without seeing Willow married? Or Drew graduate college? Or get my Will back to what we once had?" She covered her face and sobbed.

I placed my arm across her shoulder. "Rhonda, I don't think things are as bad as you believe. If Dr. Perkins knew it was cancer, she'd move things along for you. But from what she said, this is more exploratory than anything else. That's what we both need to remember."

Rhonda lifted her tear-streaked face. "You're right. I have to be brave for the kids and Will. But, Annie, I need to be able to be honest with you. I'm scared shitless."

"I understand. I'll be here for you anytime you need to talk."

Rhonda dabbed at her eyes with a tissue. "Oh, Annie, it was such a lucky day when our girls became college roommates. Otherwise, we might never have met."

"We almost met when you first came to Boston, but we didn't become friends until after I visited you here in Sabal," I said, remembering how shocked I'd been to meet her. Angela was small and quiet. Rhonda was anything but.

I stood. "I'll wait for you in the waiting room. Then, if you want, we can go to our special hiding place at the hotel and talk further."

"And have one of our special margaritas," added Rhonda.

I was pleased to see that Rhonda's natural spunkiness was showing. Margaritas at The Beach House Hotel were a special treat we sometimes shared when we needed time to talk privately.

Back at the hotel, sitting on a secret, private balcony accessed through a maid's closet, Rhonda and I faced one another. "I think of Katherine dying, unable to see how Angela, Reggie, and the kids are all doing. I don't want that to happen to me," said Rhonda. She clapped a hand to her chest. "I can feel my heart stop just thinking of it."

"It's important that you think positively about this," I said with feeling. "Dr. Perkins was upbeat; you need to be too."

"Dr. Perkins is used to the whole idea. I'm not," said Rhonda. "I need to schedule an appointment with my lawyer to review my will. If I die, I need to protect my children, and as agreed, I'll give you my shares of the hotel. Oh, Gawd! Who'll you pick for a partner?"

"I refuse to think of that now, Rhonda. If the time comes when it's necessary, we'll do it together. Right now, I'm concentrating on positive thoughts and a prayer or two." Once Rhonda had a thought in her head, it was hard to erase it, and I didn't want her to go into a tailspin over this.

"Okay, that's fair, but this is making me think of all the things I should've done to update my will as things changed." She sipped her margarita and stared out at the Gulf waters. "I've been very lucky. Maybe more than I deserve, but I swear I'll leave this world a better place than I found it."

I placed a hand on her arm. "You already have, Rhonda. You have been a very generous donor to many charities, not just one."

"I want you to handle my funeral, Annie," said Rhonda, her eyes filling with fresh tears.

"Rhonda, look at me," I said sternly. "We are going to get through this. Together. We're not talking about dying and funerals."

"I guess you're right. But I still want you to handle my funeral when the time comes," said Rhonda. "And now, no matter what, Will and I are taking the vacation we talked about."

"That's more like it. Think of the fun you'll have together."

"Yeah, we might never get a chance to do it again," said Rhonda, her eyes filling once more. "Oh, Gawd! How am I going to tell Will I might be dying."

I rolled my eyes. It was going to be a long two weeks before Rhonda's surgery. I wondered what it would take to move that appointment up. Rhonda had already agreed to fill any cancellations on Dr. Perkins' schedule, but it wasn't likely to happen.

When I arrived home, Vaughn greeted me with a kiss. "Happy you're home. I've invited Nick and Tina for dinner. I'm marinating a steak and have all the ingredients for a salad. I told him we'd keep it casual. I hope you don't mind. He wants to talk to me about something."

I glanced at the clock. I'd have just enough time to set the table and take a quick shower. After the day I'd had, I needed to wash away the stress and feel refreshed enough to face company. The thought of anything bad happening to Rhonda had burned a hole in my heart. It was a story that would have to wait until I could talk to Vaughn alone.

Standing under the water of the shower, I let a few of the tears I'd held back escape. I didn't want to imagine when

Rhonda and I would not share our days, whether at work or after, when we'd retired from the hotel business.

Later, as I was dressing, Vaughn came into the room to tell me that Tina and Nick had just pulled into the driveway. I knew how eager he was to talk to Nick and wasn't irritated that the dinner was sprung on me at the last minute. Tina and Nick were family.

I followed Vaughn into the front hall to greet them.

Tina wore a sundress and sandals and had pulled her hair into a ponytail, making her appear younger than she was, though she'd just reached thirty. Tall next to her, Nick looked the part of someone in the movie business, with gray hair pulled away from his face and tied in back with a leather string. They make such a handsome couple, I thought, reaching forward to give them each a hug.

As we headed out to the lanai, Cindy yipped hello from behind the gate keeping her in the kitchen.

Robbie appeared with Trudy. "Want to see my new puppy?" he asked Tina.

"Of course," she said, giving him a quick hug. "It's good to see you. Wow! You keep on growing!"

Robbie smiled at her and nodded.

We all went to the kitchen entrance to see Cindy. Housebroken for the most part, she needed to be supervised for her chewing on anything and everything she came into contact with.

Even now, as she wagged her tail at us, she was surrounded by chew toys that couldn't hold the interest of an electrical cord.

"How darling!" cooed Tina, picking up Cindy and laughing when the dog kissed her cheek.

"When Victor sees her, he's going to want a Dachshund, too," said Nick, stroking Cindy's head. "Guess it's about time for a dog for him."

"Why don't you let Cindy and Trudy play in the yard for a while so we grownups can sit and talk," I said quietly to Robbie.

He picked up the puppy and left the kitchen to go outdoors.

"My! He's growing up fast," said Tina as we walked onto the lanai. "He was still a toddler when he came to you."

I was filled with pride. "He's a good kid. We've all taken him under our wings, and he's turning out just fine."

"Your boys seem healthy and happy," I commented. "They must like having you around more."

"Yes, I think it's made a difference," said Tina. "And having Sydney around helps too. She's very good with them."

"She's a darling young woman," I said. "I'm not sure, but I think she will be a good influence on our football player. He's apparently now interested in learning about new foods after talking to her on the beach."

"Syd told me she met a nice guy, which is unusual for her," said Tina. "She doesn't have much use for them after her teen years with her mother. It would be nice if she and your football player became friends."

The four of us settled on the lanai. Vaughn served drinks, and I brought out cheese puff appetizers I'd heated. I listened as Nick talked about things going on in his business. New ideas were presented to him for movies and television series regularly, and I loved hearing about them.

"I have something in mind for Vaughn." Nick turned to him. "How would you like to do a limited series for streaming through Netflix or another venue?"

"It depends on what you're talking about," said Vaughn, his eyes alight with interest.

"The movie you made with Laurel Hyde, *Love is in the Air*, was such a hit that I think you should do something with her again. Something along the same lines. I've got a script I want you to look at."

"That would be terrific," said Vaughn. "Laurel is easy to work with, very professional. How many episodes are you thinking about?"

"If the first season does well, it could be renewed. The series is based on books by a well-loved author, and the possibilities are endless." Nick grinned. "I'm hooked on the idea and will do my best to make it work."

"It's intriguing," said Vaughn turning to me. "How would you feel about my doing a potentially long-term project?"

"It sounds like a fabulous opportunity. I'm pleased for you," I said honestly. "We've never wanted to hold each other back."

Nick turned to me. "I like that you support one another. I want Tina to do what she wants. Did you know she's already showing great promise with directing?"

"Maybe I should help with this project," Tina said, giving Nick the sexy smile that all her male fans loved.

He winked at her. "We'll see."

Nick and I grinned as she blew him a kiss. It was good to see them playful. Until Tina came into his life, Nick had been a very serious person. They seemed as happy as I'd ever seen them.

It wasn't until we were lying in bed that I told Vaughn about Rhonda's situation. I lifted up on my elbow and faced him. "The doctor was optimistic, but what if it is cancer? What if, God forbid, anything happened to Rhonda?"

He reached for me, and I nestled against him, trying not to cry.

Vaughn rubbed my back in comforting circles. "You told

me the doctor said this was exploratory and not to be too worried. I think it's important for you to be strong. Rhonda depends on you for that."

I sighed. "You know how Rhonda is, she's already got herself buried and me handling her funeral."

"I'm sure of that. But this is one of those times when patience is a necessary virtue. Just be kind and sympathetic, but no more than that. We don't want to feed into her fears."

"When did you ever get so smart? You know Rhonda almost as well as I do." I kissed him, grateful for his advice.

"Cancer is an awful thing," Vaughn said softly. "Ellie suffered so."

Fresh resolve filled me. "I won't let anything bad happen to Rhonda. I'll fight with her all the way."

"I know you will, and I love you for that. But honestly, if Dr. Perkins were sure of cancer, she wouldn't wait to take care of it. Maybe that's what you must keep in mind."

Vaughn made sense. I knew it. But I also knew the next few weeks would be among the hardest to face. We needed an answer.

CHAPTER FIFTEEN

W hen I walked into the kitchen at the hotel the next morning, Consuela looked up at me with tears in her eyes. "Rhonda ..."

She stopped to catch her breath, and I wrapped my arms around her. "I don't know what Rhonda told you, but it may not be cancer. They're doing a biopsy to check it out."

"Oh," said Consuela wiping her eyes. "Is she going to be all right?"

"I believe it with my whole heart. If it is cancer, it's at an early stage, and I think it's important not to panic. It'll just make things worse for Rhonda."

"*Si, si,*" said Consuela. "It was such a shock. But we need to keep Rhonda calm."

"Exactly," I said, hoping she hadn't announced it to the entire staff. They'd be rattled by such news.

I served myself a cup of coffee and headed into the office.

Rhonda was sitting at her desk, writing notes on a large white sheet of paper. "Good. You're here. I think I have someone you could ask to be your partner if anything happens to me."

I sat down in my chair and faced her. "Rhonda, enough of this dying business. We don't know if it's cancer or a cyst, and we won't know for a while. We've got to think positively and try not to scare everyone. Consuela was a mess when I walked into the kitchen. If word gets out that you're dying, which I don't believe is the case, what will that do to the staff and the hotel?"

Rhonda sank back into her chair and sighed. "I know you're right, but I'm scared to death to think of Drew and Willow without their mother."

I gave her a sympathetic look. "Why don't you call Dr. Perkins' office and see if you can talk to her? You were very upset yesterday that you might not have heard clearly."

Rhonda brightened. "You're right. That's exactly what I'm going to do."

I sat beside her while she called the office and waited for Dr. Perkins to get on the call.

At the sound of Dr. Perkin's voice, Rhonda burst into tears. "I'm sorry. I need to have a better understanding of what you told me yesterday. I was and am so upset, I can't help thinking I'm dying."

Rhonda was quiet, and then she said, "I can do that. I'll see you at three. Thank you, thank you, Dr. Perkins."

"Well?" I asked Rhonda.

"Dr. Perkins had a free time slot, and she will do the biopsy this afternoon in her office. So they're set up for something like this." Rhonda reached for my hand. "You'll come with me, won't you?"

"Of course," I answered. "It's very sweet of Dr. Perkins to do this for you."

"It really is," said Rhonda. "I'll do something nice for her and the staff. Right now, I just want to get through this day."

That afternoon, I sat in the waiting area of Dr. Perkins' office trying to keep busy playing a game on my phone. But my heart and mind were on Rhonda. She'd been given a local anesthetic for the procedure, and while she wouldn't get a lab report for a few days, she would know better what she was facing.

Dr. Perkins appeared still wearing her surgical mask. She lifted it off her face and spoke.

"I've looked closely at Rhonda's condition, inspected the lump we removed, and am confident it is simply a fluid-filled cyst. With no history of breast cancer in Rhonda's family, it is unlikely that this is anything more than that. But we'll test it, of course."

"I can't thank you enough for your understanding," I said. "We were all heartbroken at the idea of anything happening to Rhonda. And you know her, she's all in or all out in any situation, and as she told you, she was too scared to think clearly."

"Rhonda is a wonderful woman, very generous," said Dr. Perkins. "I'm glad we could take care of this for her. At this point, there's no reason for her to think she's in danger. I will go back and talk to her about it, but she wanted me to report to you immediately."

After Dr. Perkins left, I sat and slowly breathed in and out as I said a prayer of thanks. A disaster had been averted.

In the car, Rhonda was quiet as I drove her home.

"Are you okay?" I asked.

"I'm thinking of the women who aren't as lucky as I am. Women who have breast cancer and have to go through all the procedures wondering if it's going to work." She turned to me. "I want to do something to raise money for research on it. We can hold a benefit at the hotel, and I'll personally match every dollar raised."

"Great idea. Maybe we can put Lorraine in charge of a dinner and a reception where guests could meet various VIPs. Something special but easier than a large wedding."

Rhonda clapped me on the back. "I knew you'd

understand. Thanks, Annie. You're the best!"

I chuckled. It was good to have the old Rhonda back.

The next morning, after I kissed Robbie and Vaughn goodbye, I headed to the hotel, eager to get back to the financials I'd set aside to help Rhonda.

I parked the car and paused. If the upset with Rhonda was to mean anything to us, we had to follow through on our commitment to make better use of our time. I got out of the car and headed to the beach. It was a beautiful morning, and I wanted to enjoy it.

As I usually did, I walked across the sand to the water. The frothy edges of the salt-water waves looked like lace against the hard-packed wet sand. The water's surface was almost smooth, and the waves whispered as they stroked the sand like a loving hand and moved away again.

Peace wrapped me in its embrace, and I lifted my face to the sky, grateful for this moment. When I looked down, I gazed at the tiny sanderlings and other shore birds racing across the water's edge, leaving tiny footprints behind.

"Hi, Ann," came a voice behind me, and I turned to see Bobby standing there.

"Good morning! Another early day of jogging?" I asked.

"I need to keep in shape. Being able to run on the beach is great exercise." He kicked at the sand with a sneakered foot. "Any idea if Sydney might be coming down here?"

Beyond him, I could see Sydney striding onto the sand.

"I believe she's here now. Bobby, I know you're interested in her, but be careful. Sydney has been hurt in the past. You owe it to her and yourself to be kind."

His gaze settled on me, and he nodded. "Gotcha."

"Good," I said. "I hope things are going well in the kitchen."

Bobby grimaced. "Jean-Luc is a hard ass, but he's good. I'm learning a lot about what happens in a kitchen and how it's a team effort."

"I'm happy to hear that," I commented, pleased.

Bobby jogged away to greet Sydney, and I watched him thinking he'd changed a lot in the short time he'd been here. But then, this was a more realistic situation because we didn't cater to him nor allow him to believe he could act out.

I remained where I was, letting the waves swirl around my ankles, enjoying the sights and sounds around me. Rhonda's scare had made me realize how precious life was and how important it was to enjoy every moment of it.

My cell rang. *Liz.*

"Hi, honey. What's up?" I asked.

"Can you come to stay with the Ts while I go to the dentist?"

"Sure. What time?"

"Now. I lost a filling, and the dentist can see me right away. Sorry for the lack of a warning," she said.

"No problem. I'll come right away." I clicked off the call and returned to my car, relieved Rhonda and I had no morning meetings scheduled.

When I entered Liz's house, I was surprised by the quiet.

Liz walked into the living room. "It's a good morning. Everyone is happy for once. Elena will be here soon to help you get the kids down for a morning nap."

We walked together to the gated playroom and peered inside.

Emma was sitting up, pounding a red plastic ring against the carpet, Noah was lying on his back, kicking and holding onto a yellow plastic ring, and Olivia was crawling toward the stack of toys in the corner.

When they noticed us, smiles crossed their faces, and they all began to crawl toward us.

Tears blurred my vision. They were very healthy and so adorable.

"They're cute, aren't they?" said Liz, leaning over and lifting a baby into her arms.

I reached for another one, and then struggling a bit, I managed to pick up one more baby. My arms full, I laughed as little hands patted my cheeks.

"Grandma," said Liz. "That's grandma."

"GeeGee," said Emma.

Liz whooped," Yes! GeeGee." She turned to me. "Guess you've got a new name. GeeGee is cute."

Pleased, I said, "It's fine by me." I'd once thought I wouldn't have grandchildren, and now I had three of the cutest ever. They could make up any name they wanted for me.

We carried the babies into the kitchen and got them all settled in their highchairs for their morning snack before bottles and naptime.

"I've got to go. Thanks for helping me, Mom," said Liz, kissing my cheek. "I must admit that even though it means going to the dentist, I'll be thrilled to get out of the house. Alone."

I laughed. "Go. Elena and I will be here with the kids."

While the T's were eating, I called Rhonda and told her I'd be delayed.

"Not a problem," she said. "But when you get in, we've got to talk."

"Okay. See you later."

I pulled up a chair and sat facing the kids. Holding up a picture book to them, I read the simple words, as spellbound by the colorful illustrations as they were. It was something I loved to do with them.

A short while later, Elena rushed into the room. "Sorry, I'm late."

"Not a problem, but I'm glad you're here. It's time for bottles and naps."

Elena fixed the bottles, and then the two of us sat on the couch with the three babies. She held two, and I held one as we all nestled together in a comfortable group, giving each child a sense of security as they drank their milk. At lunchtime, they were learning to use cups, but using bottles was helpful in getting them settled for a nap.

When all three were finally in their cribs, I said goodbye to Elena and headed to the hotel. It was a late arrival for me, but I didn't care.

At the hotel, I grabbed my usual cup of coffee and entered the office to find Rhonda on the phone. She waved at me and continued talking. "Yes, that will be fine. Two weeks from today. Thanks. I'll reconfirm with you later today. Goodbye."

"Who was that?" I asked, sitting at my desk and taking a sip of coffee.

"That, dear Ann, was my travel agent. Will and I are leaving for a two-week vacation two weeks from today. That is just one thing I'm doing. I need to talk to you about hours here at the hotel. I'm no longer willing to work until early evening. I will be home when the kids get home from school."

I grinned. "Excellent. Because I was going to tell you that I think we need to give Bernie more authority. We pay him well to run the place; we need to back off. I don't mean to leave the hotel operation completely but to become more overseers and less active in the small stuff."

"Oh, good. I wasn't sure how you felt about it. But with the girls unable to take over for us for a while, I want to be able to give Drew and Willow a chance to have me around more. This cancer scare has made me think a lot about it."

"I understand. Robbie still needs me, and I want to be available to Vaughn when he's home. Liz and Chad and the babies too. They were adorable this morning. I don't want to miss out on their lives."

"Good. This hotel is our baby too, but like all parents, we need to let go and have others take care of it," said Rhonda.

"Are you still planning on coming in every day?" I asked. I knew Rhonda well enough to know she wouldn't simply walk away.

"Oh, yes. But on my own time. We'll have to agree on what hours we need to be here for meetings, but otherwise, we should feel free to come and go as we wish. You'll still do the financial stuff, and I'll do more of the socializing. Like usual. Sound good?"

"Sounds practical," I said. I'd always been the one to handle the details. It worked best that way.

"Oh, good. Now, when are you going on your long weekend with Vaughn?"

"We might have to put it off for a while because Vaughn is going to fly out to California to talk about starting a new, limited television series."

"But that won't be fair if I have vacation and you don't," protested Rhonda.

"Don't worry about me. Keep making plans for your trip. Our Spring Brunch is coming up, and then you'll be free to go." I set down my coffee cup. "I'm glad we had this discussion. It's been brewing for a while."

"I'm glad too," said Rhonda. "By the way, guess who will be here for the Spring Brunch?"

"Arthur?" I asked, noting her self-satisfied smile.

"Yes. I figure that's a good time to introduce him to Lorraine. "'Course, I don't want either of them to know what I'm doing."

I shook my head, knowing that was exactly what would happen. Rhonda couldn't hold back when she thought she was managing her matchmaker skills.

That afternoon, at the Department Heads meeting Rhonda and I had set up, we explained to the staff that our hours would become more flexible. "Bernie is a great general manager who deserves our respect and gratitude for the job he's doing," I said. "While we're stepping back, you will have excellent oversight and support."

Bernie then stood. "Thank you both for all you do. I believe we have a strong team to handle the hotel, and I look forward to conferring with you from time to time. The two of you mean a lot to our guests and the hotel's success. As noted in the past, your vision for the kind of hotel it has become is what makes it very special."

As applause and good wishes from everyone followed, I felt a surge of pride for all Rhonda and I had done. As she often said, it was a lucky day when our daughters became college roommates, and I'd stayed at her large, beautiful home, which became The Beach House Hotel.

She and I left the meeting and went to our office.

"It's all good, Annie," said Rhonda. "It's a new beginning for us."

"Yes," I said, unsure how I felt about it. I was the detail and numbers person and knew it would be harder to let go.

But when I left the hotel and headed home, my spirits lifted. Vaughn was waiting for me there.

CHAPTER SIXTEEN

I walked into the house and found Cindy alone in her cage. Looking through the kitchen window, I saw Vaughn at the boat with Robbie and Trudy.

I picked up Cindy and hugged her to me. "You're too little to be by the water. Once you've gotten more shots and have some training, you can be part of the sailing crew.'

She kissed me and wagged her tail.

I took her outside to go to the bathroom and then carried her down to the boat, holding onto her tightly.

Robbie ran over to me. "Hi, Mom. I can hold Cindy."

I handed her to him and kissed Vaughn hello. "We need to talk."

"Yes, I have something to tell you," he replied. He turned to Robbie. "Come on up to the house, son. We're through here for the time being."

As if making sure the puppy was well-tended, Trudy trotted behind Robbie and Cindy as we climbed the slope to the house. I watched her, feeling the same protective way toward the hotel Rhonda and I had agreed to leave in Bernie's hands.

Vaughn studied me. "Are you okay?"

"Yes, I just need a little time to think things through," I said, smiling when he laced his fingers through mine.

"I think this idea of Nick's is going to work, and I'm planning on putting some money into the deal. I'll tell you all about it when we get a moment alone."

I stood back. "Why don't I ask Elena if she's free to babysit tonight, and we have dinner alone on the boat?"

His eyes lit with pleasure. "I'd like that."

"Okay, I'll call her. Let's help Robbie feed the dogs and pack something for supper on the boat."

"Deal," said Vaughn. "We haven't done something like this for a while."

An hour later, I sat on the sailboat with Vaughn sipping champagne. He'd bought my favorite, a Billecart Salmon Brut, to celebrate his success in getting Nick to agree to let Vaughn participate in the project.

Seeing the excitement on Vaughn's face, I was happy for him, even though it might mean he'd be gone a lot for the next few months.

"What's going on with you, Ann?" he asked. "You seem quiet."

I told him about Rhonda's upcoming vacation, our talk, and our meeting with the department heads of staff. "I need to rethink how things will get done. As the financial person on the team, I need to feel comfortable checking daily sales and ensuring we have reservations coming in."

"That can be done online from home, can't it?" said Vaughn.

"You're right. I don't know why I didn't realize it would be easier that way. But then, whenever we're at the hotel, something important comes up, and we're right there to respond. It may take me a while to get used to the idea, but I value our time together and my time with Robbie, Liz, and the babies. Nell and Ty, too, when they can get away and visit us."

"It'll all work out, Ann." Vaughn pulled me closer.

I lifted my face to his and sighed happily when he bent to kiss me. His lips met mine, and a surge of desire swept through me. I loved that he made me want him so easily. But then he was a generous lover, making sure I was satisfied with his lovemaking.

The sun was beginning its descent as we pulled apart. With no one to hear or see us, Vaughn lifted my cotton top over my head and unhooked my bra.

Lulled by the waves that gently rocked us, we made love slowly and completely. After thinking of death these last few days, I reveled in the chance to feel alive, to show Vaughn how much he meant to me. As we lay together, I reached up and caressed his face. I thought this was what life should be, living every day well.

Later, satisfied, we nibbled on our sandwiches after Vaughn weighed anchor, started the engine, and headed back to shore.

I got up at my usual time, knowing there was no way I could suddenly stop going into the office. The forgotten financials still had to be assessed. Besides, the hotel was part of me. I could ease away in time, but I needed to be certain I wouldn't lose absolute control. It was my business, after all.

Vaughn took Robbie to school, and I headed to the hotel. As I pulled into my parking space behind the hotel, Rhonda drove her car into the space next to mine.

She got out of the car, stood with her hands on her hips, and faced me with mock outrage. "What are you doing here? We're supposed to be stepping away from the business."

I laughed. "I could ask you the same thing. The truth is I'm behind on going over the financials and didn't want to put it off any longer. But Vaughn suggested I do more work at home, and I'm considering setting up a home office."

"That's a great idea," said Rhonda. "I'm not ready to do that yet, but I intend to cut back on my time at the hotel after our

Spring Brunch." She winked at me. "You know how much I love Consuela's sweet rolls."

I laughed. "Okay, let's go inside and say good morning to her. I'm ready for one of those treats too."

Inside the kitchen, Consuela glanced up at us with surprise. "I thought you two were going to stay away from your usual schedule."

"In time," I said, giving her a hug. On the mornings I could greet her this way, I always seemed to feel more settled. She, with her quiet strength, was someone I adored.

Rhonda and I took our coffee and sweet rolls into the office, and I began looking over the financials. The hotel business was seasonal, but we'd been able to balance income for the months by hosting small, upscale weddings and events. In addition, anniversaries, promotions, family celebrations, and any other occasions we could think of were all promoted with special packages. And, as it had been from the beginning, the hotel served as a discreet place for high-level meetings for politicians and industry leaders.

We were in high season now, but, after Easter, a slower season would begin with fewer long-term guests and more social affairs. Rhonda and I would put on our annual Spring Brunch for the town to celebrate the end of the winter season and the snowbirds' return to their homes. Following the brunch, the staff would celebrate with their own party.

Dorothy Stern knocked on the door of the office. "Good morning. I'm here to go over the invitation list. We've had several replies, but as usual, some people are waiting until the last moment to do so." She shook her head. "I can't understand why people can't be more polite."

"The people we invite are busy with work and projects of their own. But Tina is back in town, and I'll be sure to invite her," I said. "She always adds a bit of glamour to the event."

"Oh, good. She's such a lovely young woman," said Dorothy. "I remember that she wasn't always that way."

"She's much more settled as the mother of two adorable children," I said.

"Dorothy, you'd better sit down," said Rhonda. "Annie and I are going to decrease our hours here at the hotel. I've had a scare and think you ought to know."

Rhonda told Dorothy about her health scare and how we decided to take more time off in the future.

"You poor dear," said Dorothy. "Of course, you and Ann both should take more time off and enjoy yourselves while you're young and energetic. When you get my age, everything that used to be easy is much harder. And you can't help but have a few regrets about your choices."

"We'll still want your help as long as you're willing to give it," I said. Dorothy had been a big boost to us in the past, and with Brock as a building inspector and new president of the neighborhood association, I knew we'd need her support from now on.

"Oh, I'm never giving up helping my girls. You two have done so much for other people, the neighborhood, and the city. I'm very proud to have been a part of your opening and continued success."

"We're very thankful to you," I said, hugging her.

"You're the best," said Rhonda, grinning at her. "That's another reason I wanted to talk to you. Annie and I are considering having a charity event, probably dinner and an auction, to raise money for breast cancer research. We're going to talk to Lorraine about it but would need your help too."

Dorothy's eyes lit with excitement, and she clasped a hand to her heart. "Oh! I'd love to."

Rhonda and I exchanged glances, aware that as a past

owner of her own business, Dorothy treasured her time working with us, making her feel important.

"Good. That's settled then. Stay tuned, and we'll let you know when this will happen," I said. "Now, let's go over the guest list for the brunch."

The three of us sat looking over the list of invitees and their responses.

"I see Brock Goodwin has accepted," I said. "I hope the time comes when we won't feel we have to invite him."

"Best to keep on his good side," said Dorothy. "I'll try to keep an eye on him. He's trying to get people in the neighborhood to agree to pay the association's president, even though it's always been a volunteer position."

"Next thing we know, he'll want to wear a fucking crown," grumbled Rhonda.

"We're not allowing it to become a paid position," said Dorothy with determination.

"We'll have to do our best to keep him away from the new construction site," I said. "I've alerted security, but you know Brock will do everything he can to meddle."

Dorothy nodded emphatically before returning to our task.

When we finished, we had a list of 200 acceptances. I was pleased that our newly elected mayor, Helena Naylor, would be present. We had a congenial group scheduled for this year with other city officials, a few past VIP guests, and a broad spectrum of people who provided services to the hotel.

"Oh! I forgot to add Arthur Smythe's name to the list," said Rhonda. She nudged Dorothy. "That's Angela's father-in-law. I think he and Lorraine Grace would make a great pair. What do ya think?"

"I met Arthur once at Kathryn's funeral and reception," said Dorothy, but her eyes held a hint of merriment. "Lorraine is lovely, and I think you might be onto something."

"I told ya," Rhonda said, exuding a satisfied sigh.

"We'll see. But we can't let that interrupt the goodwill shown to all who have promised to attend." I knew I sounded like my stern grandmother, but Rhonda and her matchmaking efforts could sometimes be over the top.

After Dorothy left, and I was busy analyzing a year-by-year comparison of last month's results, I was interrupted by the appearance of Lorraine.

"Hi, Lorraine. Good to see you. I hope you're all set to attend the annual Spring Brunch next week."

"That's why I'm here. I need to have that weekend off. Personal business."

"Oh, I'm disappointed. Is there any way you can change that date? People need to be able to meet you. It adds to our wedding business."

"Yes, I know. Let me see if I can change things around. It's something that came up last minute. An old family friend. But I can ask him to wait to visit me until next week."

"That would be wonderful. We're very proud of having you on the hotel staff, and when people meet you, they understand what a lovely impression you make."

"Thank you, Ann. That's nice of you to say."

"I mean it," I said. "In time, there's a special project Rhonda and I want to talk to you about setting up."

Rhonda came into the office and smiled when she saw Lorraine. "Hi. Good to see you. I hope you're all set for the annual brunch next week."

"That's why I'm here," said Lorraine. "An old family friend, a man I used to date, wants to visit me then."

The look of disappointment on Rhonda's face was amusing. "Oh, but ..." she began.

"No worries. After talking to Ann, I'll see if he can move his trip back a week," said Lorraine.

"That would be good," said Rhonda. "I have someone you should meet." She glanced at me, and at my warning look, she stopped talking.

"Well, then, I'll let you know if I can change things around," said Lorraine. "Thanks."

After Lorraine left the office, Rhonda plopped down in her chair. "What a disaster that would be if Lorraine can't be at the brunch. I figured that would be the perfect way for Arthur to meet her."

"If it's meant to be, it will work out," I said.

"That might be true in some circumstances, but I know when my special powers are needed," said Rhonda.

I rolled my eyes. "You know you're impossible when it comes to these things, right?"

"I know how good I am," said Rhonda, and we laughed.

CHAPTER SEVENTEEN

The Friday before the Spring Brunch on Sunday, Rhonda held a welcome dinner for Arthur at her house. No one in their right mind would turn down a meal that Rhonda prepared. With work and family obligations, she didn't entertain as much as she once did, so it was a rare treat to be invited.

Her idea of a simple Italian dinner consisted of antipasto, soup, a pasta dish, and a main course. No matter the time of year, her guests knew she'd serve a delicious meal.

Anticipating the evening, Vaughn and I headed to her house. It had taken a lot of juggling to arrange enough babysitters, but Angela and Reggie, Arthur, Liz and Chad, and Bernie and his wife, Annette, would all be in attendance.

It wasn't until I noticed Lorraine's car in the driveway that I realized Rhonda had upped her game by inviting her to dinner too.

Amused, I entered the house with Vaughn.

One of the staff I recognized from the hotel greeted us and said, "Welcome. Rhonda and Will have asked that you join them on the lanai for a drink before dinner."

I realized then that Rhonda had gone all out to make this a perfect evening to introduce Arthur and Lorraine to one another.

Understanding, Vaughn winked at me. "Let's do our part. Shall we?"

When we walked onto the lanai, the party was already in progress, with drinks being served and people standing about conversing. I kissed Liz and Angie hello and moved on to Arthur.

"It's nice to see you," I said, giving him a quick hug. "I bet it's a treat to get away from the hustle and bustle of the big city."

He laughed. "Well, there's a lot of what you call the hustle and bustle at the kids' house with all the children. But it is very good to be here." He glanced at Lorraine and then shook hands with Vaughn.

"Will, thank you for having all of us here," I said and then returned a kiss on the cheek. I loved Will and had since he became my financial advisor when I was trying to buy into the hotel.

"Hi, Annie," said Rhonda, coming over to hug me. "You should see the sparks flying between Arthur and Lorraine," she whispered in my ear with a definite note of triumph.

"Don't get over-confident," I warned her. "She's meeting an old boyfriend after the brunch, and I noticed Reggie frowning at Lorraine."

"We'll see," said Rhonda turning to greet Vaughn.

I went over to Lorraine. "Hi, it's nice to see you here. Dinner at Rhonda's is a real treat. She usually uses her family recipes to entertain."

"The aromas are divine," said Lorraine. "It's always a pleasure for me to go somewhere and not have to worry about details."

Arthur came over to us. "What are you lovely ladies talking about?"

"Rhonda's cooking," I answered. "You two have already met, right?"

"Indeed," said Arthur. "I'm pleased to know of Lorraine's interest in travel. It's something I enjoy."

I couldn't let the moment pass without saying, "It's always

fun when you have someone to do it with." Rhonda would owe me big time for saying that, but then I could see interest in one another on their faces and couldn't resist.

We were asked to come into the dining room. Rhonda's large home was designed for entertaining, and we all sat comfortably at the table. A server helped each of us to select from a huge antipasto platter and then placed it in the middle of the table.

"Here's to us. *Buon appetito,*" said Rhonda, lifting her glass of red wine in a salute.

"A toast to you all," said Will. "We're happy to have you here."

We lifted our glasses and then dug into our appetizer course.

The antipasto was followed by the first main course of thin spaghetti with tomato sauce topped with a large meatball. I knew from past experiences that the next main course would include meat and was pleased when Rhonda excused herself to prepare her famous veal piccata. The veal, I knew, came from the hotel and was of the finest quality.

Conversation continued as we waited for the veal. I glanced around the room, noting how relaxed Liz and Chad seemed. That wasn't the case with Angie and Reggie, and I wondered if the way Arthur and Lorraine were smiling at each other was the reason for the discord.

A simple salad with an olive oil and wine vinegar dressing followed the veal.

And then, when I thought I couldn't eat another thing, the server brought in individual servings of Tiramisu.

Though we all groaned at facing another course, we dug in and sighed with pleasure.

"I don't know how you do it, Rhonda," I said. "Everything is delicious."

"Never better," said Arthur. "Maybe you should go into the restaurant business, or better yet, the hotel business."

We all laughed.

"Sorry to eat and run, Rhonda, but Chad and I have to get back to the babysitter," said Liz. "Thanks for having us. It was delicious."

I watched the affection between them as Liz hugged Rhonda and then turned to Will. It did my heart good to see how close they were. I felt the same way about Angela.

The group broke up, and after everyone except Vaughn and I had left, Rhonda said, "Let's sit a moment, just the four of us. We need to talk about time off." She gave me a big smile. "Just before everyone came, I got a call from Dr. Perkins' office to say that the lump was a benign cyst as she'd thought."

"Great news!" I cried, hugging her.

"Yeah," said Will. "It had us worried. That's for sure." He wrapped an arm around Rhonda and kissed her.

We sat on the lanai and gazed out at the starry sky. I hoped the weather would hold for our brunch on Sunday. Even so, it would feel good to move into the next season. We made the most money in the winter season, but it was exhausting.

"As you know," Rhonda said, "Will and I have planned a two-week vacation. I want to be sure that you both are on board with that. I'm unsure what your schedule is, Vaughn, but I hope our trip won't inconvenience you or Ann."

"My schedule is up in the air at the moment. But, in any case, I wouldn't want that to influence your time away," said Vaughn.

"Nor I. We both deserve time off, and once you're back from vacation, Vaughn and I will think of a longer time away. Until then, I'm planning on taking off for a couple of days after the brunch," I said.

"That sounds good," said Rhonda. "I told the kids they will

have to find another nanny to help them when we're gone because Rita will be with Willow and Drew. It's time for them to have their own nanny anyway."

"That's something I need to talk to Liz about. Elena will be helping Troy with the spas and will work around Robbie's schedule. But she's already mentioned she can't be with the triplets as much."

Rhonda chuckled softly. "Who would've guessed this when I first met you, Annie? We were alone and sad and determined to prove ourselves. Guess we did that in all kinds of ways."

"And we were lucky at love too."

We all smiled at one another.

"Well, guess we should be going," said Vaughn rising. "Thanks for a fabulous dinner and the good company."

"Our pleasure," said Will, getting to his feet and clapping Vaughn on the back.

Rhonda and I kissed goodbye, and then I left with Vaughn, well aware of how lucky I was to have such a life. It was something I'd remind myself of as I faced the next few weeks. They were bound to be full of a few surprises along the way.

The next morning, I didn't even think of going into the hotel before I had a brisk walk along the beach. After Rhonda's delicious dinner, I needed a workout. The days were warming, and I was delighted to have this cool morning time to myself.

Holding my sandals in my hand, I stepped onto the sand. Before I could take many steps, Bobby jogged up to me.

"Hi, Ann. Can I talk to you about something?"

"Sure. I'm happy to listen," I said, motioning for him to accompany me to the water's edge.

"It's Sydney. I told her who I was, and she said, 'So'? She said she doesn't like to watch football and doesn't like the idea of grown men beating each other up for a football. What am I going to do? I'd like to get to know her better, even ask her out."

I stepped into the refreshing water and turned to him. "There's no reason you can't get to know her better. You just have to be yourself, not hide behind what you do for a living. She sounds like a very sensible woman, very unpretentious. Maybe this is a chance to think about who you are. That's what I'd tell a child of mine."

"Huh. Most women I've dated are all about my being a football star. It's pretty easy to get any date I want."

"Sydney has already shown you she isn't just any woman; she's special. So even if she never agrees to go out with you, I think getting to know her better is a good idea. You might find out a lot about yourself, too."

He kicked at the edge of the sand away from me, splashing the water, turning drops of it into small crystal-like globes. When he faced me, he said, "Okay. Thanks. That's what I needed to know. She was a lot more interested in me as a kitchen worker."

He trotted off, and I watched him thinking he was learning a lot more than kitchen duties.

I started down the beach, moving briskly. Today, I'd be busy helping Rhonda and Consuela in the kitchen, making hors d'oeuvres for the brunch. It had become a tradition for us to work together even though we could have others do the job. Sort of like an annual Christmas cookie bake with friends.

Ahead, I saw Brock talking to a neighborhood board member and turned around before he could notice me. I had no intention of talking to him about Tina, Bobby, or any other guest he might be interested in.

I was almost back to the hotel when I heard my name being called and stopped.

Brock jogged up to me. "Hey, I just wanted to tell you I'm looking forward to your Spring Brunch. I heard the mayor will be there, and I intend to talk to her about my position as president of the neighborhood association. I want her to know I'm keeping an eye on you and other hotel people along the beach. I'm going to ask her to recommend me to the City Development Council."

"I'm late for a meeting. See you on Sunday," I said and moved away.

He stepped in front of me. "I don't think you understand. I want you and Rhonda to recommend me to her."

I was so shocked I could only stand there mute, blinking with surprise.

"I mean it, Ann. It would be a great addition to my credentials."

"You've done nothing but harass us. Don't you get that it doesn't earn you any kudos from us?"

"Maybe by doing that for me, I could ease up a bit on you. Think about it. You don't want another year of trouble, do you?" He turned and walked away.

I was still shaking my head as I headed into the hotel.

Rhonda was already in the kitchen when I entered. "I saw your car and knew you must be on the beach. Anything exciting going on there?"

"You won't believe it. Brock wants us to recommend him to the mayor, hoping she'll appoint him to the City Development Council."

Rhonda, who'd taken a sip of coffee, covered her mouth and began to cough. Her shoulders shook with laughter. When she could finally talk, she said, "That ass is dumber than I thought."

"Yes, he is. He even suggested he might go easier on us if we cooperated," I said. "I didn't mention it because I was stunned by his request, but that was clearly a threat."

"Just let him try it," said Rhonda. "He'll lose his balls so fast he won't be able to do anything but squeak."

I laughed, but I knew Rhonda was serious about harming Brock if he was stupid enough to follow through on his threat.

"Okay, girls," said Consuela. "Let's get started on the work. I've frozen plenty of sweet rolls to be heated up, but we have many more things to prepare for Sunday."

What had started as a simple affair had turned into the social event of the spring. And in addition to enthusiasm, guests brought along hearty appetites. As we prepared for the onslaught of eaters, Rhonda and I enjoyed letting Consuela boss us around as if we were her daughters.

"This year, I'm going to talk to our guests about the fund-raising evening we want to host for Breast Cancer Research," Rhonda said. "They can get their food free at this event, but they'd better be willing to pay up at that one."

"Deal," I said. "I'll do my share to get guests committed to the idea. Did you tell Consuela the good news?"

"I did before you came into the kitchen," Rhonda said.

"Oh, yes! No cancer. Such good news," said Consuela. "Something every woman wants to hear for herself or people she loves."

Just then, Bobby walked through the area to Jean-Luc's kitchen. He waved a greeting at us and kept moving.

When I was certain he couldn't hear, I told Rhonda and Consuela about the conversation I had with him earlier about Sydney and him.

"He's learning," said Consuela. "Jean-Luc says he's doing better."

"I noticed that swagger of his is gone," said Rhonda.

"Maybe there's hope for him yet."

We went back to work, but I thought that meeting Sydney might be the best thing that had happened to Bobby yet.

CHAPTER EIGHTEEN

I was getting ready to leave the hotel when I got a text from Tina: I have some time. Want to meet for a glass of wine? At the hotel? You and Rhonda?

I asked Rhonda and texted Tina back: *"We're ready for some girl time and a glass of wine. Come on over. We'll meet you in the lobby and take you to our special hideaway.*

"Good," said Rhonda. "I haven't spent much time with Tina, and this will be a needed break before I go home."

We went into the front lobby and waited for Tina. When she walked into the hotel, I almost didn't recognize her. She'd drawn her dark hair into two pigtails and wore a baseball cap and sunglasses. She looked like a teenager in shorts and a T-shirt. I sometimes forgot all she'd been through at such a young age and that she was not much older now.

She gave us a little wave and joined us in bouncy steps.

"You look great," I said. "Very relaxed."

"A regular beach bum," teased Rhonda.

Tina laughed. "I love the time here. I've been able to work as well as relax. It's such a relief to know that no one can find me here, and I can do my new thing privately. I've been working online with a female producer, and we have a couple of projects to look at."

"How exciting," I said. "Come, let's get something to drink, and we can go to the secret place Rhonda and I use to relax and talk."

"Secret place? That sounds exciting," said Tina grinning.

"We sometimes have margaritas there," said Rhonda.

"Otherwise, it's coffee and, sometimes, wine."

"I feel very special to have been invited to join you," said Tina. "Two of my favorite people."

"It's wonderful how coming here has led you to this," I said as we entered the bar to order our wine.

We took our glasses up to the second floor, unlocked the door to a maid's closet, and walked through it to the balcony outside.

"Very tricky," said Tina, sitting in one of the three chairs we kept there.

The fronds from a nearby palm tree shaded the balcony from the afternoon sun and added to our privacy.

After we got settled, I said, "Rhonda has some big news. She and Will are going back to Tahiti for a vacation."

"Nice," said Tina. "I haven't been, but I hear it's gorgeous."

"Let me tell you about my health scare," said Rhonda. "It's part of the reason we're going there."

I watched Tina's face as she listened to Rhonda talk about discovering the lump in her breast. Though she was a good actress, there was no mistaking the compassion on Tina's face.

She rose and gave Rhonda a hug. "Is there anything I can do?"

"Yes," said Rhonda. "Annie and I want to hold a charity event here at the hotel. If you and a couple of other stars would participate, we could raise a lot of money. I'm pledging to match the donations we collect personally."

"I'd be happy to do that. Nick's daughter, well, my daughter too, suffered a scare like that. It's horrifying."

"Speaking of her, how is Emaline?" I asked. She'd been jealous of Tina's relationship with her father at first, but they'd ended up being close.

"She's finally decided to get her own apartment and is busy getting a graduate degree in psychology. She's a very different woman from the one I first met. My boys adore her. And so does a certain handsome doctor."

"Good for her," I said.

"Tell her any wedding has to take place here," said Rhonda. "I wouldn't want to miss seeing that."

"I've already talked to her about it," said Tina laughing. "The Beach House Hotel is the best place I know for a small, tasteful wedding."

"Has Sydney said anything to you about a football player named Bobby Bailey?" I asked.

"As a matter of fact, she has," said Tina smiling. "She's quite interested in him, but she doesn't want to be one of those women who trail after sports stars."

"She's doing a good job of not appearing that way," I said. "Bobby is taken aback by it, which is the best thing that could happen to him."

"Yeah, he arrived here acting like a brat, but I think he's getting a better idea about his place in the world. And it isn't on a fuckin' throne," said Rhonda.

"M-m-m-m. Sounds like someone I used to know," said Tina, giving us a sheepish look.

Rhonda and I glanced at each other.

"Well, now you're not only a star but a lovely mother and a businesswoman," I said. "That makes both of us proud of you."

"Thanks. I'm proud of me too, which tells you how far I've come." Tina took a sip of wine and stared out at the water.

"I hope you'll attend our Spring Brunch," I said to Tina. "That would mean a lot to us."

"Sure. I'd be happy to. Thanks for asking," said Tina. "Nick has gone back to California, and I like to keep busy when he's gone."

"You know we'll do our best to keep Brock Goodwin away

from you. Presently, he's working on the mayor to give him a job on the City Development Council."

Tina shook her head. "Why don't a bunch of women expose him for the creep he is?"

"He might be an asshole, but he stays just inside the boundary for sexual assault or harassment," said Rhonda. "I'd like to bust his balls."

"Sydney blew him off when he was trying to chat with her. She's very protective of the family and me and is careful about speaking about us," said Tina.

"She sure is a doll," said Rhonda.

"Absolutely," Tina readily agreed. "We'll have to see how the next weeks play out for her and her football player."

There was nothing like the idea of a sweet love story to make us happy.

We finished our wine, and then I suggested Tina join Vaughn and me for dinner at my house. "I can't compete with Rhonda's cooking, but Vaughn is good at grilling, and I make a mean salad."

Tina laughed. "Maybe another time. I promised Victor we'd go out to dinner at his favorite place, Burger Burger. They have an excellent salad selection which both Sydney and I like."

"Well, then, I'm glad you have plans," I said, secretly relieved to be free of company. I was exhausted from a day of cooking. Rhonda, bless her heart, looked as tired as I felt.

We left the balcony with the promise to do this again, and I left the hotel to go home.

When I walked out to the lanai at home, Cindy yapped and ran to greet me, her tail wagging. Trudy gently pushed her aside and sprinted forward to greet me. I couldn't help laughing as I patted Trudy and then Cindy.

Vaughn walked onto the lanai and greeted me with a kiss. "Where's Robbie?'"

"He's in his room," said Vaughn. "He was sent home from school for swearing in class. I've talked to him about choosing careful words. He understands that F-bombs should not be spoken at school or anywhere else."

"Oh, I agree. That's not like him. I wonder what is really going on."

Vaughn shook his head. "One of the bigger kids in the class has been teasing him and was sent home from school for bullying. I've talked to Robbie about it, and I think we've come to an understanding just to move on. The other boy was very apologetic. He apparently has an older brother who teases him all the time."

"Should I talk to Robbie about it?" I asked.

"That's up to you, but I think the issue has been resolved. He only has a few minutes more to stay in his room to think about it."

I lifted up on my toes and kissed Vaughn. "You're such a good dad."

"None of this is new behavior to me. I had to go through some of this with Ty and Nell when they were about this age. Still, it's good to clamp down on it right away."

I left Vaughn and knocked on Robbie's door. Opening it a crack, I said, "May I come in?"

"Okay," said Robbie looking glum. He was lying on his bed with a book.

I walked over, kissed him on the cheek, and sat down on the edge of the bed. "Guess you had a bad day at school, huh?"

Robbie shrugged and looked away.

"I'm sorry you did, but I hope you learned a lesson today so you don't have another bad day. I know Dad has talked to you about it, but if you want to talk to me about it, just ask."

"Okay. Can I leave my room now?" he asked.

"Dad will let you know when it's time. I just wanted to give my favorite boy a kiss." I got up and left the room, leaving the door open.

Vaughn gazed at me when I returned to the lanai. "How'd it go?"

"He's ready to get out of his room. I told him you'd let him know when he could."

"It's been long enough. He understands what we expect. I'll get him now. The worst part of being confined to his room was having Trudy and Cindy here on the lanai and not with him."

"Hopefully, he learned a lesson. We don't normally swear, and I'm not sure where he picked it up. Swearing becomes a bad habit. One I definitely don't want him to have."

Vaughn chuckled. "Better keep him away from Rhonda."

I laughed. "Especially when Brock Goodwin is around. Wait 'til you hear the latest. I'll tell you all about it later."

While Vaughn left the room, I settled on the floor with Trudy and Cindy. The puppy was growing fast but still had the adorable waddle that came with trying to control the front end and back end of her body at the same time.

Trudy gave me a longing look, and I picked her up and hugged her. "We've not forgotten you, girl." She sighed with contentment and leaned up against me. Her action made me realize I hadn't spent much time with Liz lately. Time to fix that. She'd promised to come to the Spring Brunch briefly, but I wanted some of our old mother/daughter time back. Maybe a lunch sometime soon.

Vaughn and Robbie walked onto the lanai, and Trudy bounded out of my arms to greet him. He patted her while the puppy pranced around them.

"How about some family time in the pool?" I asked.

Robbie shrugged.

"Troy is forming swim teams at the high school for kids of all ages. You can try out if you'd like."

Robbie's face lit up. "I'm a good swimmer. Troy said so."

"Well, then, let's do it." I was anxious to move on from the scolding and give Robbie something positive to think about himself. Besides, Troy had already asked me if Robbie could participate.

"We'll make it a pizza night," I said, having no desire to cook.

"Sounds good," said Vaughn.

"Remember, don't get in the pool until Dad and I are with you," I told Robbie. "And we have to keep Cindy and Trudy away from the pool. We'll gate them in the kitchen."

I went into the bedroom to change into a bathing suit. Vaughn followed me.

Inside the room, he spun me around to face him. "I haven't properly kissed you hello yet."

I sighed as his lips reached for mine. In his arms, I could let go of some of the fatigue I'd been feeling. We pulled apart and stood smiling at one another. It was sometimes difficult for me to believe that of all the women Vaughn could've chosen, he'd chosen me. But then, we were a good match. I'd known it from the moment we stood holding hands at the edge of the water in front of the hotel. The connection I'd felt with him then had grown even deeper.

"Any word from Nick when you might go to California?" I asked him.

"Not yet. I'm not in any rush. I'm enjoying my time here. I even have an idea for a story that I might try to write," he answered with an unusual shyness.

"Fabulous. That way you can spend a lot of time at home." I sent him a playful smile. "I'm sure you have a lot of material. Lily Dorio could be a villainess."

Vaughn laughed. "You never know who might appear in a book of mine." He tugged me to him. "Come here, you little vixen." He embraced me, and I felt completely at home as his arms wrapped around me.

"Ready, Mom? Dad?" said Robbie walking into the bedroom.

"We'll be right there, son," said Vaughn. "Will you check on Trudy and Cindy and make sure they're gated into the kitchen with plenty of water?"

"Okay, but hurry," said Robbie.

Vaughn turned back to me. "Later, I'll show you how slow I can be."

I grinned, blew him a kiss, and pulled out a bathing suit from a drawer, already looking forward to the evening ahead.

Outside, the air was pleasant and warm, a perfect evening for a swim and an easy dinner. Growing up in Boston, where winters were long and cold, I'd always liked the idea of living in a warm climate. This evening proved how lucky I was.

I stood by the pool, looking out at the water. The sun was heading toward the horizon. A blue heron was searching for food at the edge of our inlet. Tied at the dock, *Zephyr* bobbed in the gentle movement of the water rolling to shore. Overhead, birds called to one another, their plaintive cries a sign of the slowing pace of the day.

Vaughn came up behind me and placed a hand on my shoulder. "It's hard to believe how fortunate we are."

"My thoughts, too," I said. Observing Robbie swimming alone, I said, "I think it's time to invite Nell and her family to come for a visit."

"If we can get them away from D.C. and all the activity at the nation's capital," said Vaughn. "But I'd love to see them."

"I know Nell and Clint have been trying for a baby to keep Bailey company. Maybe a vacation is all they need to make it happen."

"Okay, set up a date so I can carve out time in my schedule," said Vaughn.

"Their visit will have to wait until after Rhonda and Will return from vacation, but I'll see what I can do."

I sat down on the side of the pool and dangled my feet as Robbie swam in laps. His long arms and legs were an added plus to his healthy, slim torso in making his way through the water. When he first came into our lives, it took me a little time to get past my anger at Robert for the way he'd told me Kandie was pregnant with his child after my trying and failing to have children before and after Liz. Yet, I'd fallen in love with Robbie from the moment I met him. I couldn't imagine not having him as my son.

After enjoying the pool with "my men," I went inside to change and order pizza for dinner, delighted not to have to do more than make a salad to go with it.

Later, after dinner, I called Vaughn's daughter, Nell. When I'd first met her, I'd been shocked by how much she looked like Liz. Though they had different personalities, I admired and loved both women.

"Hi, Ann," said Nell happily. "I've been thinking of you, Dad, and the family. Clint and I have talked about making time for a visit. I want to see the triplets and Angela's babies too."

"Great minds think alike," I said. "That's why I'm calling

you. Your father and I are anxious to see you. Let's schedule a time when you can stay for a while." I waited for her to tell me about baby news of her own, but she didn't mention it. Instead, she talked about an opportunity to work from home as a lobbyist's assistant.

After looking at calendars, we decided on a time in late April for a visit. Rhonda and Will would just be returning from vacation, and I'd need some time off. I couldn't imagine a better way to spend it than with Nell and her family. Bailey, named after Nell's mother's family, was talking, and I couldn't wait to see her. I loved when children began to express themselves. It was so interesting. Sometimes, funny.

I turned the phone call over to Vaughn and went to find Robbie. It was bedtime, and not only did I need to make sure he was ready, but the dogs were settled too. I'd forgotten how much puppies were like human babies. But overall, things were going well with Cindy. She was a good dog and felt at home with Trudy, which made things easier.

Robbie was lying in bed with a book when I went into the room. Both Trudy and Cindy were atop his lightweight blanket on a blanket of their own. After a few accidents with her, Robbie learned to get up with Cindy when she whined to go outside.

I leaned over, kissed Robbie goodnight, patted the dogs, and left the room. "Remember to take Cindy out before you turn off the lights." Vaughn and I had agreed to give Robbie as much responsibility for caring for the puppy as possible.

When I walked onto the lanai, Vaughn patted the space next to him on one of the couches.

I went over and sat down beside him. "Have a nice talk with Nell?"

"Yes, I'm happy she's coming for a visit." He drew me into his arms. "Have I told you how much I love you lately?"

"A short while ago, but go ahead, I never get tired of hearing it," I said, giving him a teasing smile.

"Okay. I love you, Ann, and the way you've made my children feel part of my family with you after Ellie died. Ty and June and their little one have promised to come sometime too."

"Your children are part of you, Vaughn, and I love them. It's that simple."

"But I know from other men that it isn't always like that. So, thank you."

His lips met mine, and my toes curled with a deep happiness.

CHAPTER NINETEEN

The morning of our Sunday brunch, Rhonda and I surveyed the arrangements at the hotel. The dining room had been cleared of some tables so a crowd could wander from one long table loaded with food to another. Two bars were set up, one at each end of the room, offering guests mimosas, strawberry daiquiris, margaritas, assorted non-alcoholic fruit punches, coffee, and a selection of hot and cold teas.

Sweet rolls, a variety of individual homemade quiches, bacon crisps, cheese puffs, a variety of salads, and a selection of various sandwiches were just some of the food items offered.

The annual brunch was a good way to thank people in the community for their support. We hoped it was a reminder to use our dining room and hotel for themselves and to suggest it to others.

The dining staff was present to serve the food and pass hot hors d'oeuvres. I was pleased to see Bobby among them, dressed in dark pants and a white shirt like the others. Bernie, Annette, Jean-Luc, Consuela, Manny, and other department heads were also ready to be part of the hosting staff. It always pleased me to see them receive kudos from the guests.

"Ready to go?" asked Rhonda, throwing an arm around my shoulder. "Remember the first one? I was scared no one would show up. Now, I just hope we have enough food for everyone."

I laughed. "We've come a long way."

"Yeah, it's sometimes hard to believe." Her eyes filled. "I'm just happy I'm here to enjoy it after thinking I might be dying."

I hugged her. "No one is happier about that than I am. We're a perfect team."

"Yeah, we need each other. Of the two of us, you're the lady, and I'm ... well ... me."

"And I love you just the way you are," I said, surprised by the sting of tears. I meant every word I said.

"Okay, let's do it," said Rhonda looking a bit teary.

We walked outside and stood at the top of the stairs as we always did to greet our guests. Rhonda had put on a peach silk caftan that looked great with her tan and the diamond jewelry she liked to wear. I was wearing a light-blue linen dress that Vaughn said matched my eyes.

Both of us were wearing comfortable sandals. We learned early on that standing on our feet greeting guests for hours could make us miserable if we wore the wrong shoes.

We'd arranged for cars to be parked at a church nearby and for shuttles to bring guests here. As the first two shuttles pulled up in front of the hotel, my heart thrummed with excitement. This party felt like welcoming people to a lovely private estate. The guests in-house were also invited to take part. Some of those staying with us were repeat guests who purposely chose to stay at the hotel this weekend so they could be included.

The mayor, Helena Naylor, was among the first to arrive. At her side and talking as usual, Terri Thomas, the news reporter for the Sabal Daily News, made her way to the front stairs. I could tell Terri was all but trembling with excitement to cover this event. She'd have enough news to fill a lot of columns. And to arrive with the mayor was a great opportunity.

Rhonda and I greeted them with hugs and then spent the next forty-five minutes greeting other guests. We'd staggered the times on the invitations to prevent everyone from arriving at once.

When we were free to mingle with our guests, I immediately went to speak to Terri. She was busy talking to a member of the Florida Senate. I waited until she was through and then took her aside. "Have fun, Terri, but remember our guests are due privacy. I expect you to honor that. If you want to set up private interviews with them, that's your prerogative."

"Okay, I understand. No personal business beyond a mention." Terri smiled at me. "This is always such a fun event. Tasty, too."

As Brock headed in our direction, I slipped away into the crowd. Though city officials and other VIPs were always part of this affair, I liked talking to our hotel guests and other true supporters, like Dorothy Stern and her group of women friends who lived in the same luxury apartment building.

"Lovely party, Ann," Dorothy said.

I kissed her cheek and said hello to her friends, telling them about the future charity event we would be holding. "It's an event important to all women."

"Yes, indeed. Even at our retirement age, we must be watchful," said one of Dorothy's friends. "I'll be happy to help however I can."

"Thank you. That's lovely of you."

"Don't worry, Ann. I'll spread the word," said Dorothy, her expression full of determination.

I grinned. "I know you will."

I left them to speak to a couple from Connecticut. Stephanie and Randolph Willis were long-time return guests who spent the month of March with us every year. The staff loved them, and Rhonda and I considered them part of the hotel family.

"You look lovely, Stephanie," I said and greeted her with a quick hug. "And, Randolph, you're looking like your dapper self."

He grinned. At seventy and in good health, he seemed to get quiet joy out of every day. He was a favorite guest of mine, as was Stephanie. I started telling them about the charity we planned to set up when Stephanie stopped me. "Rhonda told us all about it. Poor dear. Such a shame she had such a scare. You know we'll do what we can to help."

"Thanks. That means a lot to us. We want to turn that frightening time into something positive."

Stephanie beamed at me. "Yes, I know how close the two of you are."

Tina came over to us. I introduced her to Stephanie and Randolph and left them to get acquainted.

I saw Arthur talking to Lorraine and paused, studying the smiles on their faces. Maybe Rhonda was right, and something was going on with the two of them.

I checked in the dining room to ensure everything was going smoothly. I noticed Bobby acting as a runner from the kitchen, delivering food for the servers standing behind the tables of food.

I stood by as a male guest stopped him. "Aren't you 'Bugs' Bailey? What are you doing here?"

"Yeah, I'm Bugs. What of it?" Bobby glanced at me and said, "I'm just helping a couple of friends. Sorry, I gotta keep goin'." With a frown on his face, Bobby moved on.

The guest turned to me. "That's Bugs, right?"

"Yes," I admitted. "As he said, he's helping out."

The guest shrugged. "He's one helluva football player. I didn't think I'd see him here."

I let it go. Bobby would have to handle things like that on his own.

Later, as the last of the guests exited the party, the staff worked to clear glasses and dishes while others set up for the employee party that always followed. It was a way to thank the staff for their service during the Brunch and made it a great way to end the high season and move at a slower pace.

Rhonda and I flipped off our sandals and sat on one of the couches in the lobby, rubbing our feet. "Another good party," said Rhonda. "They've gotten bigger and better."

"I still like a smaller group, but this way, we get a lot of PR work done at once," I said.

Rhonda elbowed me. "Looks like our charity event is going to be a success."

One of the servers came over to us. "Can I get you anything?"

"I'd like a glass of iced coffee with a touch of milk," I said.

"Sounds good," said Rhonda. "I'll have the same."

"Are you excited about your trip?" I asked her. "You have only a couple more days here, and then you'll be off to Tahiti!"

"Before I think of that, I want to make sure Arthur gets a proper send-off. Then I'll concentrate on myself. I'm taking him to the airport tomorrow morning. I hope to talk to him about returning. I just know something is going to happen between Lorraine and him."

"Remember, part of Lorraine's job with us is making sure people are comfortable with her and the hotel. Don't read too much into it if they look like they're enjoying one another." Rhonda would never let it go if I agreed too readily to her success as a matchmaker.

Rhonda shook her head. "You know I'm right, Annie."

"I believe there might be something between them, but the minute you push it, that might change."

"Huh. Maybe you're right. I won't say anything about it."

I looked at Rhonda, and we both burst out laughing. Rhonda could never hold back, and we both knew it.

Vaughn walked over to us. "I'm going to leave. I'll see you at home."

"Okay. I'm ready too. Bernie is overseeing the hotel and the staff party, so I don't need to stay." I got to my feet, groaned, and picked up my sandals. My feet were not about to slide into those sandals until I gave them a break.

I said goodbye to Rhonda and Bernie, then Vaughn took my arm, and we walked to the back of the hotel where we'd parked our cars.

"Another successful party," said Vaughn. "Everyone seemed to be enjoying themselves. I had a chance to talk to Tina. A photographer snapped our picture. It's bound to show up in the newspaper."

"I talked to Terri about being discreet and not giving out personal details of any of our guests, so it should be fine."

We got into our cars and headed home. I couldn't wait to put on shorts and a T-shirt and get comfortable. Tomorrow would be another busy day. I wanted to make sure Rhonda and I coordinated plans for the next two weeks when she'd be gone.

At home, I rested on the lanai with the dogs. The puppy was snuggly. I liked having her nap next to me on the couch.

Robbie sat on the other side of me holding Trudy as we watched an animated movie on television. He turned to me. "Mom? Is it okay to think a bad word instead of saying it?"

"It's better than saying it out loud, but the best thing is to make up a word that doesn't offend anyone but makes you feel better."

"Like 'sh-h-h ... gar'?" he asked. "I've heard Dad say it when I know he means 'shit.'"

I held in my laughter. "Something like that."

"Okay," he said solemnly, "because Hunter makes me mad sometimes."

"Next time you feel that way, why don't we discuss it?"

"Sometimes it's too late, but I'll try," said Robbie.

I put my arm around him and gave him a squeeze. He was such a good kid.

CHAPTER TWENTY

After having gone to bed early, I got up ready for a full day at the hotel making sure all was in order for Rhonda's departure. Then, I got ready for work, and after kissing Vaughn and Robbie goodbye, I headed to the hotel. It was a beautiful morning, so I decided to take a few minutes on the beach before heading into my office.

I parked the car, took off my heels, and walked onto the beach. Lifting my arms, I felt like embracing the scene before me. Instead, the salty air brushed my face. Golden sunlight glistened atop the crests of the waves rushing to shore, making it seem as if the entire Gulf was shimmering with light. A few people were jogging; some were walking along the shoreline. I noticed two people walking hand-in-hand toward me and realized it was Bobby and Sydney. When they saw me, they dropped their hands to their sides, but I could read happiness on their faces.

"Good morning," I said. "Nice to see you up and about on this glorious day."

"It's my favorite time of day. I'm coming to the beach earlier and earlier," said Sydney. "Soon, I'll have to go back to the house to get Victor. Once he discovered where I go this time of day, he demanded to come too. This is the compromise we made. A little time for me and then time for him."

"Sounds like a good plan," I said. "How was the staff party, Bobby?"

"Good. I invited Sydney to be my date. Mrs. Swain and Mr. Bernhard said it was okay."

"That's nice. I heard a band was lined up to play earlier in the evening."

"Yeah, that was really cool. They played on the sunset deck so we could dance on the sand. But it didn't last long because Mr. Bernhard didn't want to disturb the neighbors. One of them already complained."

"I see," I said, betting that the neighbor who complained was someone named Brock Goodwin. "Well, I'm happy the party worked out well. I'm heading out for a short walk before going inside. See you later. Enjoy yourselves."

As they walked away, they held hands. In Sydney's presence, gentleness surrounded Bobby. I was pleased to see it.

I walked briskly along the water, drinking in the air, the sights, and the sounds. I knew it would be hard to have Rhonda gone, but I was pleased she could take the time off. Vaughn and I had talked again about vacation time, but he didn't want to commit to anything until he found out about the possible role he wanted to audition for. And there was still the issue of helping Liz find a full-time nanny because I would need Elena to work for me if we went away.

I hadn't realized I'd gone as far as I had and hurried back to the hotel for Bernie's weekly department head meeting.

Just before I reached the hotel, Brock Goodwin blocked my way. "Ah, just the person I wanted to see. You didn't tell me that Bugs Bailey was working at the hotel. I found that out at your party. And Tina Marks is back here with her family. I didn't realize she was staying for the entire month."

"What is it you want, Brock? You know I can't and won't talk about our hotel guests."

"I asked you nicely to speak to the mayor about the position I want. She turned me down. But if you ask her for me, she might listen to you. I overheard her rave about all the work you and Rhonda have done with the hotel."

I held up my hand to ward him off. "You know I don't get involved in politics."

"That's not true," he said. "You get involved in the neighborhood association all the time."

"Only when Rhonda and I have to defend ourselves against your silly harassment." I turned on my heel and jogged onto the hotel property wishing there was a way we could get rid of him in our lives.

I went into the conference room for the staff meeting and took a seat. Rhonda arrived and slid into the chair next to me.

"Arthur is coming back for our charity event. He told me he wanted to get to know Lorraine better." She gave me a triumphant look. "How do you like them apples?"

I laughed and then quieted as Bernie began the meeting.

During the meeting, Bernie explained how he wanted things to run with the shoulder season about to happen. "While reservations will naturally slow down, service and attention to detail are more important than ever. For the next several months, weddings and private events will become normal."

"And may I remind everyone that weddings and events often involve publicity, and it's important for us to keep our stellar reputation," I added.

"And just like the party yesterday, we need staff to realize they must honor their agreement to keep private details of our guests private," said Rhonda.

"It makes it hard when some politicians want attention from the press during their stay," countered Ana Gomez, head of Housekeeping.

"True," I said. "But if we don't waver from what we ask of

our staff, that will minimize any such problems."

The meeting continued pleasantly, and before Bernie closed the session, he said, "Rhonda, you're taking off tomorrow and hopefully won't even think of us and the hotel for the entire time you're gone."

"You know I'll be thinking of you all, but I will try and rest after such a personal scare. Gawd! I can hardly believe Will and I are returning to Tahiti. I'll take plenty of pictures of everything but me in a bikini." She let out a raucous laugh, and the staff joined in.

"We wish you and Will a wonderful trip," said Bernie diplomatically, and the meeting ended.

In the office, Rhonda and I went over figures from the party. Our annual Spring Brunch cost us several thousand dollars, but Rhonda and I agreed it was well worth it from a PR point of view for locals, guests, and the staff at their party following the event.

"We have only one wedding between now and when I return. Then I'll be here to help plan the charity event before we host a whole slew of weddings," said Rhonda.

"Yes, it's good timing for you to be away," I said. "But you know I and everyone else will miss you."

"Aw-w, that makes me happy." Rhonda grinned. "Wait until you see the lingerie I ordered online. If that doesn't add a little sizzle to bedtime, I don't know what will."

I laughed. Will had no idea what he was in for. "Let's hope it works."

Rhonda grew serious. "Will and I have needed this time alone. I can't wait to be able to talk to him or go somewhere without interruptions. With Reggie working with him, the business has grown, which means long hours. Then when he comes home, he's tired, and so am I. It was much easier when I had Angela at a young age."

"I know the feeling, though having Vaughn at my side makes such a difference. He's a good dad. Robbie was sent home from school for swearing when he and another boy got into a fight."

"That doesn't sound like Robbie," said Rhonda. "But boys are very different from girls. Something I'm learning with Drew. No need to worry, though. Robbie is a good kid."

"I'm excited for you that you can take this trip. I'm sure Reggie will do a good job for Will when he's gone."

"Though he and Will are good partners, I think Reggie likes being the boss while he's gone," said Rhonda.

We went back to reviewing the expenses for the party and then did a quick check of the upcoming reservations. We were 80 percent full but with a lower average room rate, a sign of the coming months.

"I think we're all set," I said. "Why don't you go home and pack?"

"You're sure?" Rhonda said, already standing. Smiling, she grabbed hold of her purse.

"Go. Have fun! And as Bernie says, don't think of us at the hotel. Relax and enjoy yourself." I hugged and kissed her. "We'll do a good job for you. I promise."

Tears welled in Rhonda's eyes. "I know you will. Remember, write down any details to share when I return." She pulled out a tissue from her purse and dabbed at her eyes. "It's the leaving part I hate."

"I know. But go!" Tears blurred my vision. We spent almost every day working together, and I'd miss her.

After a sleepless night in which I questioned myself about

details I hadn't discussed with Rhonda, I got up early, dressed, and slipped out of the house.

At the hotel, I parked and went down to the beach, which always brought me a sense of calm.

I saw Sydney standing in the lacy-edged water, staring at the scene.

"Mind if I join you?" I asked, coming up behind her.

She turned and smiled at me. "That would be nice. Tina told me how she and you used to do this. As she said, it's a good way to pause and think about things."

"Yes, it is for me, too," I said. "I thought you might be here with Bobby."

"He's going to meet me a little later," she said happily. "I'm just enjoying my time before I go back to the cottage to get Victor."

"It looks as if it's going to be a beautiful day. Cool in the morning and evening but pleasant during the day."

"Every day is beautiful here," said Sydney. "I'm happy Tina brought me along."

"She thinks the world of you, you know."

"She's been a lifesaver for me," said Sydney. "I hope to repay her one day."

"You repay her every day by taking good care of her children," I said, smiling at her.

Her eyes brightened. "I try my best."

"Good talking to you," I said. "I need to check something at the hotel."

I left her and went to find Manny. Because of the mid-day heat, he always got an early start to the day.

I found him out front trimming some bushes by the building. "Good morning!" I said cheerfully. "I wanted to thank you and Paul for the help you gave us in giving brunch guests a tour of the garden. I think we have some interest in weddings from a couple of them."

"No problem. I'm always glad to show it off. Since Paul has been back, the garden is looking even better."

We looked up as a white limousine stopped in front of the hotel. The backseat window rolled down, and Rhonda stuck her head outside. "Hi, Annie! Hi, Manny. I just needed to get one last look at the hotel before we head to the airport."

"Have a fantastic trip," I said, smiling and waving to her. Leaving was hard for Rhonda. This place was much more than the seaside estate she'd bought after winning the Florida lottery.

She waved and blew several kisses to us as the limo pulled away.

We watched quietly as the limo left the hotel property, and I knew Manny was feeling the same sense of loss as I was.

I decided to take another walk on the beach to settle my feelings. It was still early, and I wouldn't be needed for a while. A breath of fresh air would do me good. The scare of Rhonda having cancer and dying felt very real when she blew kisses to us.

Inside the hotel, I noticed Bobby and approached him. "I saw Sydney earlier. If you're headed to the beach, I'll walk you out. This gives me a chance to thank you again for your help with the brunch the other day. I overheard your conversation with a fan and can't help wondering if you're anxious to return to football."

Bobby shrugged. "I'm not as excited about it as I once was. But yeah, I need to get back and practice with my team when it's time. I owe that to them."

"You're someone all the sports people are watching."

"Yeah, I guess," he said.

We walked out the back of the hotel.

As we stepped onto the beach, we saw Sydney half-running, half-falling away from us, crying, "Help!"

In the distance, I could barely make out a man running along the water's edge.

Bobby sprinted to Sydney with me trailing behind.

He knelt beside Sydney. "Are you alright? What's happening?"

Sydney collapsed onto the sand. "Go!" she said, pointing to the man in the distance. "He's got Victor."

Bobby took off running.

I reached for her. Sydney was sobbing so hard that she could hardly get her breath, then she leaned over and retched onto the sand.

"Sydney, sweetheart, what is happening?" I asked, putting my arm around her.

"It's Victor! He took Victor!" she managed to say. "Oh, God! I'm going to be sick again."

I held her head as she threw up. "What happened?"

"A guy bumped into me on the beach while I was playing with Victor. I think he drugged me. Oh, God! I feel dizzy." She gripped my hand.

When she stopped retching, she looked up at me. Tears streamed down her cheeks. "I couldn't stop him. He took Victor. What are we going to do? Bobby will never be able to catch him. He's too far away."

"I'm calling 911 now," I said, pulling my phone out of my pocket. Trembling, feeling sick myself, I told them what I could about the kidnapping and asked them to send an ambulance for Sydney.

"I'm okay, I think," said Sydney. "I want to go to the house."

I gave them the address and clicked off the call. "Do you think you can make it?"

"I don't know, but I have to tell Tina. She trusted me to take care of Victor." She began to cry heart-rending sobs that added to my terror.

"Let me help you up," I said, trying to get her on her feet.

Her legs wobbled, and she sank to the ground. "Give me a minute."

Sydney clung to me as I lifted her to her feet.

After walking a bit, I saw where Sydney had left towels and a small cooler. We left them alone for the police to check for clues and headed toward the house.

We'd almost made it to the path to the house when Bobby showed up, dripping sweat and breathing hard.

"Did you find him?" asked Sydney.

Bobby shook his head. "I'm guessing he had a car waiting to take them away from the parking lot down the beach. I didn't see him or Victor or anything suspicious. I'm sorry, Syd."

"Oh God! Oh God!" Fresh tears rolled down her cheeks, and terror filled her face.

"Sydney thinks she was poisoned somehow," I said as Sydney collapsed again. "The EMTs are going to meet us at the cottage, along with the police."

"I've got her," said Bobby. He picked Sydney up as if she weighed nothing, and she nestled against him.

I followed them as we hurried to the house to tell Tina some of the worst news a mother could hear.

CHAPTER TWENTY-ONE

Tina met us at the door. Her eyes widened when she saw Sydney in Bobby's arms. "What happened? Where's Victor?" She opened the door.

"You'd better sit down," I said, a tremor in my voice, my stomach roiling with shock.

"Victor! I want to know where Victor is," cried Tina, grabbing my arm so hard I thought she might have bruised it. "Tell me."

Bobby laid Sydney on the couch, and I held Tina's hand, knowing she deserved the absolute truth. "Victor has been kidnapped. We've called the police. Sydney has been drugged, and EMTs are on their way, along with the police."

Tina's body stiffened with horror, and then her whole body seemed to melt, and she collapsed into a heap on the floor. "No! No!"

I knelt beside her and wrapped my arms around her. "We're going to do everything we can to get him home quickly and safely."

"Victor! My baby! I want my baby," she wailed, her voice full of such anguish that the tears in my eyes spilled down my cheeks.

I rocked Tina in my arms. "I'm so sorry. Sydney and Bobby did their best to catch the man who did this. The police will help us. Hang on. We're going to get him back."

Bobby grabbed a bowl and brought it over to the couch where Sydney lay, sobbing hysterically before she was sick once more.

"I'm sorry I couldn't catch him," Bobby said to Tina, fighting tears. "I tried my best. Honest. But he was too far away."

Tyler, hearing all the noise, began to call from his room. "Syd, Syd! Mommy! Mommy!"

"I'll get him," I said as Tina cried, "Victor! Victor! My baby! Dear God, bring him home."

Blinded by tears, shaking from disbelief, I went into the baby's room and picked him up. Seeing me, he started to cry.

I tried to soothe him as I brought him to Tina.

She sat up on the floor and shook her head. "I want Victor. I want my Victor."

"Tyler wants his mommy," I said firmly.

Tina blinked as if coming out of shock and held her arms out to Tyler. "Come here, baby."

"I'm going outside to make sure the police and EMTs know where we are." I needed to call hotel security and Bernie to let them know what was happening.

As if in a dream, I made myself lift one foot, then another, leaving the hysteria behind as I walked to the edge of the driveway and made the calls.

Saying the words out loud made the circumstance all too real. Unable to stop myself, I emptied my stomach into the bushes beside the driveway. I couldn't stop the shaking that wracked my body.

I saw the ambulance and waved to the driver. It was followed by a police car. "Do you know what kind of drug was given?" asked one of the EMTs stepping out of the ambulance and reaching for a bag inside.

"No, I don't," I said.

Two policemen passed us and hurried into the house.

We arrived together at the door together, and Bobby ushered us inside.

Sydney was still lying on the couch, and Tina had collapsed into an overstuffed chair nearby, holding Tyler, who was sucking his thumb and leaning against her. All faces were wet with tears.

The EMTs hurried to Sydney's side and began checking her over, talking quietly to her. One of them signaled for me to come over.

"Can you help Sydney to the bathroom? We want to get a urine sample for testing. That will tell us a lot. It appears that something was injected into her."

A policeman was standing by, taking notes.

The other policeman said, "We'll need one of you to show us where the incident occurred. We'll need photographs of the child and as much information as possible." He turned to Sydney. "After you take care of the sample, we need to get a description of the man."

"I'll do anything I can to help. I just want Victor back," she said, lowering her head between her legs after she sat up. "God, I feel as if I can't move."

"I'll help you," I said, lifting her to her feet and walking her to the bathroom.

We returned to the living room with the sample a few minutes later. "What drug do you think it is?"

The EMT said quietly. "I suspect it's an opioid of some kind. Possibly heroin from what we're seeing."

"Oh, my word! Is Sydney in danger of ..."

He held up his hand. "If it is heroin, her body should get rid of it within 4–6 hours. We'll need someone to stay with her to make sure she's all right. And we're not going anywhere until we know what we're dealing with. We carry drug tests in our vehicles. So chances are we'll know something shortly."

I stood aside as one of the policemen approached Sydney. "What can you tell us about the man who took Victor?"

Sydney shook her head. "Not a lot. He was just an average guy. He was wearing a red Buccaneers hat. His face was scruffy, and he was wearing sunglasses, so I couldn't tell much about him. It all happened very fast." She bent over and dry-heaved.

"Can you tell us more? When did you realize you'd been drugged?"

Sydney said, "I don't do drugs, so I was confused at first. But my limbs felt as if I couldn't move them. I might've blacked out for a few seconds, and then I felt as if I couldn't open my eyes. I tried to get up and run, but it felt like I had weights on my feet, and I couldn't catch my breath because my heart was racing. Then I felt sick." She covered her face and sobbed. "I saw him pick up Victor and run away, but I couldn't catch him."

Bobby rubbed her back in comforting circles. "I tried to catch him, but he was too far away for me to get to him. I suspect he might have had someone waiting for him in the parking lot down the beach. When I got there, I didn't see him or Victor. It was pretty quiet because of the early morning hour."

"Will one of you show us where this happened?"

"I will," I said, eager to keep the public from touching the area. I prayed Brock Goodwin wouldn't be around.

As I walked beside a policeman toward the beach, I was aware that Rhonda and I couldn't keep all of our guests safe. Yet, I felt a sense of guilt over this. I'd invited Tina to our Spring Brunch, knowing others would be thrilled to meet her. Did that somehow contribute to the knowledge that her family was here, and her nanny liked early morning hours on the beach?

I led the policeman to where Sydney had placed towels, a canvas bag, and a small cooler. Beyond them, we could see disturbed sand, and then a few steps beyond that spot, we spied a syringe.

The policeman pulled on plastic gloves and took out a plastic bag where he placed the syringe.

We walked down the beach. The way the sand was disturbed told the story of a struggle until we followed the signs to the hardpacked sand at the water's edge. We scoured the area for footprints, but the waves had come in and washed them away.

"You can go back to the house. I'm going to continue to see what I can find," said the policeman.

I was anxious to see how things were there, so I trotted back to the house.

Two more police cars had arrived.

Inside the house, computers and other equipment had been set up. The television in the living room was on and showed a photograph of Victor. A drawing of a man wearing a Buccaneers baseball cap and a scruffy beard was also shown. Victor's clothing was described, and a brief description of the kidnapper was given.

"The boy and his captor were last seen on the public beach near The Beach House Hotel," said the newsman. "If you have any information regarding this, please call the number shown on your television screen. A $50,000 reward is being offered for any information leading to the man's arrest and recovery of Victor."

Staring at the television screen, I thought the facts were all too real, and I felt tears roll down my cheeks. It felt as if I was in the middle of a nightmare and couldn't wake up. I could easily imagine what Tina was going through.

A middle-aged man wearing tan slacks and a navy sport

coat introduced himself to me as Detective Joe Mariano. With brown hair and blue eyes, his appearance was ordinary except for the bulge of muscles I noticed in the sleeves of his jacket. He obviously worked out. Somehow, that made me feel hopeful.

Sydney was sitting up on the couch wrapped in a blanket. Bobby sat beside her. Tina was pacing the room, holding onto Tyler.

I went over to her. "What can I do to help?"

She shook her head. "We have to hope and pray the policemen can get Victor back to me safe and sound. I called Nick, and he's taking a private jet here."

"Would you like me to change Tyler and settle him in his highchair?" I asked, noting his wet diaper.

Tina clung tighter to Tyler. At his squeak of discomfort, she sighed and handed him to me. "Thanks, Ann. I don't know what I'd do if you weren't here. I can't bear the thought of anything happening to Victor." She began to cry.

I rubbed her back, wishing I could magically end this horrible scene. "We're going to get him back," I said, putting all my hope into it.

Tina plopped down into a chair and covered her face with her hands.

I carried Tyler into his room and spoke softly to him as I changed his diaper, playing a little game with him though my heart was breaking at the thought of losing Victor.

He studied me with big, blue eyes. His solemn expression made me wonder if he understood what had happened.

I hugged him to me. "It's going to be all right," I said, praying it would be so. I took him to the kitchen and put him in his highchair. Searching in the cupboards, I found the box of Cheerios and sprinkled a few on his tray.

"I'll get his breakfast." Sydney tried to stand and fell back against the couch.

One of the EMTs said to her, "You're going to feel better in a few hours, but until then, we want to keep an eye on you until you get this opioid out of your system."

Tina got out of the chair and said, "I'll take care of Tyler. I need to keep busy, or I'll go crazy waiting for any word."

The telephone the detectives had set up started ringing. We all stopped, and a hush filled the room.

Joe Mariano answered the call with a calm voice. "Good morning. Yes, this is the right number. What can you tell us?" After a pause, he said, "You're sure? It was ten o'clock last night. Okay. Thank you. I've got your name and number. If needed, we'll get back to you. Thank you."

"Well?" Tina said, clutching her hands.

Joe shook his head. "A crank call. I'm sorry, but this happens a lot. People want the reward and make up a story. This person said she saw Victor with the man last night at Disney World."

"I'm adding $50,000 to the reward," I said, knowing Rhonda would agree with me. "Maybe that will help."

"Okay, we'll get that information to the news sources." Joe called over a second detective, a younger man called Mike. "Get that information out quickly."

Mike bobbed his head and went to a table he'd set up in the living room. Another policeman was working on a computer at the kitchen bar.

I called Bernie and asked to meet with him immediately and to please send someone from hotel security to the house, so they could know what was happening.

"I must leave briefly, but I'll be back," I told Tina. "Hang in there." I hugged her and left before we both started to cry again.

CHAPTER TWENTY-TWO

When I entered the hotel, I saw several people in the lobby staring at the television and talking about the kidnapping.

"To think it happened right here," said one guest.

"Do you think it's safe for us to be on the beach?" another said.

I walked up to the group. "Hi, I'm Ann Sanders. For those of you who don't know me, I'm one of the owners of the hotel. I want to assure you that the beach is safe. This is a horrible, isolated incident of a man taking a child for what we believe is a ransom." As awful as it sounded, I hoped that was the reason behind the kidnapping and not something worse.

"What if the man comes back?" asked an older woman.

"I doubt that would ever happen, but to make everyone feel comfortable, we'll have the beach in front of the hotel patrolled by our security team. We do ask that you don't interfere with any markings left by the police."

"Thank you," the woman replied. "That makes me feel better."

I left them and went to Bernie's office. After greeting him, I told him about the conversation in the lobby. "We must make our guests feel safe and comfortable about being here. In addition to sending a security team member to the house, we must have security patrol the area at our beach front. As news spreads throughout the state and nation, we need to protect the hotel's image."

"I agree," said Bernie solemnly. "I've already protected the entrance to the hotel. Unless someone is registered at the hotel or has a reservation, they will be turned away."

"Good idea," I said. "We don't want to do anything to complicate the situation. If the man is looking for a ransom, we don't want to make it seem as if it can't happen. So, a look of normalcy is important."

Bernie shook his head. "I feel terrible for Tina and Nick. Like you, I feel as if they're family."

I let out a long, painful sigh. 'I'll be spending my time with her, but if you need anything from me, please let me know. I've added a $50,000 amount to the reward given for information leading to the arrest of the man and release of Victor."

"Rhonda would want you to do that," said Bernie. "Should we call her?"

"No," I said, thinking how excited she'd been to go on vacation. "There's nothing I nor anyone else can do except let the police do their job while we keep the hotel running."

"Yes, that's what I thought," said Bernie.

"At different times of the day, we'll need food sent to the house. "There are two detectives, a couple of policemen with Tina, Sydney, and Bobby. That reminds me, please let Jean-Luc know that Bobby won't be in today. It's much more important for him to be with Sydney. He and I discovered Sydney on the beach, and Bobby tried to catch the man." I told him all I knew and then rose. "I'm going to my office to call Vaughn, and then I'm returning to the house to be with Tina. Nick is taking a private jet here. I'm not sure when he'll arrive."

Bernie stood. "Don't worry. I'll take care of things here. Give Tina my best wishes."

"Will do," I said and headed to my office.

Vaughn had phoned several times. I sat at my desk to

return his calls.

He picked up right away. "Ann, I've heard the news. Tell me everything."

I began with Bobby and me walking onto the beach seeing Sydney in distress and gave him a detailed accounting of what had happened since then.

"We're guessing a ransom will be requested because everyone knows how wealthy Tina Marks is. Nick has already offered a $50,000 reward for information, and I've added $50,000 to it, hoping someone will provide information leading to the man's arrest and Victor's release."

"Where are you now?" Vaughn asked.

"At the hotel to take care of security with Bernie. But I'm going back to the house with Tina. You can imagine what she's going through." I started to cry. "I can't believe such an awful thing has happened. I'm worried that Rhonda and I are somewhat to blame because we asked her to come to the Spring Brunch. Maybe that's when the news got out that she and her family were staying at the hotel."

"Wait a minute," said Vaughn calmly. "You don't want to put yourself in that kind of position. Maybe Tina mentioned she was at the hotel with her family. We might never know. The thing to concentrate on now is the return of Victor."

"I know you're right, but the thought still bothers me. I'll stay with Tina until she no longer wants me there."

"Is there anything I can do?" Vaughn asked.

"Nick is flying into Sabal on a private jet. You might try to see if you can pick him up. I'll try to get information to you."

"Okay. I'll wait to hear from you. Call me for any reason and keep me informed about Victor. I have to say, the thought of this happening is enough to make me sick. Give my regards to both Tina and Sydney. They must be devastated."

"Yes," I said. "It's the most awful, helpless feeling to know there's nothing you can do about it but pray."

"At some point, I want to see Tina, but I'll leave it up to you to tell me the best time to do that."

"I understand. I'll keep in touch. But, understandably, I don't know when I'll be home. Will you do me a favor and call Liz? I know she must be concerned."

"No problem," he said.

I ended the call feeling no better than when I phoned him. Vaughn was as helpless as I was to do anything about this awful situation.

Things were pretty much the same when I returned to the house. Sydney was on the couch with Bobby. The policemen were sitting at desks or milling around talking. Tina was nowhere to be found.

"Where's Tina?" I asked.

"She's getting changed. She's going to make a plea on television for the abductor to release Victor," said Bobby.

I knocked on the bedroom door.

Tina opened it and threw her arms around me. "Come in. I'm going to go on television. I didn't know if I could do it when I was asked. But then I told myself I'd do anything to help Victor." She held up two dresses. One black, the other a colorful turquoise. "Tell me which one I should wear."

"How about something navy blue? Black indicates you've given up. Turquoise isn't serious enough."

"Oh, good thinking," said Tina. She pulled a navy sheath out of the closet and put it on.

"There," Tina said, smoothing down the dress's fabric. "The television cameraman is going to shoot it at the front of the hotel, if that's all right."

"I'll let Bernie know, and we'll clear the area. We want to

present a calm but strong presence," I said.

"Will you stand beside me?" Tina asked, giving me a pleading look.

"Of course," I said, even though I dreaded that kind of attention.

We left the bedroom, and I called Bernie. He asked for a little bit of time to prep the area.

"Let's give Tyler his lunch. And then, hopefully, he can go down for a nap," said Tina.

I helped her cut up some slices of cheese, set aside a dish of applesauce, and placed a few pieces of cooked carrots on his tray, things the triplets liked.

Tyler was already showing signs of nodding off as he fingered his food.

Mike, the detective who worked with Joe, came over to us. "I've got a kid this age. Need help with him?"

"Could you help watch him for a few minutes?" Tina told him. "I've agreed to make the televised plea for Victor, but I don't want to be gone long. So when I get back, I'll put Tyler down for a nap."

"Okay, I can do this," Mike said.

Tina took my arm. "C'mon. Let's get this over with."

We broke through the throng of newspaper people at the end of the driveway waiting to talk to Tina.

"We're going to be speaking from the front of the hotel," I said, causing several to rush ahead of us as we headed there.

Just as we stepped onto the pavement of the front drive, a white limousine pulled up. Rhonda climbed out, ran to Tina, and enveloped her in a bosomy hug.

"I heard the news and had to come back to help. What can I do? Any new developments?"

Will joined us. "What's the latest?"

I was so happy to see them that I could hardly speak with

the lump in my throat. "Tina is going to make a plea on television to the abductor to return Victor."

"You poor dear," said Rhonda, holding onto Tina. "I've been praying every minute since I heard the news." Tears flowed down Rhonda's cheeks. "There was plane trouble, and our flight stopped in Tampa. So when the news about Victor came on the television, Will and I skipped our flight and caught one back here."

Tina stood back and let out a shaky breath. "I'm trying to be brave for Victor, but this is going to be my best performance ever. After that, I want to shrivel up and die when I think I might never see him again."

"We need to be positive," said Rhonda. "What can I do for you?"

"Ann has agreed to stand with me while I speak. I want you there too," said Tina.

"You got it," said Rhonda. She turned to Will. "I'm going to stay here with Tina and Ann."

He bobbed his head. "I'll walk over to the house for an update. See you there. Good luck with the television spot."

He paid the limo driver and then headed to Tina's house.

"Okay," said Rhonda. "I know you need to speak calmly to the asshole who did this, but I promise you that if I ever have the chance, I'll take him down."

"Rhonda, you can't say a word at the press conference," I said, knowing how outspoken she could be.

"I won't. I promise. But my mind will be full of really ugly thoughts," she said.

"Thanks," said Tina. "I need the two of you with me. Nick is on his way, but I don't know when he'll get here."

"We're with you all the way," I said, realizing how helpless that sounded.

CHAPTER TWENTY-THREE

While television crews set up cameras outside the hotel, I sat with Tina and Rhonda in Bernie's office. Though I was jittery at the thought of being in front of the cameras, I tried to tell myself I could do this without breaking down. Tina appeared to be in her own world, staring out the window motionless.

At a signal from one of the television crew, Tina, Rhonda, and I walked out to the front of the hotel, where a lectern on a small dais had been set up by the entrance. After one of the news reporters made a few remarks, she turned to Tina.

I saw Tina stumble as she stepped forward and rushed to her side. Rhonda steadied her other arm and stood like an angry warrior next to her.

As I listened to Tina beg her abductor to return Victor, I felt as if my body had separated, a part of me had risen, and I was looking down at the surreal scene from above. I forced myself to remain calm, but I wanted to rail against what had happened.

"Please, anyone, if you have any information, call the number that has been given," Tina ended.

"That's right. A $100,000 reward is offered for such information," said the reporter as we turned and entered the hotel.

We made it as far as Bernie's office before Tina broke down completely. "Let's get you away from the crowd," I said after we let her cry. "We'll go out the back and take the private path to the house."

"Thanks. I want to get back to Tyler. He may wonder where I am."

Rhonda and I helped Tina back to the house, relieved to escape the reporters still lingering at the front of the hotel.

When we entered the house, Joe Mariano waved us over. "We've just received a ransom note via text to our number. Doubtful we can get the phone number. I assume the kidnapper is smart enough to use one of the disposable phones you can purchase. But we'll do our best to track down its location. We'll follow any lead we can."

"What does the note say?" I asked, holding onto Tina.

"The kidnapper wants one million dollars in cash dropped off at a location he will choose. He'll let us know where to come. He doesn't want Tina to deliver the cash. He wants the small, dark-haired woman standing with her in front of the cameras to do the drop in exchange for Victor. He says she appeared to be the calmest."

"Me? I was doing my best to hold everything inside," I said.

"No matter what he says, Annie is not going there alone, and I'm providing the one million dollars," said Rhonda in a tone that no one dared to question.

"We must follow his instructions. If we don't, he could panic," warned Joe.

"Okay, I'll just drive the car," said Rhonda. "But if he tries anything, no promises as to what I'll do."

"And where are you going to get the money?" Joe asked.

"Don't worry. I have it. We'll deal with my bank," said Rhonda. "Believe me. They love me."

"Okay, we'll want to identify the bills somehow," said Joe. "You'd better go with her, Mike."

Rhonda, Will, and Mike left the house.

"Did he say if Victor is all right?" Tina asked Joe, her voice thin with worry.

"No, but I've asked for proof that he's alive," said Joe. "I've told him the deal is off unless he can show us something to indicate that."

A text message came across the computer screen hooked up to the phone number. "Victor says his favorite toy is Piglet."

'Oh-h-h, yes! He loves his stuffed Piglet," said Tina and burst into tears.

Just then, we heard a commotion outside, and Nick entered the room.

Tina let out a cry and went into his arms. "He's got Victor, and now he wants a million dollars."

Nicholas held her tight and turned to me. "Fill me in," he said crisply though his eyes had filled.

Tina sobbed in Nicholas's embrace as I gave him what details I could. "This is Joe Mariano, the head detective working the case. I'll let him explain further."

After Joe had shown Nicholas what they were doing, Sydney and Bobby approached him.

Tears streamed down Sydney's face. "I'm so sorry, Mr. Swain. I didn't realize I was drugged. I tried to get to Victor and couldn't."

"I'm sorry, too, sir," said Bobby. "I tried to catch him, but he was way ahead of me."

Nicholas studied him. "Bugs Bailey? If you couldn't catch him, nobody could." Giving Bobby a nod of approval, he put an arm around Sydney. "I'm sorry this happened to you. Are you going to be all right?"

"The EMTs said I will. I feel better than I did."

"Well, let's see if we can bring my boy home," said Nicholas.

Joe waved me over. "We need you to wear a loose-fitting dress for the drop-off. We'll have you wear a bulletproof vest and have you wired. Can you call your husband and have him bring a dress here? I don't know how much time we have."

A thread of fear wove through me, but I picked up my cell and called Vaughn. When he heard my request, he said, "Ann, I don't like this. You could be killed."

"I know," I said, my heart pounding. "But that's what the abductor requested. Rhonda is getting the money now and insists on driving me to the drop-off spot. Policemen will be around. I'm not sure where, but they'll be there to protect Victor and me."

"Okay, tell me which dress or dresses you want, and I'll be right there. When Robbie gets home from school, Elena will be here, so we're covered there."

I requested two dresses, hung up, and told Joe, "My husband will bring them right away."

"Okay," said Joe. "I want you to be aware of what you need to do. When you get out of the car, you must do exactly as you're told. But you cannot deliver the money until you see Victor and make sure he's away from the kidnapper and within reach of you. We'll wait to see what the kidnapper or kidnappers have to say and proceed from there."

"Okay." I swallowed hard. "I don't know why he wanted me to do this part, but I will. Anything for Victor." My voice grew wobbly. "I'm his godmother."

A short while later, Vaughn arrived with two dresses. He kissed Tina and shook hands with Nicholas, who was holding Tyler. "I'm very sorry about what's happened. I'm here to help in any way I can."

"Thanks, Vaughn," said Nicholas. "It's hell waiting for news. I don't understand how this person knew Victor and Sydney." He turned to Joe. "What do you think?"

"He could've known he was your son and Tina's child, or he could've been watching people at the beach and come to the conclusion that Sydney was a nanny and Victor came from a rich family." Joe's lips thinned with anger. "We'll find out. The faster we get the money to the kidnapper, the better the chances are of Victor being safe."

"He said he'd call," I explained as a technician attached wires to me. I'd chosen to wear a cotton print dress with puffy sleeves and a high waist which Joe thought would work best with a bullet-proof vest.

Seeing me in the vest and wired, Vaughn's forehead creased with worry. "I wish you didn't have to do this," he said into my ear as he gave me a hug.

"It's going to be all right," I answered, surprising myself at the confidence in my voice.

Just then, Rhonda, Will, and Mike returned.

"Got the money," said Rhonda. "What's new?"

"We're just waiting to hear from the kidnapper about where to meet him," I told Rhonda.

"Let's call Jean-Luc and have some food delivered. Who knows how long that will take," said Rhonda. "We need to keep everyone alert."

A couple of hours later, another text came:

"Meet me at the County Nature Preserve off I-75 within 15 minutes. If you don't show up, you won't get the kid. And don't be stupid and try to have cops there. The area is blocked off. Go around the barricade. Put a sign on your dashboard that says Victor, and we'll go from there."

Rhonda and I looked at one another. "Time to go," she said.

"Not without a bulletproof vest for you," I said.

Mike quickly put one on Rhonda, and we headed to the door, scared we'd miss the deadline.

"Remember everything I told you, Ann. You can fill in Rhonda on the way," said Joe. "Stay calm and collected. Listen to everything the kidnapper says and do everything exactly as he wants. The fact that he's after the money is important. You won't know we're around, but we will be. The car is loaded with the money, and we've hooked up some recorders."

I kissed Vaughn, wishing I didn't have to let go of his embrace. Rhonda clung to Will for a moment before she got what I call her "tough face" on. Seeing that made me feel stronger. Rhonda didn't take shit from anyone.

Carrying a sign that said "Victor" that Mike had drawn, we raced to Rhonda's black Mercedes GLE Coupe, and she took off with a roar of the engine.

Once we reached I-75, Rhonda put the pedal to the metal, and with a couple of minutes to spare, we reached the turn-off for the nature center.

"Okay, slow down," I said. "I don't think he knows there will be two of us. So stay in the car and don't react to anything."

We drove along the road. I checked my watch—3:45 PM. "I know why they wanted to meet us here then. They clear the walkways by three o'clock. It's one of their rules."

"With all the gators here, that makes sense," said Rhonda, driving slowly so we could look for any sign of them.

Rhonda drove around the barricade and stopped in the empty parking lot.

A young man emerged from behind a tree next to the registration area. He was holding a gun.

"Where's Victor?" hissed Rhonda.

"That's what I have to find out," I said, emerging from the car. I turned back and pulled out the canvas duffle bag holding the cash.

"Okay, I'm here," I called to him as he approached.

Though he wore a ski mask, I could tell from his shape and clothing that he was young. Surprisingly, his sneakers were expensive ones like Chad wore.

"I thought you were driving yourself," he said, his voice gruff, anxious.

'She's my business partner, the one you saw standing with Tina and me. She wouldn't let me drive her car."

"Okay. Gimme the money," the man said, holding out his hand.

"Not until I get Victor. Where is he?" I said, forcing myself to be calm. I don't know what I'd do if he wouldn't cooperate.

"I said, 'Gimme the money,'" he snarled. He lunged toward me, but I easily sidestepped him, making me realize he was under the influence of some drug.

"Look, I have the money right here," I said as he whirled around. "But I can't give it to you until I see Victor and know he's safe." I braced myself for another attack.

"Shit. Follow me, then no more stalling. C'mon. We have to hurry."

He led me through a gate that he had unlocked by force, it appeared. Then, we followed the wooden trail to the first rain protection structure.

Victor lay on the ground. His mouth, hands, and feet were bound with silvery tape.

"Okay, gimme the money, and let's go," the man said, pointing the gun at me.

"I can't leave Victor," I said, holding the money behind my back.

"I'll get the kid," the man said after a moment's hesitation when I wondered if he would shoot me. "We gotta hurry."

He picked up Victor and held the gun to Victor's head as he trotted to Rhonda's car.

I followed behind.

He set Victor down and grabbed the bag of money. "Get in the front seat."

My body stiffened with fear. Was he going to shoot us there?"

"Wait, I need Victor. I lifted him into my arms and slid onto the passenger seat.

"I'm going to get in the backseat, and you're going to drive," he told Rhonda. "My gun will be pointed toward the three of you. Do as I say, and nobody will get hurt. Get it?" He climbed in the back and kept the gun pointing in our direction.

"Where are we going?" Rhonda asked, her eyes wide.

"You'll see," he replied. "Just follow my directions."

While they talked, I made sure my microphone could pick up the conversation and removed the tape from Victor's mouth. Then, I hugged him and kissed him on his cheek. "Auntie Ann and Auntie Rhonda are here to help you."

He gazed at me wide-eyed, and I held him close as he began to cry.

"Shut the kid up!" cried the kidnapper.

"Sh-h-h," I whispered, rubbing circles on Victor's back, holding him tight to me. I heard the panic in the man's voice and prayed Victor would be able to stay strong. I whispered in his ear that Mommy and Daddy were waiting to greet him, but that we had to do what the man said."

He quieted.

We were back on I-75.

"Here, just ahead, take a right," the man said.

"Are we stopping at the county rest area?" I asked, hoping the police would pick up on it.

"Shut up!" From behind, the man struck me on the head so hard I saw stars. Victor whimpered in my lap.

Rhonda pulled into the rest area and parked beside a gray car at the far corner of the parking lot. There was just one other car around, and a woman was walking a dog.

"Turn off the engine," the man said to Rhonda. "Everyone

needs to stay inside the car, facing front. Any attempt to get out and you're all dead."

Rhonda stopped the engine, and we all faced the front.

He got out of the car, and then we heard a loud bang.

Shocked, wondering what had happened, I felt the jolt of the car.

"I think he's shot one of the tires," said Rhonda quietly.

We waited for what seemed an eternity, and then we turned around.

The small gray sedan was exiting the parking lot. The lady walking her dog was gone.

I spoke into the microphone to tell the police what they were looking for. "First of all, Victor is here and okay. Sorry, we couldn't get a license number or a good description of the man. I could tell he was young even though he wore a ski mask. He was dressed in a dark, long-sleeved T-shirt and blue jeans. And, Joe, he seemed as though he was on something."

"Ann, put Victor on," said Joe. "His parents need to hear him.

I hugged Victor to me. "Say something to Mommy and Daddy."

"Mommy, I want to come home," said Victor.

"I know you do," said Tina. "We're right here waiting for you. Auntie Ann and Auntie Rhonda will bring you home." She choked on the last words.

"He's okay," I said. "He was bound at his hands and feet with tape. Rhonda is using a small pocket knife to try and free him. Otherwise, he seems in good condition."

While we waited for help with the car, Rhonda and I worked to get the tape off Victor. Once his hands were free, I offered him a cookie. He took it eagerly.

While he nibbled on the treat in my lap, Rhonda kept working on the tape around his ankles.

"Did the man hurt you?" I asked Victor, making sure any responses could be heard through the microphone.

"No, but he told me he had Piglet for me, and he didn't."

"Did he feed you?" I asked.

"Uh, huh. McDonald's. I told him that's what I wanted."

"There was another man with him, right?"

"Yeah. Tony."

'Who was the man who took you away from the beach?" I asked, realizing Victor would be a great resource for the police in catching his kidnapper.

"Glenn. Can I have a drink?"

I opened a bottle of water and handed it to him.

As he sipped it, a police car rolled up beside us, and Tina and Nicholas emerged and ran to us.

Freed now, Victor allowed Nick to lift him out of my lap and into Tina's arms. They both sobbed, and seeing them cry, Victor began to wail.

Joe got out of the car, and when things settled down, he said, "You've already gotten good information from Victor, but we need to ask him a few questions while things are fresh in his mind."

An unmarked car rolled up beside us. Mike, Will, and Vaughn emerged.

"Good news. They've caught the guys heading to the airport," said Vaughn, sweeping me into his arms. "Thank God you're safe. You were right. We've been told they were on something, which is why they didn't even search you for wires." I felt a shudder go through him. "I never want you to have to do this again."

"Me either," I said, snuggling against him. Now that it was over, I thought about how bad it could've been and felt my body go weak.

"As it turns out, they're not hardened criminals, just two

young druggies with big ideas," said Mike. "Looks like one of Rhonda's tires had a big shootout."

"When we heard that noise, we feared the worst," said Will, rocking Rhonda in his arms.

Nick came over to us. "How can we ever thank the two of you for helping Victor? It was a brave thing you did."

I accepted his hug and turned to Rhonda as he hugged her.

"I don't know if I could've done it without Rhonda," I said. "We've fought together against so many naysayers in the past that I knew I could count on her to help me no matter what happened."

"Yeah. We're a team," said Rhonda.

Nick turned back to Tina and Victor.

I went to her and kissed Victor's cheek. "Thanks for helping me, buddy. I love you, little guy."

Rhonda kissed the three of them goodbye before Joe left with them.

Watching them go, Rhonda and I stood with our husbands and Mike.

"So far, this has been the worst vacation I've ever had. I'm just glad that everyone is safe," said Rhonda.

Nervous laughter left me, and soon we all were chuckling, happy for a healthy release of the tension we'd all gone through. The. Worst. Vacation. Ever.

CHAPTER TWENTY-FOUR

The next morning, Rhonda and I sat in our office.

"So, you're not going to go to Tahiti after all, not even a couple of days late?" I asked her.

Rhonda shook her head firmly. "Nope. After all that happened with Victor, Will and I decided to spend time with the children instead. You won't believe it, but we've even promised them a trip to Disney World. Gawd! You know how I'm not too fond of that place. All those crowds. All those lines. But a promise is a promise, and I will make it a fun day with them."

"Good for you. Last night Vaughn and I had dinner with Robbie, and then we all went to see Liz, Chad, and the babies. After hearing beforehand what I'd gone through, Liz cried when she saw me. I realize how much she needs me. I've been thinking about how lucky we were that the kidnappers were so inept. It could've gone the other way —overreacting and shooting."

"I've thought of that too. And I think of how cooperative Victor was," said Rhonda. "My Willow would've fought everything and everybody. But Victor seemed to understand how important it was for him to do as the man said."

"I know. He was terrific. I'm grateful that Tina and Nicholas are staying at the house as planned rather than going home. They don't want Victor to be afraid of being here or near the water in the future. Tina called Barbara, her old psychologist, and they talked about it."

"What about Sydney?" Rhonda asked. "She was

traumatized and devastated by all that happened."

"Funny you should ask. I saw her this morning while taking my daily walk on the beach. She and Bobby were together. When I asked how she was doing, she told me Tina and Nicholas insisted she stay with them as part of the family, that they all love her, and don't blame her for anything that happened. As she spoke to me, Bobby had a protective arm around her. I have a feeling that sharing the trauma of this has made them even closer. Before you can say anything about it, I predict they will be married someday."

"What? You didn't even give me a chance to do my magic on them," said Rhonda, huffing. "No fair."

Laughing, I said, "Let's walk over to the house together to say hello. We can also check on the house under construction."

We found Tina and her family in the pool at the house that had once been my pride and joy. Nicholas held the baby on the shallow-end steps, letting him kick and splash. Tina was in the pool with Victor, pulling him around in the water. Sydney was sitting on the edge of the pool at the deep end. To anyone who didn't know what the family had gone through recently, it appeared simply to be a peaceful scene.

Off to the side, sitting on a chair, a woman in long, khaki pants and a blue-denim, short-sleeve shirt wore a gun in a holster at her waist. Nicholas had insisted on having an armed guard from our security force stay with them until they flew home. I couldn't blame him for feeling that way.

When Tina saw us, she hoisted Victor onto the side of the pool. "Better go say hi to Auntie Ann and Auntie Rhonda," she said to him from the water.

I held out my arms, and Victor ran into them. "Hi! Did you

see me swimming?" he asked.

"Yes, I did." I hugged him so hard that he laughed. But I couldn't keep myself from hanging on tight to him after what we'd been through together.

"Now give Auntie Rhonda a hug," Tina said, and Victor eagerly went into her embrace.

Tina climbed out of the pool and wrapped a towel around herself. "I'm very happy to see you two. We just got word that both men have appeared in court and won't be released on bail at this time. So, we can all rest easy." She indicated the guard with a nod of her head. "But I feel even safer with her."

"It's the least we could do," I said. "We've added more people to our security team, but, in truth, there was no way we could've prevented the kidnapping. Sydney and Victor were on a public beach away from the hotel's beachfront. Even then, we can't patrol the beach."

"Of course not," agreed Tina. "It's just one of those awful things that can happen."

Sydney walked over to us. "Thank you both for all you did. I can't stop thinking about it, how helpless I felt."

Tina put an arm around Sydney. "We're going to have another session with Barbara this afternoon. It's doing us all good to talk about it."

"Bobby is going to talk to her, too," said Sydney. "He feels very bad about not being able to catch the guy. I keep telling him he tried, and that's what matters."

"Bobby has learned a lot while he's been with us," I said, reminding myself to have a good talk with him. He was quite a different man from the arrogant star he was when he'd arrived.

"When is your charity event?" asked Tina. "I want to be here to support it."

"In two weeks," said Rhonda. "We're holding it here at the

hotel and limiting the crowd to 150 people, though other people can go online and bid on some items being auctioned off."

"Sounds like it's going to be fun as well as worthwhile," said Tina. "I wouldn't miss it for the world." She turned to Sydney. "And you can have that evening off after the party so you can meet up with a certain football player."

Observing Sydney's bright smile lighting her face, I shot a triumphant look at Rhonda. She wasn't the only matchmaker.

After chatting a few more minutes and spending time with Nicholas and Tyler, Rhonda and I left and walked to the corner of the property where the second house was being built.

Seeing it under construction brought back the time when my home was being renovated. I was such a beaten-down person when I first met Rhonda. Building the house was as much about creating a new life as it was about owning my first home after Robert had cheated me out of the house we'd shared for years.

"Remember how it was when you were having your house renovated? You've come a long way, baby!" said Rhonda, tuning into my feelings.

"Yes, thank goodness. Seeing this reminds me so much of those early times together."

We walked around the structure. The foundation had been poured, and the exterior concrete-block walls erected. Inside, workmen were framing walls with wood studs. I could see that the layout of this house was very close to the one that had been mine, and I liked it.

We saw a figure walking down the long driveway toward us as we went outside the house. Before Brock Goodwin could reach us, a security guard stopped him. I didn't know what was said, but Brock stormed away.

Rhonda shook her head. "That bastard must have parked outside the barricade and walked around it."

"He's persistent. I'll give him that," I said, disgusted by Brock's continual harassment. "I'm going to call the County Inspection Office and ask that they make it clear to him that he has no official business trying to inspect the house."

"Better you than me," said Rhonda. "You know I can't talk about Brock Goodwin without a lot of four-letter words. That man drives me crazy."

"I know," I sighed. "While you're saying those four-letter words, I'm thinking them. I've been trying to talk to Robbie about how to handle a situation that makes you want to swear by imagining nice words to replace them."

"With Brock, there are no nice words," grumbled Rhonda as we returned to the hotel.

"I hope you have fun on your days off," I said as we walked along. "Things seemed to have calmed down."

"I will, but you must call me if I'm needed. I will try to stay away from the hotel, but it won't be easy. The hotel is like a child we have together. Ya know?"

"Oh, yes. I feel the same way. I don't want the kidnapping to make the hotel feel unsafe to our guests. That's why I've agreed for us to sit down this afternoon with Terri Thomas for an exclusive interview. In all the talk of the kidnapping this morning, I forgot to mention it to you."

"This afternoon? Sure. I can do that," said Rhonda. "My so-called vacation doesn't begin until tomorrow."

At the hotel, we'd just finished going through the invitation list for the charity with Lorraine when Terri Thomas arrived.

Lorraine knew Terri well and talked to her for a few minutes about the upcoming charity event. "We're almost booked for the event itself, but for several days before the event, we're allowing people to bid online for various items," Lorraine explained.

"What a fun idea," said Terri. "Can you make one of the auction items delivery of The Beach House Hotel's cinnamon rolls every morning for a week? Or several free breakfasts here?"

Lorraine turned to Rhonda and me.

We both nodded. "That's easy," I said. "We'll count on you to keep bidding on that one, Terri."

"I will. You know how much I love them," she replied, laughing.

"I'd better go. We have a small but lovely wedding coming up this weekend," said Lorraine. "Nice to see you, Terri. We'll talk later about the wedding edition of the newspaper."

"Speaking of weddings," said Rhonda. "Arthur told me he's coming for the charity dinner."

"Oh, I know," said Lorraine. "He told me that too."

Lorraine winked at me as she left the room, and I couldn't hold back a chuckle. The look of surprise on Rhonda's face was too funny.

"What was that all about?" asked Terri, looking from Rhonda to me.

"Nothing," Rhonda and I said together.

"We'll give you this story and coverage of the charity event, but you know we don't talk about guests," I said, trying to throw Terri off the trail to Lorraine and Arthur's romance. "Now, let's talk about the kidnapping. You've promised to emphasize the safety of the hotel and the quick response from our management and our security team."

"Ah, yes. That's the story I'm here to report." Terri wagged a finger at us. "But you know I'll eventually track down the story behind Lorraine."

"If it's a story to tell, we'll let you know," I said, silently warning Rhonda not to say anything about it. "Would you like a cinnamon roll?" I asked Terri. It was a bribe that worked most times to keep on the good side of Terri.

"That would be lovely, along with a cup of your fabulous coffee," said Terri, sitting in a chair in front of my desk.

As we unwound the story of the kidnapping, I felt my mouth go dry. It felt as if Rhonda and I were talking about two strangers, not two friends who'd done what they could to help rescue a little boy we all loved.

"Please turn off that recorder," I asked Terri, shaken by the experience all over again. I pulled out a tissue and dabbed at my eyes, holding inside the renewed terror I felt.

"You two are real heroes," said Terri looking wide-eyed. She was writing on a tablet as fast as she could. "Tina gave me a short interview earlier, and she couldn't say enough about what you did to save Victor."

"I hope I never have to do anything like that again," said Rhonda. "Do you know how nerve-wracking it is to drive with a gun pointed at you?"

"I was so worried about getting Victor free I didn't dwell on it. But when he shot the tire on Rhonda's car, we all screamed, thinking we might be next," I admitted.

"How are you going to deal with the aftermath of this?" Terri asked.

"We've been talking to a counselor about it. Dr. Barbara Holmes is well known here in town. She has devoted a lot of time to each of us to help process the experience. We're very grateful to her."

"Yes, I know Barbara. She's wonderful," said Terri, becoming solemn. "Let's list things you want me to cover for the hotel, promoting its security."

The three of us made a bullet listing of what we wanted to

be included, and then Rhonda rose.

"Thank you for coming," said Rhonda. "I leave for a staycation tomorrow, and I need to

take care of a few things here."

"Yes, thank you," I said. "Hopefully, the newspaper will give the hotel excellent coverage."

We walked Terri to the front of the hotel and waited while she went down the steps.

"I had to stop talking about it," said Rhonda. "Ya know, it might be good for me, after all, to go to The Magic Kingdom. A nice escape."

"We all need a little magic," I said, placing a hand on her shoulder. "I think I'll stop by and see Liz and the kids on my way home."

"Talk about magic," said Rhonda, grinning. "We were so excited to learn she was pregnant, but we never dreamed she'd have triplets."

"They're so adorable that I don't want to miss anything," I said. Now, more than ever, I wanted to enjoy my family. It meant the world to me that Vaughn and Robbie would be waiting for me at home.

From the vantage point at the top of the hotel stairs, we gazed out over the property, and I knew how lucky Rhonda and I were to have survived what could've been a tragedy.

CHAPTER TWENTY-FIVE

I drove into the driveway at Liz's house, parked, and hurried toward the front door, anxious to see Liz and the babies. But, before I could knock, the door flew open, and Liz stood there, a finger covering her lips.

She stepped outside. "They're still napping. They must be tired. I let them loose in the kitchen, and they had the best time. I think Noah is going to be musical, like Chad's mother. He loved pounding on a pan with a wooden spoon. The girls loved putting things in bowls, then taking them out again."

"That sounds adorable," I said. "Nice that you can let them experience that."

"The kitchen is still a mess. Instead of cleaning up, I took a shower and washed my hair. Elena will come later, and I'll clean up then."

"Have I told you lately how proud I am for how you handle the three children at once? I don't think many people could do such a good job."

Liz's eyes watered. "Thanks. That means a lot." She sighed. "I wasn't going to say anything, but I thought I was pregnant again. I'm not, but the worry sent me into a tizzy. That would be way too much for me to handle."

"I'm happy you didn't have to face that problem."

"Me, too. It was enough to scare Chad into having a vasectomy. We decided three children were enough."

"They are three beautiful children," I said. "I adore each one."

"I'm lucky to have your love and support, and they are too,"

Liz said. "I'd invite you in, but I can't take the chance of waking them. Hope you don't mind, Mom."

"Not at all," I said. "Give me a call, and let's plan lunch together—just the two of us. I've missed that. Love you."

"Me, too. Maybe next week." Liz threw her arms around me. "I'm so lucky to have you for a mom. The thought of what you and Rhonda went through has made Angela and me realize we've got to know more about the hotel and how to manage it. If we're to take it over one day, we should know all about it."

"You're right. We'll try to set up training sessions once a week or something like that. Right now, Rhonda is planning to tour the Magic Kingdom with her kids."

I didn't say another word, but then I didn't have to. Liz's expression said it all. We both grinned at the thought. We'd gone to Disney with Rhonda and Angela, and sometimes Rhonda was like a kid herself.

When I pulled into the garage of my house, I sat in the car for a moment, thinking how lucky I was to be alive.

I got out and walked into the kitchen, laughing when Cindy yipped and wagged her tail to greet me. Trudy trotted over to me, eager for her share of attention. I picked her up. "Don't worry. You're still my big girl."

I set her down and petted Cindy, cooing sweet nothings to her.

Vaughn came into the kitchen and curled his arms around me. "Hey, beautiful! Glad you're home. It's a good time for a quick sail. Robbie and I have planned a little surprise for you."

"Oh? Anything I should know about?"

He grinned at me. "It wouldn't be a surprise if I gave anything away. Just get ready for a sail."

"It sounds wonderful. I won't be long," I said, kicking off my shoes and heading into my bedroom.

Moments later, I was in sneakers, jeans, and a knit shirt and heading down to the *Zephyr*.

Robbie greeted me with a hug. "Don't go below, Mom. We have a surprise for you."

"Okay, I'll sit right here while you and Dad get the boat out on the water." I noticed how much he'd grown in the last few months. He was going to be tall like his father.

I sat back in the cockpit and gazed out at my surroundings as Vaughn and Robbie motored the boat out onto open water. Moments later, with the sails hoisted and the engine cut off, I felt like I was becoming one with the wind as the boat skimmed the water's surface.

The salty tang of the air and the boat's motion washed away the tension I'd be carrying. "This feels good," I said, smiling at Vaughn.

He grinned. "Thought you might like this. It's been a few rough days."

"And how," I said, lifting my face to his as he bent over me.

"Can I give Mom her surprise?" asked Robbie.

"Sure," said Vaughn. "Go ahead. In addition to having dinner ready for you, Robbie and I bought you a little gift. Something we think you deserve. It was Robbie's idea."

Robbie came up on deck holding a colorful paper bag tied off with a silk ribbon.

"Open it," cried Robbie, handing it to me.

I took off the ribbon, peeked into the bag, and started laughing as I pulled out a Wonder Woman cape. "For me?" I asked.

Robbie nodded. "My teacher said you're a 'superhero.' Right, Dad?"

"Right," said Vaughn.

"Thanks so much," I said. I hooked it around my shoulders and hugged Robbie. "I did a brave thing. That's true. But in a way, we're all superheroes when we're afraid to do something and go ahead and do it anyway to help someone."

"Can I be a superhero too?" Robbie asked.

"Absolutely. When the time is right, I'm sure you will be."

"How about a glass of bubbly? I bought your favorite blush champagne," said Vaughn.

"That sounds delightful. I want to celebrate being with my 'boys.' And, Vaughn, before she returns to California, I want to invite Sydney and Bobby to go out on the boat with us for a supper cruise."

"It sounds like a little matchmaking going on, but sure, why not?"

I grinned. "I'm ahead of Rhonda on this one."

He chuckled. "Tomorrow, I'm taking Nick out on the boat. I'm hoping to be able to find out more about the role he has in mind for me. But after that, we can do your matchmaking cruise. Now, Wonder Woman, let me get the champagne. The wind has died a bit, and we can sit and relax."

As Vaughn went below, Robbie took the wheel. He was becoming a good sailor, watching the sails to make sure they were catching the wind. For a moment, he looked like Robert, and I couldn't help thinking what a treasure my ex gave me when Robbie became ours.

Later that night, after Robbie and the dogs were asleep, Vaughn and I slipped out of the house wrapped in towels. It was a perfect night for skinny-dipping. The moon was a silver globe in the sky, shedding subtle light around us. I'd vowed never to take our relationship for granted. The rewards for not doing so were priceless.

Two days later, I made a point of rising early and getting to the beach. As I'd hoped, Bobby and Sydney were there, strolling together along the sand.

I called them, and they turned around and headed toward me.

"Good morning. I'm glad I saw you. I want to invite you both to come for a sail with Vaughn and me this evening. I understand, Bobby, that you'll be leaving us soon, and we wanted this time with you and Sydney. It's casual. Just bring yourselves to our house at five o'clock, and we'll have a light supper aboard the boat."

"That sounds like fun," said Sydney. "I'd like that very much."

"You can count me in, too," Bobby said, looking surprised. "Thanks."

"Don't worry about having a night off," I told Bobby. "I'll speak to Jean-Luc. "

"Thanks again," said Bobby looking even more surprised. He had no idea what I was hoping to happen between the two of them. They were good for each other.

I left them and went inside the hotel to talk to Bernie about Bobby having a night off and leaving us right after the charity event. I'd received an email from Bobby's coach that he was due back for some pre-arranged personal training sessions.

In the meantime, I planned to treat myself to a cinnamon roll and a short talk with Consuela.

I found Consuela putting the finishing touches on a second batch of sweet rolls. Some would have a buttery white icing coating; others would be left plain with just a swipe of butter across the top.

"Good morning, Annie," Consuela said. "How are things with Rhonda on vacation?"

"So far, so good," I replied, giving her a hug. "I'm just

wondering how long Rhonda can stay away. We've only allowed ourselves a few days away except when Will and Rhonda went to Tahiti for their honeymoon."

Consuela shook her head. "You both work too hard, but I understand. The hotel is your baby."

"Yours too," I said. "We wouldn't have made it through our first year and beyond without you and Manny helping us."

"We owed Rhonda, and then, as you said, The Beach House Hotel became like our baby too."

She handed me a plate with a sweet roll on it. "Fresh out of the oven."

"Thanks, Mom," I said, bringing a smile to her face at my teasing. I poured myself a cup of coffee and took it and the sweet treat to my office.

I was sitting at my desk when I received word that Bernie had arrived. I went to see him.

As I approached the lobby, I saw Brock Goodwin enter.

"Hello, Brock," I said coolly.

"Ann, just the person I want to see. I read in the newspaper about the charity party you're putting on, and I want to be sure I'm on the list."

"You'll have to check with Dorothy Stern. She's in charge of the guest list. The last I knew, we were full for the event itself, but for five days before it, anyone can go online and bid for auction items."

Brock shook his head. "No, that won't do for me. As president of the neighborhood association, I should be among the invited guests."

I shrugged. "As I said, you'll have to speak to Dorothy about it. Sorry, but there's nothing I can do for you."

Brock let out a puff of anger and walked away. I knew I'd put him on the spot because he and Dorothy were declared enemies. Heaven knew what Dorothy would say to him, but a plan was forming in my mind.

I went on to Bernie's office. Rhonda and I were lucky to have him as the hotel's general manager. He knew the hotel business inside and out and was a consummate gentleman, representing the hotel in its best light.

Bernie greeted me with a stiff little bow and offered me a seat. "I understand you wanted to talk to me."

"Yes. I received an email from Bobby's coach. He's due back for some personal training that was arranged some time ago. I'm requesting that he stay here until after the charity event, but we'll need to find a replacement in the kitchen. I've been pleased with the changes in him. Jean-Luc seems happy with him. What do you think?"

"I believe being here working in a menial position has brought home a lot of life lessons to him. I'm actually surprised but very pleased. Jean-Luc doesn't put up with any nonsense from anyone, and working in the kitchen has proven to be a good plan for Bobby."

"Good. I'm glad we agree. How's your new puppy?"

Bernie grinned. "He's appropriately named King, as he truly is the king of the castle. I thought I was, but I can't compete with a Dachshund puppy."

I laughed. "Cindy is trying to take over Trudy's spot, but Trudy is staying strong."

"Annette and I have just learned we're about to become grandparents. Her daughter, Babette, phoned us last night." He gave me a proud smile. "King might have some competition in the future."

"Congratulations! I'm happy for you. Grandparenting is the best."

"Annette is beside herself with joy. She's already starting a campaign to get Babette and her husband to move here."

"I don't blame her," I said. "Thanks for taking the time to

meet with me. I'll talk to you later about the charity event. Brock Goodwin just asked why he wasn't invited."

Bernie rolled his eyes. *"Dummkopf."*

I didn't speak German, but I knew exactly what Bernie had said.

I went back to my office, called Rhonda, and after she agreed with what I had in mind, I called Dorothy.

CHAPTER TWENTY-SIX

That evening, I stood ready to greet Bobby and Sydney. I'd come home early to make sure the dogs were fed, and Robbie was next door for an evening with his best friend. I wanted this sailing trip to be perfect.

Bobby and Sydney arrived on time. Watching them get out of the car and walk toward the front door, I was struck again by how big Bobby was. Sydney looked small next to him. They wore jeans and T-shirts and carried light jackets.

Vaughn came up behind me, and we waited for them to reach us.

"Hello, welcome," I said and opened the door.

"Thank you for having us," said Sydney, handing me a bottle of red wine.

"We're glad you're here. It's a great evening for a sail, though you'll probably need your jackets when the sun goes down," said Vaughn.

Trudy barked for attention, and Sydney squatted beside her. "Hi, there."

Bobby leaned down and petted Trudy—a good sign.

"Come on in," said Vaughn. "The puppy is in the kitchen."

Sydney and Bobby followed him to the kitchen. I watched as they fussed over Cindy, in sync with one another. Another good sign.

"Our son, Robbie, is next door for an overnight treat," I said. "So, if it's okay with you, we'll go right down to the boat and take off." We'd already loaded our supper on the boat and prepared her for the sail.

"I can't wait," said Sydney. "I've sailed once before in San Diego, and it was fantastic."

"I've never been on a sailboat," said Bobby. "You'll have to tell me what to do."

"No problem," said Vaughn, clapping a hand on Bobby's shoulder. "I'm pleased to tell you all about it. The number one rule is that the captain of the boat is in charge, and what he or she says goes. Otherwise, you'd have chaos. I think you're going to love it."

"Vaughn loves getting someone interested in sailing," I said.

We gated Trudy in the kitchen with the puppy and headed down to the boat.

"This is a beauty," said Bobby, admiring *Zephyr.*

"Thanks. She's a great family boat. With our time commitments, we haven't made overnight trips, but it's roomy enough and well-equipped for that. In the meantime, we love taking her out for a day or evening sail."

Vaughn stood in the cockpit and helped Sydney aboard and then Bobby. I stayed on the dock to take care of the lines.

"I was told you're both good swimmers," said Vaughn. "The cushions you're sitting on are all safety flotation devices, so if you or anyone goes overboard, they have something to hang onto until we can reach them."

"Okay," said Bobby.

"When I say, 'we're coming about,' it means we're reversing direction, and this boom will swing the opposite way. Be sure and duck your head."

Vaughn started the engine.

I tossed the dock lines aboard the boat and hopped on.

Vaughn steadied me, and I sat in the cockpit next to Sydney.

"I'm glad we could do this," said Sydney. "Nick loves to sail and keeps saying he will get another boat after selling the one he had."

"It's been a wonderful way for Vaughn and Robbie to bond. They love working on the boat as well as sailing it," I said.

We motored out toward the open water. Just as we went through the pass, a dolphin playfully rose out of the water and followed us.

"Look, Bobby!" cried Sydney. "That's good luck for us."

Bobby grinned. "Very cool."

I took over the wheel out on the open water as Vaughn hoisted the sails. The wind caught the mainsail, and we heeled to one side before I got the boat righted.

"Whoa! What was that?" Bobby said.

"The boat is going to heel from time to time. Don't be alarmed," said Vaughn taking over the wheel from me. "Some of the fastest and best sailing is done with the boat heeled to one side, close to the water. But be assured. It's safe." He checked the sky. "I'm afraid the wind isn't strong enough for that to happen tonight. It'll be a nice, gentle sail."

"I love the quiet," said Sydney. She leaned over the side of the boat and trailed her hand in the water.

"Come on over here, Bobby," said Vaughn. "You can handle the wheel with me for a while. I'll show you how to keep the sails full."

The look of delight on Bobby's face was telling. For a man his size, he moved quickly to Vaugh's side.

"How are you feeling?" I asked Sydney.

"Much better mentally. I realize I wasn't in any condition to go after Victor, that I was even lucky to be able to talk to you and Bobby and point to where Victor was. So medically, I've recovered. But I promised myself never to get into the drug scene. It was scary as hell."

"Yeah, it was never my thing. When I was growing up, we

didn't have the exposure to drugs that you kids have today. For that, I'm grateful." I studied her, and then, unable to stop myself, I said, "It seems as if you and Bobby have established a nice relationship."

Sydney smiled shyly. "I like that when I met him, I didn't know what he did for a living. It's allowed us to get to know one another as people. I'm not thrilled he's a football star, but I understand it's a game he loves. And he's good at it."

"Did he tell you why he's here working at the hotel?" I asked her.

"Yes. He said he was a real jerk in the past, and being here has taught him a lot." Sydney glanced at him. "For such a big, tough guy, he has a gentle heart. He was devastated not to have caught up with the kidnapper."

"He's a good man who's had to learn how to handle being famous. It's not easy. Vaughn is an excellent example for him to follow. Looking at the two of them now, I think they might become friends."

"Oh, I hope so. If we get married ..." Sydney stopped and covered her mouth. "I shouldn't have said anything."

"You and Bobby are that serious?" I asked, knowing that's exactly what Rhonda would've asked.

"Please don't say anything about it, but we've talked about getting engaged someday. I told him I had to see what it was like to go through a football season with him."

"I won't say a word."

"Hey, galley slave, how about a cold beer?" teased Vaughn looking at me.

"Aye, aye, captain," I said, saluting him.

"Wow! If this is what it's like sailing a boat, I'm all for it," said Bobby, laughing at the two of us.

"This happens only once in a while," I said. "So don't get your hopes up."

I went below, pulled a couple of beers out of the cooler for the men, and handed them to Sydney. "And what'll you have? I have a nice Chandler Hill pinot noir if you'd like a glass of red wine."

"That sounds perfect," said Sydney.

I opened the bottle of wine, poured some into two plastic glasses, and handed them to her.

The sun was edging to the horizon, and a burst of color filled the western sky. Finally, the wind had died down, and we all settled in the cockpit where Vaughn could keep one hand on the wheel.

"Here's to us! Health, Happiness, and Go, Buccaneers!" I said, lifting my glass.

"Yes, to all of it," said Sydney smiling at Bobby.

"To us!" said Vaughn and turned to Bobby. "If you can't make a go of it in football, you could apply to be first mate on my boat. You're going to be good."

Bobby laughed. "First mate is much easier than playing football, but thanks."

"We do wish you a good season," I said. "Rhonda and I have already talked about seeing some of your games."

Bobby's cheeks grew pink, and his eyes grew suspiciously moist. "Thanks. That means a lot. Jean-Luc told me the same thing. He's been great."

"We all had our doubts about you when you first arrived some weeks ago, but you've proved to us what a good man you are. It couldn't have been easy working for Jean-Luc. He doesn't give praise often."

"He's a real badass, but a gentleman too," admitted Bobby. "The best part of working at the hotel is meeting Sydney." His lips curved as he put an arm around her.

Sydney looked up at him, and it seemed natural that he kissed her quickly.

I glanced at Vaughn, and he winked at me.

Later, after Sydney and Bobby left, Vaughn said, "Let's have a cup of coffee on the lanai. It's a beautiful night."

We each fixed our cup of coffee and carried it to the lanai.

Vaughn sat on the couch and patted the cushion next to him. "I need to tell you something."

I sat, sipped my coffee, and set my cup down. "What is it?"

"It's actually two things. First, I'll leave right after the charity event to go to Canada for a few weeks. I've got the male lead in Nicholas' latest project, a smart rom-com that will be a hit, I think."

"Wonderful," I said, hugging him. "I know it's something you wanted. Congratulations."

"Thanks. I must admit I was starting to get restless."

"What's the second thing?" I asked.

He grew serious and pulled a small velvet box out of his pants pocket. "I can't stop thinking of how I felt as I watched you take off with Rhonda to do what you had to do to bring Victor back. They were among the worst moments of my life. I felt so damn helpless. I want you to know you carry my heart wherever you go." He opened the box.

Inside was a white-gold necklace with a small heart pendant whose open shape was outlined with sparkling diamonds. It was stunning in its simplicity.

"I didn't want it to be overly large, but small enough that you can wear it all the time without ever having to take it off," said Vaughn. He tilted my face and lowered his lips to mine. "I love you so much."

Tears filled my eyes at the thought of our ever being broken apart by violence. I put on the necklace and patted it, loving the feel of it close to my heart. "Thank you, my darling. It and you mean the world to me."

Later, lying in bed, we showed each other exactly what we meant.

CHAPTER TWENTY-SEVEN

Two days later, Rhonda was at the office when I walked in. "What are you doing here?" I asked. "You have another day of vacation."

"A staycation is far different from a vacation. I'm exhausted. I had to come back for a rest. Besides, with the charity dinner and auction coming up, I couldn't stay away. This event is my way of giving thanks for being spared from breast cancer. I want to be part of getting it ready."

"You're right. We should both be part of each step of this celebration. It's good to have you back."

"What's been going on while I've been gone?" asked Rhonda.

"We had a sweet, small wedding over the weekend. And Sydney and Bobby went sailing with Vaughn and me. Very interesting."

Rhonda rubbed her hands together. "Oh, yeah? What's the deal? Is your matchmaking working?"

"I don't know if it's my matchmaking skill, but I have tried my best to allow them to be together in a romantic setting. I think it's working. Sydney told me they've talked about getting engaged, but she wants to go through a football season before giving him an answer."

"Smart girl," said Rhonda.

"I think it's making Bobby work hard at getting and keeping Sydney's affection. It couldn't happen to a better guy," said Rhonda. "Let's see what the football season does to him."

"I told him we're planning to come to one of his games," I said.

"If he acts like a pompous big shot, I'll wring his neck," said Rhonda. "But I admit he's come a long way since his arrival."

"He's a sweet guy who got off on the wrong foot with his stardom. Being unable to catch the kidnapper has made him more determined than ever to be in shape and do a good job. It's obvious he adores Sydney."

"Well, let's hope we don't have to do any more favors for anyone. It's hard enough making sure the hotel has an excellent reputation without having to take care of problems for the Vice-President and her friends."

"I agree. The hotel business always brings interesting guests. We'll be busy no matter what."

"Is Operation Brock working?" Rhonda asked, letting out an unladylike laugh.

"Okay this far," I said. "Dorothy called to tell me she's invited Brock to be her date for the evening, that that was the only way she could placate him."

"Very nice," said Rhonda grinning.

As the day of the event drew near, we met with Lorraine and Dorothy to make sure all the seats were full and that online bidding was taking place. Lorraine had Terri Thomas give a shout-out to the event with a nice article about how online bidding helped build the beginning of a nice fund for cancer research.

The morning of the event, Rhonda and I worked with Lorraine to make sure the dining room was set up as we wanted. Hotel guests who weren't going to attend the dinner and auction were given special discounts to eat at other restaurants in town, a marvelous suggestion from Dorothy. That made hotel guests a little more understanding about not being able to eat in the dining room that night.

We'd gone with a pink and white theme, and seeing tables, rounds of eight, covered with bright hibiscus-pink linen table clothes, I sighed with satisfaction. Crisp white-linen napkins looked stark and pure against the pink background. Crystal glasses and sparkling silverware were offset by centerpieces of fresh lilies, adding to the pink theme.

"Gorgeous," said Rhonda. "Worth the $300 ticket per seat, don't'cha think?"

"Yes. With the special food, the wine, and the chance to mix with a couple of famous people like Tina, Nicholas, Vaughn, and others, it's a lovely evening for a good cause."

We left the hotel at four and would return at six when cocktails would be available for purchase, and free wine would be offered. Rhonda would match the amount we'd raised, but she didn't want to lose out on raising any money at the bar.

At home, I sat with Robbie watching the end of a movie with him. Though the film was cute, I paid attention to him, cuddling him as much as I could. I knew the time would come when he wouldn't want to cuddle on the couch with me. Until then, I intended to enjoy every minute I could with him.

After the movie, Elena arrived. We talked about dinner for Robbie and her, and then I asked how she and Troy were doing with the new spa.

"It's going well," she said. Then frowned. "I need to talk to you about getting someone to replace me in caring for Robbie."

My heart sank. Elena had been helping me from the time Robbie came into our lives. She knew him almost as well as I did. "Any ideas?"

"Actually, I do. My younger cousin is looking for a position and loves the idea of working for you part-time." She chuckled. "She can't believe I work for you and Vaughn Sanders, the star. She's a good kid, a hard worker. I think you'll like her."

"Sounds good. When can I set up a time for an interview?"

"Let me check with her," said Elena. Her eyes filled. "I hate to think I won't be as much a part of the family, especially with Liz and the babies. You've all been very generous with me. I never could've taken those college courses without your support."

"You and Troy were an early part of The Beach House Hotel, working long hours, doing a good job. I'm thrilled you could help me with Robbie and Liz with the Ts. We'll miss you like crazy. But, Elena, you'll always be part of the family." I, who grew up a very lonely child, loved being able to add to my hotel family.

We hugged, and then I went to get ready for the evening.

I was in the shower when I felt someone beside me. I opened my eyes. "Fancy meeting you here," I said, smiling at Vaughn.

He hugged me. "I haven't seen much of you all day, and with going away to Canada for a few weeks, I want to take advantage of spending time with you."

I hugged him and later got out of the shower and raced around to get ready. I'd bought a new blue dress with a sweetheart neckline and a filmy skirt in a shade Vaughn told me matched my eyes.

As I stood in front of the mirror, making sure my hair was satisfactory, I studied the simple heart necklace Vaughn had given me. As he wished, I never took it off. Now, it lay against my chest, all but hidden by the large heart with five diamonds he'd given me before we were married. It was a symbol of the family we were forming before Robbie came into our lives. It was as striking now as it had been then.

"A bejeweled princess," Vaughn whispered into my ear before kissing my cheek.

I turned to him. In his tux, he looked every bit like a movie star. "And a handsome prince for an escort. I have a feeling it will be a very interesting evening."

"What have you and Rhonda planned now?" he asked, cocking an eyebrow at me.

"Wait and see," I said demurely. "It should be a lot of fun."

"Okay, but I have a feeling it's going to cost me money," he said.

"Maybe. Hopefully not." If I mentioned anything more, it would ruin our plans.

When I walked into the kitchen to say goodnight to Robbie, he looked up at me wide-eyed. "You look like a princess."

I blinked rapidly so I wouldn't ruin my mascara. "Thank you, darling. You say the sweetest things." I kissed him. "I love you so much."

"Yeah, me too," he said, giving me a sweet embrace.

I didn't care if he crushed my dress. I hugged him to me.

At the hotel, the valet service was in full swing. We'd hired extra men for the job,
and our wait in line didn't take very long.

Getting out of the car, I heard the buzz of anticipation as guests entered the hotel dressed in their finest. The invitation was for dinner, but I knew how much people enjoyed getting fancy for an affair like this.

As Vaughn led me up the hotel's steps, it seemed surreal to think I was part owner of this beautiful place.

Bernie, looking dapper in his tux, greeted everyone at the door. This was one evening I was happy to hand over that task.

Other staff members directed people to the dining room, where bars were set up at each end of the room. So, naturally, a crowd gathered near them. Waitstaff mingled among the other guests offering hors d'oeuvres.

I searched for Rhonda. She looked radiant in a shimmering gold caftan. At my short stature, I would look awful in a caftan, but on Rhonda, they were perfect, and she delighted in having them made in luscious fabrics. Will, still a somewhat shy man, stood beside her, content to let her speak.

Next, I scanned the crowd for Dorothy. Wearing a black dress, she'd gone fancy with her jewelry, wearing a tasteful diamond necklace and a wide gold bracelet around her wrist. She saw me and gave me a thumbs-up sign.

I smiled when I saw the mayor talking to a group of avid listeners. All was set.

Rhonda and I and our spouses were seated with the mayor, who'd come alone, Arthur, Tina, and Nicholas. Rhonda had tried to work it out that Lorraine would be seated with us, but because Lorraine had organized the evening's event, she told Rhonda she wouldn't be comfortable eating dinner with us. I had noticed, though, that Lorraine and Arthur had looked as if they were enjoying talking to each other during the cocktail hour.

"Everything looks fantastic," gushed the mayor as she spread her napkin across her lap. "I'm hopeful that we can raise a lot of money."

"Me, too," said Rhonda. "It's such a good cause."

"Anything these two undertake will be a success," said Tina, giving Rhonda and me affectionate smiles.

The food service began, and I was as impressed as everyone else with each course. A consommé with mushrooms was served first, followed by a fresh green salad with unique blue-cheese croutons and a wine vinegar and olive oil dressing. The main course was a "surf and turf" presentation of petite filet mignon and salmon, each with an accompanying sauce, served with grilled asparagus and roasted potatoes. We were offered slices of lemon chiffon pie garnished with red raspberries for dessert.

"I don't know how Jean-Luc does it," said the mayor, dabbing at her mouth with her napkin. "Every meal I've had here has been delicious, and to be able to serve this crowd all at once is fantastic."

"We're very lucky to have him," I said.

"And our entire crew," added Rhonda.

"With her sister married to Jean-Luc, I suppose the Vice-President will be making another trip here soon," said the mayor.

"Probably. But, of course, such trips are kept confidential," I said. Secretly, I hoped Amelia Swanson wouldn't come and ask us to do another favor for her. So far, her favors had meant a good deal of trauma to Rhonda and me.

After dinner, a buzz of excitement filled the air as the mayor rose and walked over to the dais. "Ladies and Gentlemen, time to open your wallets in gratitude for such a lovely event to help the cause of research for breast cancer. I'm sure we're all aware of someone who has had breast cancer. Let's see what we can do to conquer this horrible disease. Thanks to Rhonda Grayson and Ann Sanders for hosting this affair. Now let's begin."

Lorraine slid into the mayor's empty chair next to Arthur,

and the happy look he gave her touched me. I glanced at Rhonda, and her smug look made me laugh.

"Is everybody ready?" The mayor asked, tapping the top of the lectern for attention.

I focused on the mayor and checked the table close to the dais. Rhonda and I had purposely placed Dorothy and her "date," Brock, where they could be seen easily.

One item after another was auctioned off. A young woman paid $2,000 for a picnic sail with Vaughn. People happily won stays at various hotels, private vacation homes, and other things. As we'd promised Terri Thomas, we offered one breakfast at the hotel, plus fresh sweet rolls delivered for seven days. She bid on that one and won. A couple of paintings and other art pieces were auctioned off, bringing in good money. But the items that earned the most money for the cause were a couple of trips to various locations in the U.S.

"And now, ladies and gentlemen," announced the mayor, "we have a special offering for you to bid on—a trip to Tahiti. Brock Goodwin, I've heard that you've always wanted to travel to that area. So now, you can show your support for this cause by bidding on this. Let's start at one thousand dollars. How about it, Brock?"

I watched his face. Knowing how much he wanted to be on the mayor's special board, I wasn't surprised when he nodded and raised his hand.

"Okay, folks, we'll keep the bidding at thousand-dollar increments. With all the extras attached to this offer, including a stay in Hawaii and a 7-day Tahiti cruise, this offering is worth well over twenty thousand dollars. So who's going to bid two thousand dollars? Brock?"

Dorothy raised her hand before Brock could respond.

Brock looked at Dorothy and sneered. "Ten thousand dollars."

"Eleven," said Dorothy, giving him a triumphant look.

Someone else called "Fifteen."

"Brock?" asked the mayor.

"Twenty," he answered, but after saying it, he looked upset.

"Okay, that does it," said the mayor. "The giver of this item has signaled the end. Congratulations, Brock. You're going to Tahiti!" She handed him an envelope.

Amid the applause, Brock stood and took a bow. But as he sat down, I saw a look of panic cross his face.

Rhonda gave me a satisfied look. Brock's ego had run away with him. We doubted he'd be able to pay twenty thousand dollars for that trip. He didn't know it, but we'd make it easy for him to back out. All he had to do was stay off the property until the house under construction was finished.

"Attention," said the mayor. "To those of you who've won prizes, further information will be given to you by those who've offered it. Thank you all for coming and participating. According to my sources, we've raised over $75,000, which Rhonda Grayson will match. Thank you one and all for this successful evening."

Guests got up from their tables and mingled before heading out the door. Everyone at our table stayed put.

Brock Goodwin walked over to us, waving the envelope in his hand. "I need to talk to the two of you about this. I was pushed into bidding."

"We'll be pleased to talk to you tomorrow. Shall we say ten o'clock?" said Rhonda. "I can give you all the details then."

"But I don't know if I can do this," protested Brock.

"We'll talk tomorrow," I said, remembering how Brock had sneered at Dorothy, who could easily pay for that trip.

He shook a finger at me. "Why do I get the feeling I was set up?"

"Why would you say that? You bid and won the trip fairly.

Isn't that what you wanted?" I knew we were being mean, but we had to get his attention somehow, and this would hurt no one.

"See you tomorrow," said Rhonda. "And don't be late. We've got a lot going on."

After he left, the mayor and Dorothy came over to our table.

"How'd I do?" the mayor asked.

"You were perfect," said Rhonda.

"You have a nice way of getting people to increase their bids," I said smugly.

"A certain someone couldn't resist," said Dorothy. "It went so quickly that I couldn't do more bidding, but it all worked out."

"It was a fabulous evening," said the mayor. "I'm very glad I could help out. We raised a lot of money for a good cause."

Rhonda and I shook hands with her and promised her lunch anytime she came by.

Tina and Nicholas said goodnight to us and left, arm in arm.

"We'll drop you off, Dorothy," I said. "Thanks for your help."

"Anything for you girls," she said. "But did you see how Brock looked at me when I tried to outbid him? He's such an ..."

"Rat bastard?" Rhonda said.

"Exactly," said Dorothy with an emphatic nod of her head.

CHAPTER TWENTY-EIGHT

At home, Vaughn and I got out of our fancy clothes and slipped on our bathing suits. We were both in need of exercise after that abundant meal.

There was something special about swimming in the soft glow of lights around the pool or on clear nights by the moon's light. It always made me feel part of nature.

After swimming several lengths of the pool, Vaughn and I sat on the steps at the shallow end to talk.

"Do you want to tell me about the story with Brock?" Vaughn said. "You and Rhonda were looking at him and grinning all evening."

I filled him in, and he let out a laugh that crinkled the skin at the corners of his eyes. "Brock is such a buffoon. He deserves this little lesson. So, after you let him get out of the deal, are Will and Rhonda going to use those tickets for another try at Tahiti?"

"Or give them to Arthur and Lorraine."

"Whoa! Arthur and Lorraine? When did that relationship come about?"

"It's something Rhonda has been working on. I'm not saying anything will happen right away, but I saw how they looked at one another, and there's definitely something strong between them. And I know that he stayed at Lorraine's last night and will stay there again tonight. Reggie isn't quite ready for his father to move on, but Angela, like her mother, thinks they're perfect together."

Vaughn shook his head. "It amazes me how the two of you

operate sometimes."

"It's just that we want to see other people as happy as we are," I said, wrapping my arms around him.

"How about your showing me how you feel instead of telling me?"

As Vaughn pulled me closer, I thought it was an excellent idea.

The next morning, Rhonda and I waited in our office for Brock to show up. I thought he might brush us off or be late, but then we knew he didn't have the money to pay twenty thousand dollars for a vacation he couldn't afford to take.

Ten o'clock came and went. By ten-fifteen, I was annoyed and got up to go see Tina. She wanted to talk about returning for the Christmas holidays, and I needed to confirm that with her before putting the reservation in our system.

Brock knocked on the door, and I sat down, picking up some paperwork to look busy.

"Come in," Rhonda called.

Brock stepped into the room. I noticed the dark circles under his eyes and suspected he must have spent a restless night.

Brock looked down at the floor for a minute before lifting his face and glaring at us. "I'm not going to pay for the trip that I bought. I can't prove it, but I think the two of you set me up. Even Dorothy bid against me. She can't afford something like that."

"Really? That's what you think?" I asked, genuinely surprised. "Dorothy can buy as many trips to Tahiti as she wants."

"But she works for you part-time," he protested.

"Things aren't always what you think, Brock. Especially

when it comes to money. She works here at the hotel to keep busy and productive."

"We're not talking about Dorothy," said Rhonda. "We're talking about you. You made a big show of buying my travel package. So, what's the real problem?"

"I'd rather not spend my money on a trip I don't need to take. But, in case you haven't noticed, I'm needed here in town with my job and running the neighborhood association," Brock said, his face growing red.

We all knew he was lying.

"How about we make a deal?" said Rhonda. "I'll take back my travel package, relieving you of the need to buy it, but only under one condition."

Brock's expression brightened. "What are you talking about?"

"In exchange for taking the package deal back, you will not appear on the hotel property until the construction of the new house is completed," said Rhonda.

"No way," said Brock. "It's my responsibility to know what's happening in the neighborhood."

"Okay. No deal. Have the check to me by five o'clock, or I'll announce to everyone who attended the event that the package is now available due to non-payment," said Rhonda.

"You wouldn't..." scoffed Brock.

Rhonda's smile was almost happy. "But I would."

"Listen, Brock," I said. "You continue to harass us every opportunity you get. We're tired of it. This is the best way I know for all of us to be winners on this occasion. You get out from under the debt, and we have no harassment from you over something you have no business being involved with. Win, win. Get it?"

"But I give you a lot of business by coming here for drinks and meals," Brock said.

"Not enough to matter," countered Rhonda.

"How about I never leave the main building, just come for food and drink?" said Brock.

Rhonda and I glanced at one another.

Rhonda shrugged. "Okay, but if you're caught, we will announce the deal we made."

"How long is it going to take to finish the house?" Brock asked.

"Longer than you think," I said.

Brock let out an exaggerated sigh. "Okay. Here are your tickets. But don't think you can keep me away indefinitely. I have my contacts, you know."

"Oh, yes. And so do we," said Rhonda, accepting the envelope from him.

Brock wagged a finger at us. "You'd better stick to the bargain. My reputation would be ruined if you didn't."

"Exactly," said Rhonda, smiling like the cat who'd just dined on a big, fat canary.

Brock turned and stormed out of the office.

"We did it, Annie!" said Rhonda, getting out of her chair and doing a little jig. "We finally got the best of Brock." She pulled me up, and I danced with her. But I knew that Brock, like other problems of running the hotel, wouldn't go away. But I couldn't think of anyone else I'd rather face them with.

"C'mon, Annie. Let's go find Consuela," said Rhonda, throwing her arm around me. "There's nothing better than coffee at The Beach House Hotel to prepare for another day."

I gave her a high-five, and together we left the office.

As we entered the kitchen, I studied Consuela. Her black hair was graying now, but she was as active as usual. I wondered what it would've been like to have a mother or both parents alive when I was growing up. My grandmother was a cold woman with many rules. Perhaps that's why partnering with Rhonda in business was so good for me. She was a free spirit while I fought old habits. It worked well both ways.

I gave Consuela a warm hug for being the kind, loving woman she was. Smiling at me, she shook her head. "Oh, Annie, what would we have done if anything had happened to you and Rhonda? When we learned what the two of you did to save Victor, I had to sit down and catch my breath. It was terrifying."

"It was scary," I admitted.

"Aw, she has nerves of steel," said Rhonda grinning at me.

"At least I wasn't driving," I said. We were an unlikely team, but as I'd thought a moment ago, it worked.

"Wait until we tell you what we did to Brock," Rhonda said, lifting a sweet roll onto a plate.

By the time Rhonda finished the story, the three of us were laughing so hard that we had to set our coffee mugs down.

"And what about Lorraine and Arthur?" Consuela asked. "Is your plan working?"

"Oh, yes. I knew it would," said Rhonda giving me a self-satisfied look. "It'll just be a matter of time before it becomes very serious. I'm sure of it."

"Then who will you get to replace Lorraine?" Consuela asked.

"That's the part I've got to work on," said Rhonda. "We must convince Arthur to move to Florida. He's kind of a big shot in New York, so I don't know if he'll agree to it. But we can't lose Lorraine."

"Right," I said. That was a problem I didn't want to face. I checked my watch. "We need to go talk to Tina and Nicholas. They're getting ready to leave, and we need to confirm Christmas arrangements with them."

We left Consuela and headed to the house. Normally, we'd stop and look at the one under construction first, but we didn't bother. At this point, we didn't care how long it took for construction to be finished.

When we got to my old house, Tina greeted us at the door with open arms. "Come in. I'm pleased we have a little time together before we leave for the airport. Victor has been waiting for you to arrive. He has a special thank you gift for you."

As soon as we walked into the living room, Victor saw us. Grinning, he left the room and returned proudly holding a picture frame. He looked adorable as he struggled a bit with its size.

Rather than help him, Tina encouraged him. "He wanted to do this all by himself."

He stepped in front of us, and I accepted the thin black frame he handed me and turned it over.

Victor had drawn a crayon picture of Rhonda and me standing by a car. He'd given each of us a stick figure and faces with eyes and smiling mouths. Rhonda's hair was blond, and mine was dark. Above our heads, he'd drawn a circle and lots of stars.

"What is this?" Rhonda asked.

"It's you," said Victor. "My angels."

Teary-eyed, I glanced at Rhonda, whose eyes had already leaked tears down her cheeks. "This is a wonderful drawing. Let's hang it in our office at the hotel. Would you like that?"

Victor nodded.

"It's a very special drawing because everyone will know how much we love you, Victor," I said, squatting and pulling him into my arms.

Tina stood aside, dabbing at her eyes with a tissue. "He wanted to do something for you, and I suggested a drawing. I had no idea what it would be, but it couldn't be more appropriate. You two will always be his angels, as you are mine for me."

Rhonda silently handed me a tissue, and I let my tears flow. Everything with the kidnapping had turned out well, but I never wanted to go through something like that again.

Nicholas walked into the room, followed by Sydney, holding Tyler. "Guess we missed the presentation. It looks like it was a success."

"Such a beautiful, thoughtful gift," I said.

"Tina and I want to talk about reservations for Christmas," said Nicholas.

"Yes, we want to be sure that all of you will return to The Beach House Hotel to celebrate."

"Oh, yes," said Tina. "We'll be back and maybe share a cup of coffee or two."

Our eyes met, and I knew Tina meant sharing time as loving families do.

Rhonda looked at Sydney. "So, I heard last night at dinner that you would come back to Florida occasionally to see a certain football player. When you do, you've got a place to stay with me anytime."

Her cheeks blushing brightly, Sydney said, "Thanks."

"Okay, everyone. The limo is here to take us to the airport. Let's go," said Nicholas.

I hugged Tina and held on a moment longer than usual. She'd become like a daughter, and I hated to see her go.

Sydney stood by so I could say goodbye to her and the baby. As I hugged Sydney gently, not to squeeze Tyler, I whispered in her ear, "I'm rooting for you and Bobby. Let me know how it goes."

"I will," she said, smiling. "That sailing trip meant a lot to us, seeing how you and Vaughn handle your different lives."

"Sailing trip? What sailing trip?" asked Rhonda overhearing us.

I grinned. "I'll tell you later."

Having said goodbye to all of them, Rhonda and I stood by as the limo carried them away.

She turned to me. "Okay, spill. What sailing trip was Sydney talking about? Is that your   maneuvering a little matchmaking trick?" She cocked an eyebrow at me.

Grinning, I said, "It might be. But, as you say, wake up and smell the coffee if you think I will let you get ahead of me."

"I knew it!" said Rhonda, chuckling and throwing her arm around me. "Best. Partner. Ever."

We strolled back to the hotel, aware that running The Beach House Hotel together meant more adventures to come.

Thank you for reading *Coffee at The Beach House Hotel*. If you enjoyed this book, please help other readers discover it by leaving a review on Amazon, Bookbub, Goodreads, or your favorite site. It's such a nice thing to do.

And for your further enjoyment, here are links for the other books in The Beach House Hotel Series, which are available on all sites:

Breakfast at The Beach House Hotel:
https://www.amazon.com/dp/B00YD5X6NG

Lunch at The Beach House Hotel:
https://www.amazon.com/dp/B01F6LRPAA

Dinner at The Beach House Hotel:
https://www.amazon.com/dp/B01MFCEC1Q

Christmas at The Beach House Hotel:
https://www.amazon.com/dp/B075CBZ21S

Margaritas at The Beach House Hotel
https://www.amazon.com/dp/B08Y83FX9V

Dessert at The Beach House Hotel:
https://www.amazon.com/dp/B097CFLPQ8

Sign up for my newsletter and get a free story. I keep my newsletters short and fun with giveaways, recipes, and the latest must-have news about me and my books. Welcome! Here's the link:

https://BookHip.com/RRGJKGN

Enjoy a synopsis of *High Tea at The Beach House Hotel*, Book 8 in The Beach House Hotel Series, which will be released in 2024:

Guests can be surprising...

Ann and Rhonda continue their work at The Beach House Hotel, always striving to make their upscale property the best on the Gulf Coast of Florida. As they've learned, not all guests are easy. When they receive a request from Hilda Hassel, a member of the Bavarian royal family, for a two-week stay at the hotel in January, demanding the best room and High Tea every afternoon, Ann is uneasy. Other Hassel family members cancelled a large, fancy wedding at the last moment leaving a mess behind. But Rhonda convinces Ann that having a royal guest could increase important European business, and Ann agrees.

After deciding to give Hilda the Presidential Suite for two weeks during their high season and welcoming her to the hotel, Ann and Rhonda are left to wonder if they've made the biggest mistake of their lives when Hilda arrives with her "nephew," and strange things begin to happen.

Another of Judith Keim's series books celebrating love and families, strong women meeting challenges, and clean women's fiction with a touch of romance—beach reads for all ages with a touch of humor, satisfying twists, and happy endings

About the Author

A *USA Today* **Best-Selling Author,** Judith Keim is a hybrid author who both has a publisher and self-publishes. Ms. Keim writes heart-warming novels about women who face unexpected challenges, meet them with strength, and find love and happiness along the way. Her best-selling books are based partly on many of the places she's lived or visited and on the interesting people she's met, creating believable characters and realistic settings her loyal readers love. Ms. Keim loves to hear from her readers and appreciates their enthusiasm for her stories.

Ms. Keim enjoyed her childhood and young-adult years in Elmira, New York, and now makes her home in Boise, Idaho, with her husband, Peter, and their lovable miniature Dachshund, Wally, and other members of her family.

While growing up, she was drawn to the idea of writing stories from a young age. Books were always present, being read, ready to go back to the library, or about to be discovered. All in her family shared information from the books in general conversation, giving them a wealth of knowledge and vivid imaginations.

"I hope you've enjoyed this book. If you have, please help other readers discover it by leaving a review on Amazon, Goodreads, Bookbub, or the site of your choice. And please check out my other books and series:"

The Hartwell Women Series

The Beach House Hotel Series

Fat Fridays Group

The Salty Key Inn Series

The Chandler Hill Inn Series

Seashell Cottage Books

The Desert Sage Inn Series

Soul Sisters at Cedar Mountain Lodge

The Sanderling Cove Inn Series

The Lilac Lake Inn Series

"ALL THE BOOKS ARE NOW AVAILABLE IN AUDIO on Audible, iTunes, Findaway, Kobo, and Google Play! So fun to have these characters come alive!"

Ms. Keim can be reached at **www.judithkeim.com**

And to like her author page on Facebook and keep up with the news, go to: **http://bit.ly/2pZWDgA**

To receive notices about new books, follow her on Book Bub:

https://www.bookbub.com/authors/judith-keim

"Sign up for my newsletter and get a free story. I keep my newsletters short and fun with giveaways, recipes, and the latest must-have news about me and my books. Welcome! Here's the link:

https://BookHip.com/RRGJKGN

"I am also on Twitter @judithkeim, LinkedIn, and Goodreads. Come say hello!"

Acknowledgments

And, as always, I am eternally grateful to my team of editors, Peter Keim and Lynn Mapp, my book cover designer, Lou Harper, and my narrator for Audible and iTunes, Angela Dawe. They are the people who take what I've written and help turn it into the book I proudly present to you, my readers! I also wish to thank my coffee group of writers who listen and encourage me to keep on going. Thank you, Peggy Staggs, Lynn Mapp, Cate Cobb, Nikki Jean Triska, Joanne Pence, Melanie Olsen, and Megan Bryce. And to you, my fabulous readers, I thank you for your continued support and encouragement. Without you, this book would not exist. You are the wind beneath my wings.

Made in the USA
Middletown, DE
10 October 2023

40538642R00158